praise for dave duncan and the enchanter general series

"Enjoyable characters, a detailed setting, and atmospheric adventure intertwine in this multilevel mystery. Durwin is a congenial and persistent investigator, and readers will look forward to his future adventures."—*Publishers Weekly*

"An entertaining, fast-paced read that will please readers looking for mystery and enchantment."—*Kirkus Reviews*

"*Ironfoot* is gritty, magical, at times brutal, but above all humane. This is historical fantasy pulled off spectacularly well."—Greg Keyes, author of *The Briar King* and *The Reign of the Departed*

"A fantastic murder mystery firmly anchored in real history, plus a generous mix of arcane magic."—Glenda Larke, author of *The Lascar's Dagger*

"I was surprised by how compelling it was . . . I would recommend this."—*Milliebot Reads*

"An enjoyable easy read . . . hopefully there's a sequel in the not too distant future."—*Cannonball Read*

"[Duncan has] rich, evocative language and superior narrative skills . . . one of the leading masters of epic fantasy."—*Publishers Weekly*

"Dave Duncan writes rollicking adventure novels filled with subtle characterization and made bitter-sweet by an underlying darkness. Without striving for grand effects or momentous meetings between genres, he has produced one excellent book after another."—*Locus*

"An exceedingly finished stylist and a master of world building and characterization."—*Booklist*

"Duncan writes with unusual flair, drawing upon folklore, myth, and his gift for creating ingenious plots."—*Year's Best Fantasy and Horror*

"One of the best writers in the fantasy world today. His writing is clear, vibrant and full of energy. His action scenes are breathtaking and his skill at characterization is excellent."—*Writers Write*

"Duncan's prose avoids the excessively florid in its description and the archaic in its dialogue, opting instead for simpler narration and contemporary parlance . . . serves as a refreshing reminder that epic fantasy need not always be doorstops filled with manly men speaking in overblown rhetoric and grasping their swords."—*SFF World*

"Duncan produces excellent work in book after book . . . a great world-builder. His fantasy worlds are not mere medieval societies with magic added but make organic sense."—*SFReview*

"Dave Duncan has long been one of the great unsung figures of Canadian fantasy and science fiction, graced with a fertile imagination, a prolific output, and keen writerly skills."—*Quill and Quire*

Merlin redux

by dave duncan

The Seventh Sword
The Reluctant Swordsman
The Coming of Wisdom
The Destiny of the Sword
The Death of Nnanji

A Man of His Word
Magic Casement
Faery Lands Forlorn
Perilous Seas
Emperor and Clown

A Handful of Men
The Cutting Edge
Upland Outlaws
The Stricken Field
The Living God

Omar
The Reaver Road
The Hunters' Haunt

The Great Game
Past Imperative
Present Tense
Future Indefinite

The Years of Longdirk (as Ken Hood)
Demon Sword
Demon Rider
Demon Knight

The King's Blades
Tales of the King's Blades
The Gilded Chain
Lord of the Fire Lands
Sky of Swords

Chronicles of the King's Blades
Paragon Lost
Impossible Odds
The Jaguar Knights

The King's Daggers
Sir Stalwart
The Crooked House
Silvercloak

Dodec
Children of Chaos
Mother of Lies

Nostradamus
The Alchemist's Apprentice
The Alchemist's Code
The Alchemist's Pursuit

Brothers Magnus
Speak to the Devil
When the Saints

The Starfolk
King of Swords
Queen of Stars

The Enchanter General
Ironfoot
Trial by Treason
Merlin Redux

Standalone Novels
A Rose-Red City
Shadow
West of January
Strings
Hero!
The Cursed
Daughter of Troy (as Sarah B. Franklin)
Ill Met in the Arena
Pock's World
Against the Light
Wildcatter
The Eye of Strife
The Adventures of Ivor
Irona 700
Eocene Station
Portal of a Thousand Worlds

the Enchanter General

Merlin redux

dave Duncan

Night Shade Books
NEW YORK

Night Shade books may be purchased in bulk at special discounts for sales promotion, corporate gifts, fund-raising, or educational purposes. Special editions can also be created to specifications. For details, contact the Special Sales Department, Night Shade Books, 307 West 36th Street, 11th Floor, New York, NY 10018 or info@skyhorsepublishing.com.

Night Shade Books® is a registered trademark of Skyhorse Publishing, Inc.®, a Delaware corporation.

Visit our website at www.nightshadebooks.com.

10 9 8 7 6 5 4 3 2 1

Library of Congress Cataloging-in-Publication Data is available on-file.

Hardcover ISBN: 978-1-949102-03-1
Paperback ISBN: 978-1-949102-04-8

Cover illustration by Stephen Youll
Cover design by Shawn King

Printed in the United States of America

This book is dedicated to its author, our beloved Papa. We are so grateful your fantastical worlds and clever words will live on forever.

—The Duncan Family

1189

i
t began on St. Theodore's Day—Tuesday, July 4th. That unhappy day was when I first sang the ancient enchantment I called the *Myrddin Wyllt*.

Many years earlier, I had found some pieces of rat-chewed, mildewed vellum amid the rubbish in a castle cellar. Although the words on it were almost illegible and written in a very old dialect, they appeared to be parts of a single poem, and since then I had stumbled on more scraps of verse that I identified as being from slightly later copies of the same work. I had tried several times to fit it all together, filling in gaps with some hopefully inspired guesswork, but meeting with no success until the spring of 1189. Then, just before leaving for France, while hunting for something else in my "miscellaneous fragments" collection, I found two other pieces of what were obviously yet other copies, which I had previously overlooked. The fact that even traces of so many versions had survived for so long suggested that it must have been a highly valued work. Manuscripts of that age are very rare indeed, and I spent every moment I could spare trying to reconstruct the original version. That was a very busy time for me, between meetings of the king's privy council, the betrothal negotiations for my younger daughter, Royse, and the annual college budgetary conference.

When I had fitted it all together, the ancient song at last began to make sense. By convention, we use the opening words of an incantation as its title, and this one began, "Myrddin Wyllt beseeches thee," so *Myrddin Wyllt* it became in my files. I knew that a man called Myrddin Wyllt had been a sixth-century prophet and madman in what we would now call southern Scotland. I was soon to wish that I had never set eyes on it.

It was midsummer before I could find enough time to get back to the work I enjoy most—repairing ancient spells that have become corrupted by time or the efforts of their original owners to keep them secret. I had invented this craft and was still better at it than anyone else. Early on that fateful morning, I went down to my workroom and eagerly read over what I put together the previous evening. I made a couple of trivial corrections, and then decided I would attempt to sing the whole song through, which I had never done before. Basically, the text was a prayer to Carnonos, the ancient antlered god of many names, lord of forests and good fortune. It was a hunter's plea for guidance, and was obviously meant to be sung. I had no desire to go stalking venison through the streets of Oxford, but I dearly wanted to hear how the song would sound. The rhythm was obvious, but I had to guess at a suitable melody. I began to chant, and was soon caught up in the imagery, the invocation of trees and summer flowers, insects and peaceful wildlife, far from the muddling cares of mankind.

To my astonishment, I felt myself sliding into trance. Many of our enchantments require two voices, and it is quite common for the supporting cantor to be entranced during the rite. I had never met a spell that entranced the enchanter himself, though. My voice seemed to fade away, and yet I could still hear myself in the distance, as if someone else were singing.

By then I was standing on a hay meadow under a cloudless sky of deepest blue. The hills were richly clad in vineyards, but in the distance, I recognized the Vienne River and the distinctive mass of Chinon Castle, near Tours, in Touraine. This was the very heart of King Henry's French domains.

A party of about twenty horsemen was making its way slowly up the gentle slope in my direction. They were riding destriers—warhorses—but none bore weapons or armor, which meant that they were either going to a parley, or coming from one. The hay-scented air was absolutely still and the noon sun blazed pitilessly overhead, although thunder clouds were building in the north. The cavalcade's snail-like pace was due to more than the summer heat, which might be hard on the horses and was certainly good for the grapes, but must feel like the breath of hell to the dying man leading that procession.

As they went by me, I barely recognized him: Henry by the Grace of God, king of England, duke of Normandy, Aquitaine, and Brittany, count of Anjou, Touraine, and Maine, lord of Ireland. He seemed to have aged ten years in the six weeks or so since I had last seen him. He sat astride his horse, but it was being led by a mounted squire. A knight rode very close on either side of him, each ready to catch him if he started to fall. Obese and white-bearded, he was clearly in agony. For a third of a century he had ruled the greatest empire since Charlemagne's, extending for a thousand miles from the Scottish border to the Spanish. I had a strong suspicion that it was not going to survive this parley.

The men supporting him I recognized as Sir William Marshal and Geoffrey Fitzhenry, Bishop of Lincoln, commonly known as Geoffrey the Bastard, big men both. The last horse to go by me was a sumpter, bearing a bundle of poles and canvas that might be a small tent, but I guessed was a litter. Until very few years ago, the king had been an avid hunter, able to outride almost any man in his retinue. *How are the mighty fallen!*

And up ahead, in the shadow of the towering plane tree? Three men were waiting there, two of them on horseback, with an entourage of supporters and horses standing nearby, out of earshot.

One of the mounted men was unmistakable, a giant, well over a fathom tall, with a red-gold beard and icy blue eyes—Lord Richard, known as the Lionheart, the elder of Henry's two surviving sons, a mighty warrior and a shameless traitor. The other beside him was a much less impressive person—Henry's nemesis, King Philip of France, thirty-two years his junior, his liege lord for all his holdings in France, and now his master. Philip was short, ruddy, and seemed utterly insignificant, especially alongside the titanic Richard. He was reputed to be a clumsy and reluctant horseman, and certainly not a warrior, but he had no equal when it came to intrigue, scheming, and subterfuge.

Standing beside the two horsemen was a tonsured clerk, clutching a satchel. I could see no fussy clerics in the background group, which meant that the parley had been set up by the participants themselves, not forced upon them by the Church, and so it was a genuine effort to achieve something, not just another of the futile brothers-in-Christ holy rituals that buzz like blowflies around all quarrels.

I moved my point of view closer, hoping to hear what the horsemen were saying, but they were studying the approaching party in silence. So Henry was about to die? Triumph for Philip, but what of his companion? Did Richard feel no guilt?

The agenda would almost certainly include the English king's abject surrender. The feud had been long and complicated. Its ultimate cause was that Henry's duchies and counties covered the entire western half of France, but France was Philip's kingdom, so Henry was his vassal, owing him homage for all those lands. Henry paid lip service to the principle, but he was not a man to truckle to an overlord. Nor could he see any contradiction in the fact that he demanded absolute obedience from his own vassals, the earls and barons of England.

The immediate cause, boiling up over the last year or so, was that all three—King Philip, King Henry, and Duke Richard—had sworn to go on Crusade, to help wrest the holy city of Jerusalem back from the Saracen heathens. Henry was now far too sick to think of going, but he stubbornly refused to name Richard as his heir. Many years ago he had so honored his oldest son, another Henry, even having him crowned, so that he became known as "the young king." The result had been feud and rebellion. Ultimately the young king had died in a tournament, and King Henry had not made the same mistake again, keeping Richard in doubt, constantly hinting that he might leave his empire to John, his youngest son. So Richard dared not go on crusade, lest his father die during his absence and his brother steal the throne. Likewise, Philip dared not go and leave Richard behind—he no longer feared the ailing Henry, but Richard had been a notable warrior since he was sixteen, aiding the young king's rebellion.

Henry advanced with only his two supporters, leaving the rest of his retinue behind. All three halted.

Philip spoke and beckoned to a shadowy follower to come forward with a cloak to spread on the grass for the invalid. Philip's show of pity failed to hide the delighted mockery beneath. Henry refused the mercy angrily.

The king of France turned to his clerk and ordered him to read out the terms. They were even worse than I expected. Henry must do homage in person to Philip, an act he had long managed to shun by sending sons in his place. He must acknowledge Richard as his heir throughout his empire, must pay a huge indemnity to Philip, and must give up certain key castles. And, of course, in the final insult, he must pardon all the nobles who had rebelled against him, and the list that the clerk handed to William Marshal was several pages long.

Henry had been my mentor. He had made my life. Seeing me first as a gawky youth, a crippled Saxon nothing, he had recognized my skill at enchantment and financed the rest of my education. The first task he had set me when I graduated as a sage had seemed to be a trivial matter, but turned out to be a major conspiracy. He had rewarded my success with a knighthood and the office of enchanter general. Now I watched my liege being destroyed, a once-mighty monarch being robbed of everything by a pair of greedy nobodies. I wept, but my tears fell far away.

Stone-faced, Henry heard the sentence, and then just muttered, "Agreed."

But, as he gave his son the kiss of peace, I heard him whisper something that sounded very much like a promise of revenge.

Then I heard someone calling my name from a great distance, felt someone shaking me. I fell out of my trance and was back at my desk in Oxford.

Lovise was beside me, holding my hand and regarding me with concern. "Darling! What were you doing? You were weeping, I was frightened. I thought I would never manage to waken you."

Feeling as if I had been beaten about the head with iron rods and then strangled, I scooped up my scattered wits. Such aftereffects show that a trance-inducing enchantment is badly worded and needs more work. A raging thirst burned in my throat.

"Need a drink," I mumbled.

She ran over to the table where I keep a carafe of wine and one of water. She filled a beaker with half of each and brought it to me as I struggled to sit up. I drained it.

"How long have you been gone?" Now she had jumped from worried to angry. "Lucky I found you! I brought down some invoices for you to approve."

Lovise not only supervised the healing classes in the College, but was herself the most sought-after women's healer in Oxford. She was no longer the sylphlike maiden I had married. Twenty-three years and four children had made her buxom, but she was still tall and blonde. Her eyes were still as blue as sapphires. And in my eyes, she was still the loveliest woman in England.

"I don't know," I said. "I didn't mean to go into a trance, I was just trying to hear how it sounded." I was babbling. "It's a very old enchantment, so it's oddly structured."

She peered at the vellum. "What does 'Myrddin Wyllt' mean?"

"It's a man's name." I recounted the horrors I had seen, and Lovise listened in amazement. She knew as much about enchantment as I did and could tell when rules were being broken. Only very rarely had we met a spell that could show visions, certainly none so detailed and credible. We had certainly never found any magic that could reach across the Narrow Sea.

"How far can you trust that vision? If it was a sending from Hell, you ought to burn the fair copy and all your notes immediately."

"But if I was seeing real events, then I have been shown a page of history turning, for obviously King Henry is very close to death."

And then we should have a new king—Lord Richard, surely. Please God, never his brother, Lord John!

Whether the vision had been sent from Heaven or Hell, I must decide what I should do about it. If that sounds like the peak of arrogance, coming from a former stable boy, then consider where time and fortune had brought him. Once a crippled Saxon in a land where anything of importance was spoken in French, I had risen to the office of Enchanter General of England. In Oxford I had founded and nurtured the finest college of purely secular knowledge in Christendom, and had collected the greatest library of what we still discreetly called "Ancient Song" but was in fact enchantment. My colleagues and I had driven the devil-worshiping Sons of Satan out of the country. We had organized the beneficial uses of enchantment throughout England.

I continued to enjoy the trust and approval of King Henry, who had later raised me to the peerage as Baron Durwin of Pipewell and appointed me to his privy council—me, the crippled son of a Saxon hostler, debating with the greatest lords of the land! What magic could top that? But the years were starting to tell on me, also. Harald, our eldest, was playing country gentleman now in Pipewell Manor, the estate the king had given me. Both girls, Iseut and Royse, were betrothed and gone to live with their future parents-in-law until they reached marriageable age, as is customary among the gentry. We missed them greatly.

That Henry was sure to die soon was barely a secret. Back in late May, as his health continued to deteriorate, he had flattered me with a summons to France in my capacity as a healer. I had known from the start that I would be unable to help him, because French enchanters were just as competent as English in the healing arts. I took Sage Wilbor of London with me as my cantor, and we did what we could to prescribe for the king, but his body was simply wearing out, and the war he was currently fighting was certainly not helping. Among his many troubles, he had an anal fistula that was starting to fester. What he should do was give his crown to his son, Lord Richard, and retire to die in peace in a monastery somewhere, but to tender that advice would be both useless and foolhardy. The king's rages were legendary.

When in doubt, I usually sought my wife's advice. "What do I do now, dear? The privy council already knows the king's health is very bad. Do I ride off to Winchester and inform the justiciar that it is much worse, and he has just surrendered to his foes?"

"I think," Lovise said with a fearsome frown, "that you should go straight back to bed. Your news is not urgent, because nothing will change until Henry actually dies. He is as tough as horseshoes, and you are in no fit shape to ride anywhere."

As usual, she was absolutely right.

I had been entranced longer than I realized, and needed the rest of the day in bed to recover. Even on the next day, Wednesday, I was not at my best, but I was still official master of the college, so I had to put on my finery and preside at a graduation ceremony, handing out sheepskin scrolls to newly qualified sages, cantors, and healers. The ceremony held a special joy for Lovise and me, because Lars, our younger son, was now a qualified cantor. When his familiar grin arrived before me, I repeated the customary congratulations, shook his hand, and muttered, "Don't celebrate too much; I may have an important job for you tomorrow."

He just smiled—down—at me, and said, "Whatever it is, I can do both, Lord Enchanter."

I made excuses and left the celebratory dinner early to go home and wrestle with the *Myrddin Wyllt* problem. I might need months of study to determine how trustworthy it was, and I would need to locate the flaws in it before it could be used without inflicting such painful aftereffects. Nevertheless, after long discussion, Lovise and I decided that I could not just ignore the warning. If Henry was near to death, then it was my duty to tell the justiciar, Ranulf de Glanville, who acted as regent when the king was out of the country. I knew that he was currently in Winchester, and so was Queen Eleanor, who had at least as much right to be informed.

I spent a couple of hours hunting for defects in the wording, and made some corrections. Another problem, of course, and a very common one with old manuscripts, was to know what melody to use. The words provided the rhythm, but after that we had to rely on experience—which means guesswork.

But just before we retired, I felt sufficiently recovered to ask Lovise to come back down to the workroom to help me with another enchantment, one that took much less toll of the chanter.

We still lived in the home that Queen Eleanor had given us when we were married, a modest house in the grounds of Beaumont Palace, outside Oxford. There we had raised our children, of whom only Lars was still at home. I had since developed part of the ground floor into a spacious workroom, thirty feet long. One entire wall of it was covered from floor to ceiling by shelves angled at forty-five degrees to make a collection of diamond-shaped boxes. In those were filed almost two thousand parchment scrolls, recording hundreds of incantations. Hobbling on my cane, I hunted down the one I wanted.

I untied it and handed the cantor's part to Lovise. She smiled when she recognized the opening words, *Loc hwær*, "Look where." This was the spell that elevated me to grandeur, for I had composed it myself, the first time anyone had created a new spell in centuries. Few people knew of its existence even yet, but it was a family treasure. It was a much simpler work than the *Myrddin Wyllt*, for it merely reported a person's present location. It showed no visions, but was powerful magic nevertheless.

"So who are we going to spy on this time?" she asked.

"Lord John." He and Richard were the last survivors of Henry's five legitimate sons. His many bastards were not eligible to inherit the crown. I did not know whether John had joined Richard's rebellion or remained loyal.

"You want to tell him the news also?" Lovise asked, with a hint of doubt that both amused and pleased me. Even then, Lord John's name smelled of perfidy.

"No, I'm hoping he will remain in ignorance for some time yet."

Loc hwær is a short incantation and we were both familiar with it. When we finished, she closed her eyes for a moment and then croaked, *"Nottingham heall,"* in the ancient cracked voice of a Wyrd, a voice that I knew well. Then she opened them and asked me what she had just said.

The news was welcome, and not surprising. Lord John owned not only Nottingham Castle but the whole county. What mattered to me was that he was a long way from both Oxford and London. Even tidings of great importance could travel no faster than a horse. By the time he heard of his father's death, it would be too late for him to make any effort to usurp the throne.

I was up before dawn preparing for the journey—tidying up some business that would not wait until I returned, and chanting a few Release spells. Most incantations are Repeat spells, which have to be chanted afresh every time, but Release spells can be sung beforehand and invoked with a word or two when needed. In effect I was loading arrows in my magical quiver, a practice I had found advisable back in the years when I had traveled all over England, collecting all the ancient spell books I could find. Although King Henry had made the roads of England much safer than they had been before he came to the throne, travel still had its risks. I had never had the misfortunate to meet up with highwaymen, but I always included at least one defensive spell, a weapon that could hurt more than a blow with my cane.

As soon as Lovise was available, I asked her to watch over me while I invoked the *Myrddin Wyllt* enchantment again. Knowing now that it would put me into a trance, I played safe and stretched out on the leather-padded couch I keep in my workroom for just that purpose. Then I began to chant my appeal to Carnonos, lord of forests, and soon the cool shadows of woodland closed around me. With them came forest dampness, the scents of moss and pines. My own voice faded into the sighing of wind in high treetops, and then gradually into the faint, distant singing of a choir. Towering trees had become the pillars and arches of a crypt.

I peered around in uncertain candlelight, and made out a group of men kneeling alongside a bier, on which lay a body already swathed in cere cloth. I recognized Sir William Marshall again, and Geoffrey the Bastard, still in faithful attendance on his father, but others were too deep in shadow for me to recognize. Geoffrey was murmuring a prayer. Although he was bishop-elect of Lincoln now, he was always referred to as the Bastard to distinguish him from the king's legitimate son of the same name. That other Geoffrey, the duke of Brittany, was dead by then, but the Bastard's name endured. Unlike Henry's legitimate sons, he had always stayed loyal.

The chill of the crypt seemed to cool even more, as a sense of loss ate into my soul. A world without Henry II would take a lot of getting used to.

But now I had a clear message to carry to Winchester: *The king is dead, long live the king.* Yet I lingered for a moment. The prayer ended, followed by a rustle of amens. The mourners began to rise and then stopped to listen. *Tap, tap.* . . . Like the tolling of some Tartarean death watch, the sound drew closer, louder, and gradually became recognizable as the noisy clank of sollerets on stone. Out of the darkness emerged a giant, huge and grim, pacing ever nearer. Candlelight glinted like frost on his hauberk, for even there he was wearing chain mail, although he had shed his sword and helmet before entering the church. Gog, Magog, Goliath . . . ? No, for this titan wore a surcoat adorned with three lions, *gules passant*, and everyone knew whose charge that was.

Nobody spoke. He stopped and stared down at his father's corpse. If he prayed, he did not move his lips, nor make the sign of the cross. After several ice-cold minutes, he nodded to Geoffrey, beckoned to Sir William to follow him, and walked away. Clink, clink, clink . . . into the darkness.

My question had been answered. I hauled myself out of the trance.

"That was quick," said a depressingly cheerful Lovise. "Didn't you get acceptance?" She handed me a beaker of water as I struggled to sit up.

I drank. I had the same raging thirst as before, but the headache was merely a vague throb behind my eyes, so my changes to the text had improved it. "I did. I saw all I needed. *The king is dead, long live the king!*" Belatedly I crossed myself and whispered an Ave.

Lovise did the same. "So you and I are the only ones in England who knows this! Isn't it treason to spy on the king?"

"If I say it is, will you report me to the justiciar?" Brief though the trance had been, I still needed a few moments to settle my wits.

"What will you do now?"

"Take the word to Winchester."

My wife inspected me critically. "You're getting old for breakneck long-distance trekking. Send a courier."

"The matter is too important." I stood up. "I shall present Lars to the queen, to celebrate his graduation."

She smiled. "He was very late coming home. Can you imagine the hangover he must have?"

"I can," I said. "But at seventeen he's indestructible."

I kissed my wife and went upstairs. Lars, understandably, was fast asleep, invisible except for a tangle of barley-pale hair on the pillow. I gave him a "God bless!" somewhat louder than usual.

The coverlet moved to expose one normally sky-blue eye, presently seeming more like a carmine sunset. People often commented how much Lars resembled me, but I could see little likeness between a dewy youth innocent of the world's malice and the wrinkled forty-five-year-old face that scowled at me out of my mirror every morning.

"And thee also, Father." He spoke in a hoarse whisper.

"Sorry to wake you when you've just gotten to sleep. I'm going on a very important outing and need a cantor. Are you capable of staying awake?"

The rest of his face appeared, unshaven and not a little haggard. He nodded, then winced as if he wished he hadn't. "Yes, sir."

"Are you capable of spending all day all the saddle?"

"All day?"

"Sixty miles or so."

His face twisted in horror. *In one day?*"

I laughed. "I think we can stretch it to two. We're going to Winchester to get the queen out of jail."

He threw off the cover. "How soon?"

"I'm just going to send for the horses."

"Do I have enough time to put some clothes on?"

Juvenile humor, but he was seventeen.

Sixty miles in two days is a heroic exploit, which I was secretly dreading. No knight rides out without a squire or two, and no enchanter without a cantor. There were many men in the College

I could have taken with me, but none I would trust as much as I trusted my own son. Besides, this would be a treat for Lars, to celebrate his graduation.

As soon as we had cleared the town and could ride abreast, he asked why I was in such a rush to visit Winchester.

"To inform Queen Eleanor that King Henry is dead."

He looked at me in shock. Before he could ask the obvious question, I blocked it. "I can't tell you how I know that, but I do. It's the greatest secret in England, and you are the second man in England to hear it. God save King Richard!"

"Amen. He died in France? But no enchantment will work across the sea . . ."

"Sorry, son. I mustn't tell you. Maybe one day."

He nodded, an adult now. We rode on through the summer fields and a morning already growing hot. Then Lars reasonably asked, "Father, *why* is the queen being kept in prison?"

It was a good question, and should have been asked years ago, but youngsters growing up tend to accept everything they see as normal. The sun rises in the morning, the king is fighting in France, the queen is in jail . . . Politics is the king's business.

"Because she bore too many sons."

"Huh? Woman are usually faulted for not bearing enough of them."

"Five in all, and five daughters—two daughters for King Louis when she was married to him and three for Henry—but girls just get married off. Sons cause trouble. Plantagenet sons do, anyway. Five: William, Henry, Richard, Geoffrey, and John. William died as an infant, but all the rest grew up as typical Plantagenet males, worthy of the lion, the family symbol: bellicose, greedy, and lecherous. Every one of them wanted his piece of their father's great empire, which he was never willing to give. He dispensed lots of fancy titles, but he never relinquished any real power. All four in their time curried favor with the king of France, who was always happy to make trouble. Henry died of camp fever while campaigning against his father. Richard is now our king. Geoffrey was trampled to death in a tournament three years ago, or so the French claim. And then there is Lord John."

I had cast his horoscope when he was born, and it was a horror.

"And the queen?"

"About sixteen years ago the Lords Henry, Richard, and Geoffrey—John was still a child—rose in rebellion, with the support of their mother. The king won in the end. He forgave his sons, but he could not forgive his wife, and she has been a prisoner, more or less, ever since."

Silence for a few minutes, as we went in single file past a loaded hay wain, then, "The new king isn't married, so Lord John is now his . . . um, heir presumptive?"

"Maybe. Geoffrey was older than John and he left a posthumous son named Arthur, who succeeded him as duke of Brittany. He must be two years old now."

Lars said, "Mm . . ." thoughtfully. A lot of people were going to be saying that now. Lord John was in his early twenties and the worst satyr of them all. The sooner King Richard married and produced a few sons of his own, the better for baby Arthur and the peace of England.

The urgency of the news we bore drove us like invisible whips. We could not have reached our destination in two days without changing our mounts several times at monasteries or priories on the way, for in those days every religious house was required to stable a few of the king's horses, and my rank let me claim what I needed. Lars had never seen me do this before and was impressed.

By noon I was feeling my age. Had I ever been a fresh-faced, jeweled-eyed kid like him? Had the world ever looked so glorious to me back then as it did to him now? Probably not. His legs were the same length. My father had been a Saxon hostler working for Norman monks; his was enchanter general for England, and a peer of the realm. Lars had won his cantor's cape at seventeen, which was younger than I had been, and now he was racing off with me on a mission of historic importance, carrying news that would change the face of Europe. The dust, the flies, the heat of early July—none of those meant anything to him. Lars was ready to pick up his horse and run with it.

We spent Thursday night in the chantry in Reading, roughly halfway. By sunrise on Friday, we were on the Winchester road again.

The summer sun was setting as we spurred our mounts to a gallop so we could reach the city gates before they closed, which we managed only because the guards saw us coming and waited for us. Perhaps the quality of our horses impressed them more than our dusty, disheveled selves. I knew Winchester well, and from there I led Lars by the fastest street to the castle. The curfew was still ringing.

But the castle gate was closed.

Lars said, "Oh-oh!"

We reined in. In a sling on my back I carried my favorite walking cane, a stout oaken one with a silver handle, given to me by Queen Eleanor herself. I now drew this and pounded the ferrule on the studded timbers of the gate. The spy hole opened and a whiskery face appeared behind the grill.

"Who goes there?"

"Baron Durwin de Pipewell and his son."

"Come back in the morning."

"I bring urgent news for the queen."

"Come back in the morning."

"Varlet! I am a member of the king's council."

"And you'll still be that in the morning."

He might have yielded had I told him I must see the justiciar, not mentioning the queen, but it was more likely that his orders excluded me specifically. The justiciar and I were old foes, and he knew I favored the queen whenever I could.

"Open this gate or you will regret it!"

His reply was fortunately cut off as he slammed the spy hole shut.

I was bone weary and now red-hot furious. What I should have done was to go around to the postern gate at the rear of the castle complex and open that with the Release spell, *Cambrioleur*. I had done that before. This time I didn't. Instead I again struck the gate with my staff, only this time I gave it three strokes for effect, and then declaimed the trigger for a spell I had discovered years ago and often found useful: "*Geat, opena!*"

The castle gate was wide enough and high enough to admit a loaded hay wain, so its instant obedience was dramatic. Bolts and hasps and hinges tore loose from the timbers, and the whole great edifice toppled inward. Half a dozen men-at-arms screamed in fright and leaped back to avoid being crushed. The impact when it hit the ground was louder than thunder and must have been audible throughout all Winchester.

Lars said, "*God's legs!*"—a foolish, if not blasphemous, expression that had become popular because the late king had favored it.

We fought with our horses for a moment. As soon as we had them calmed, I said, "Come!" and urged mine across the flattened gate. The shocked guards stared at us owlishly, and made no effort to stop us. Doubtless they were wondering who was going to pay for the damage. I was relieved to see that none of them had been hurt, for we would have had to waste time chanting healing spells for them. I headed in the direction of the King's House.

"Your mother," I told Lars, "will skin me if she hears that I have set you such a bad example. Understand that I can get away with such nonsense once in a while, just so long as I don't hurt people, but that's because of my title. Other sages cannot. Those who display their powers in public can be torn to pieces for being devil worshipers."

He grinned. "I'm trying to imagine Mother opening a door that way."

The image of the imperturbable Lovise ever doing any such thing made me laugh, as he had intended. "Your mother is a very competent sage. She could perform the enchantment, and so could you, if you knew the spell. But neither of you could get away with it as I can."

To be honest, I was already feeling ashamed of that grandiose display, and sought to excuse it. "The justiciar and I are not on the best of terms, and he may try go keep me from access to the queen tonight. He will be less inclined to do so since I have demonstrated my . . . let's just say since I have shown the strength of my feelings in this matter."

Suitably impressed, Lars nodded.

Winchester Castle is quite new, having been built by King Henry himself, and is a favorite royal residence—or prison, as it was then. It includes a chapel, herb gardens, and so on; it lacks the grimness of most fortresses. Already the ruckus I had caused had brought scores of people out to look at the wreckage.

As we dismounted at the door of the King's House, a fancily dressed flunky appeared to greet us. His tonsure showed that he was some sort of cleric, probably a deacon, for he was not garbed as a monk or priest. Although I did not recall him, he clearly knew me.

His bow was barely more than a nod. "Peace be with you, my lord."

"And with you," I said. "I bring an urgent message for the queen."

"The lord justiciar has ordered that any communications for Her Grace will be passed through him."

"You are aware that I, too, am a member of the king's council?"

"Yes, my lord."

"Then fetch Lord de Glanville. I know he is in residence at the moment."

Before he could respond, the man in question appeared at his back. His smile was sweet as lemon juice. "I'll deal with this, Patrick. Have someone see to their horses. Enter, my lord."

I followed him, Lars came hurrying after, and I did not forbid him. Glanville led us to the St. George Room, a pleasantly appointed meeting place, growing dark as twilight faded.

Ranulf de Glanville was elderly now, white-bearded and starting to stoop, but still subtle and sly. He was a distinguished lawyer, although he had led armies in his day, having notably accepted the surrender of the king of Scots at the battle of Alnwick. As chief justiciar of England, he acted as regent whenever the king was in France, fighting against King Philip and whichever of his own sons happened to be rebelling at the moment—which had been the case for much of the last seventeen or so years. Ranulf and I clashed often in the council and detested each other; his current expression showed that the situation had not changed.

The hot day had left the room as stifling as a warm blanket. He went over to the window and threw back the shutters to let in some air, then turned to face us with his back to the light.

Discounting Lars with a glance, he directed his attention to me. "I am minded to throw you in the dungeon for damaging crown property." Had the justiciar been on the bench and I in the box, his expression would have signaled a coming death penalty.

"Singlehandedly sacking a royal fortress? The king of France will be amused to hear of it."

Having no answer to that, he bared his teeth. "So what brings you here, devil worshiper?"

"I have news that must be imparted to Her Grace before anyone else."

"As you very well know, the queen is not allowed to receive visitors, and the king specifically forbade her to have any communication with you."

"Nevertheless, my news be must delivered in person."

"And I forbid you to see her."

That was the opening I had been hoping for. "On whose authority?"

"The king's."

"No, my lord. *That you do not have.*"

His expression was hidden in shadow, but he crossed himself. I nodded, and he would see my smile.

"Wait here." He strode across the room and out.

"Clever," Lars murmured. "You haven't actually told him, but now he knows. Why must the queen hear it first?"

"Because she is the queen, and because Lord de Glanville is, and always has been, lickspittle trash."

Two pages hurried in with tapers and began lighting candles all around the room. Dawn followed. Lars looked around, studying the padded chairs set against the walls and the paintings, nodding to himself. My son fancied that he had an eye for art. He went over to the tapestry of the dragon slaughter that gave the room its name.

"Very fair," he said.

"However fair, a cage is still a cage."

More pages brought washing water and towels so we could refresh ourselves. Next came wine and ale and a small table already laden with food and drink. I discovered that I was hungry. Lars always was. We did not sit, just stood by the table and gobbled. We both chose ale over wine to quench our thirsts.

Suddenly she was there, ennobling the whole room—Eleanor, Queen of England, hereditary duke of Aquitaine, duchess of Normandy, countess of Maine, Anjou, Nantes, Poitou, and several other places. Leaning on my cane, I sank to my knees. Lars was there before me.

In her youth she had been a legendary beauty. Now she was, incredibly, sixty-seven years old, and yet she looked thirty years younger. Part of that was artifice, for a wimple concealed her neck and a French cap her hair, but few lines marred her face, and her onyx eyes were as quick and bright as ever. Her gown had once been bright scarlet, but too many years and too many washings had worn it threadbare, and it had never had the trimmings of lace and ermine that a queen's should have. She had probably retired before I arrived, because a captive has little use for evenings, and if so she must have dressed with great haste, yet that did not show.

"Baron Pipewell!" she said. "My faithful Durwin! This is a great and most unexpected pleasure."

"For me just seeing you is an overwhelming joy, Lady Queen, but I come bearing very sad news."

"How wonderful! I can't wait to hear it. Do rise, both of you. Lovise is well, I hope? Present this handsome young man!"

"Lars, madam, my younger son and today my cantor."

"Lars. How beautiful he is! He looks very much like you did, that evening when you burst in upon us in Beaumont Palace, breathing fire and raving about treason and Satanism." She

22

smiled at Lars, who was turning as red as her gown and seemed as tongue-tied as I had been when I first met her, in Burton, a quarter of a century ago. "Does he sing as melodiously as you do, Enchanter General?"

"Better than I ever did," I said. "And he is quite facile on the gittern." Lars shot me an angry glance, guessing that one of us might be required to perform shortly and I had just passed the honor on to him.

"Now to business," the queen said. She crossed to a chair and sat, adjusting her robe. I realized that her long-time companion, Amaria, was present and gave her a brief smile of acknowledgment. In Eleanor's presence other women always seemed irrelevant.

Ranulf de Glanville had followed her, and was standing just inside the doorway.

She glanced at him under her suggestive black lashes, then back at me. "I presume," she added, "that what you have to say also concerns the justiciar?"

"It does, Lady Queen."

"Then he may remain to hear it. Now break my heart, Enchanter General."

"Lady Queen, your husband has been called to judgment."

"That won't take long. He's in Hell already—I'll vouch for it. When and where did this gratifying manifestation of Our Lord's benevolence occur?"

"In bed, in Chinon. He had been failing for several days."

"Chinon? So he truly managed to die in bed? Justiciar, do you accept Lord Durwin's news?"

Ranulf had shrunk. "This is truth, upon your honor, Baron?"

For me, that was the highlight of the evening—that I, born into poverty, a despised Saxon, crippled in childhood, had risen so high that the current ruler of England must accept my word on a matter of state.

"Upon my honor, my lord, King Henry breathes no more."

He bowed to Eleanor. "Then you are no longer a prisoner, Lady Queen. By your leave?" He turned and walked out.

She beamed in delight and turned to me. "How came you so soon by this wisdom?"

"Your Grace may recall that long-ago day when you so graciously received a very young Saxon cantor with a game leg? You charged me to cast a horoscope for your son, the Lord Richard, as he then was." Who now was so much more.

"And a very sound horoscope it was. Yet I directed you to leave nothing out. When you predicted that he would become a king, you did not specify what realm he was to rule." Her coal-black eyes had a trick of looking straight through to a man's soul. "But you knew, didn't you? You knew it would be England."

"With respect, madam, I did not. The stars are never so specific. He might have been elected king of Jerusalem, or German Emperor, or have married a great heiress." Besides, at that time Lord Richard's elder brother, Henry, had been alive, and I had not dared to predict his early death. Now he was dead, their father was also dead, but King Richard lived. I had known for years—everyone knew—that Richard was, and had always been, Queen Eleanor's favorite son, just as John, the youngest, had been his father's.

I was relieved to see her smile creep back. "That was what I told him when he grew up enough to read your convoluted Latin. Nor did you say *when* he would receive this unnamed crown. Did you know that also?"

"Not the exact day, madame. The planets' movements among the spheres are not predictable so many years ahead, and horoscopes can only predict dark times and bright times. We all have those, until in the fullness of God's plan for us, we enter a dark time that we do not survive."

She frowned, suddenly wary. "But you do have more information now than just the stars? You are quite certain that I am now a widow?"

"I am. I assure you that the information I give you came from an extremely reliable source and will be confirmed by mundane means within a day or two. King Richard . . ." I paused, hearing myself utter that strange combination of words. "His Grace has heard the news. I expect his couriers are already on their way to you." I wasn't about to disclose how I knew all this, even if she asked directly, but she knew better than to do so. Queens must not be seen to meddle in the occult. Everyone accepted and believed in horoscopes, so those were safe. Even the Pope employs astrologers.

She clapped her hands in delight. "Wonderful! You are Merlin Redux, Lord Durwin."

"I have always ranked Your Grace ahead of Queen Guinevere." Queen Eleanor's fondness for Arthurian romances was well known. Nor had she lost her skill in steering banter along safe lines. She had not called me Lancelot, who had been the one to rescue Guinevere from captivity.

"And to be flattered again! I had almost forgotten how much I enjoyed flattery. Amaria, bring me some of that wine, and then we'll all drink the new king's health! After that," she added mischievously, "Cantor Lars de Pipewell will sing something joyful for us."

Mourning was not in her nature.

Aware that both Lars and I were exhausted, Eleanor neither kept us long nor made him sing for her. We were granted a fine room, with a bed that any innkeeper would have considered large enough for four. It was comfortable enough, except that the straps squeaked. Lars, who would normally sleep until noon if permitted, began to thrash about just before dawn, anxious to explore a new place—and a castle, yet!

Still aching from the previous day's long ride, I growled like an angry bear. That stilled him for about two minutes. Then he decided he needed the chamber pot and bounced out of bed with excessive energy, making the straps scream. I gave up hope of more sleep.

The queen, we were informed, would receive well-wishers at Terce, which gave me a couple of hours to show my son around the castle and some of the town. Inevitably that led to visiting the town's chantry, which was one of the first I had licensed to teach and qualify adepts, healers, and sages. It was ranked very close behind Oxford itself.

The dean of Winchester Chantry was my old friend and companion, Sage Eadig, so this was almost like a family gathering. I asked after Enid, he after Lovise. I proudly showed off Lars in his cantor's white cape, and Eadig checkmated me by sending for his eldest daughter, Gwynda, who had been awarded hers a month ago. I explained that we had come to make an official inspection of his establishment, starting with the quality of the ale. He led us to the refectory, which was currently empty, except for a couple of servants preparing the tables for dinner.

Lars and Gwynda had played together as children, but had not met for four or five years. Since then, both had undergone changes that interested the other, and they settled off in a corner together to engage in what appeared to be a profoundly engrossing conversation.

Eadig and I exchanged amused parental smiles and carried our ale out of earshot. He had never been tall and now was close to tubby, with his flaxen hair thinned to a mist, but he was ever quick-witted, courageous, and trustworthy.

"I was expecting you," he remarked, "because I heard you sneaking into the castle yester-eve. I sent a novice to find out if this was the end of the world, or if something more important might be happening. By all the suffering saints, what did you think you were doing? It's the talk of the town. All England will . . . no?"

"No. England will have more important things to talk about." I raised my ale. "Long live King Richard."

My long-ago assistant nodded. "That's what the gossip says this morning—that the king's wizard came galloping to tell the queen. So it's true? Henry has . . . when?"

"King Henry died in his bed, in Chinon Castle."

When I did not add more, Eadig's steel-colored eyes silently dissected me. He knew me too well. "When?"

"Very recently."

"Then you must know how to fly? Or you have a spy at court and communicate with *Despero in extremis*?"

"*Despero* doesn't work across the Narrow Sea. I've tried it."

"Then you must have a new incantation, none I ever heard of."

"As the old adage says, two can keep a secret if one of them is dead." I grinned to show I was teasing. I knew I could discuss this with Eadig as I could with almost no one else, but I would not dare trust even him with the incantation itself. If it ever escaped into the world at large, it would create chaos. "Not new, very old. That's why it is so powerful, of course. It purports to be written by Myrddin Wyllt."

With his ale almost at his lips, Eadig paused long enough to say, "God's legs!" before taking a drink.

"Quite. I'm still discovering what it can do, but I already know that it could almost be considered black magic, because if anyone could spy on anyone else at any time, the world would go insane. Lovers, merchants, soldiers—none of them could hide anything from anyone. This is one of a very small collection of extremely dangerous enchantments that I will pass on to my successor as enchanter general and to no one else."

"No need to apologize. I wish we could call back some of the spells we teach our pupils. To King Richard! Long may he reign."

We drank.

"You are a marvel," Eadig said, wiping foam. "So you're digging into old Welsh lore now?"

"No. Myrddin was Scottish. Why are you grinning, friend?"

A stranger would not likely have detected the alleged grin, and he removed it at once. "I was going to say I hope you didn't pay too much for it, but it sounds as if you didn't."

Now I was mystified and it was his turn to read my expression.

"'Myrddin' is pronounced 'Mirthin'. I can't say it right. I'll get Enid to pronounce it for you. It's the old Welsh name for Merlin. 'Wyllt' means 'wild' and refers to the wild woods."

I was stunned. Had I known that meaning of Myrddin, I would have thrown the old vellums away as worthless fakes. But an incantation that could look across the Narrow Sea was certainly not that. A spell composed by the genuine Merlin was an amazing find.

"I paid nothing for it," I said, "except many hours of translating it into a legible text. I found it in a ruined fort at Rhuddlan."

"In North Wales."

"Right. The first time I tried chanting it, it showed me King Henry himself. He was obviously at death's door. I already knew that he was entering a very dark time."

"Casting the monarch's horoscope is high treason, Enchanter."

I didn't deny that I had done that. "There was always a chance that he would make it through the dark time, as he had survived so many others in the past, but two days ago I learned that he had yielded up his soul. I called for Lars to hasten with me here, to Winchester. I enjoyed the journey with him. He's grown up so suddenly that I feel I hardly know him now."

Eadig noticed my clumsy effort to change the subject, but did not object. "Children always do."

"True. And the size of him! Takes after his namesake, Lovise's brother."

"Gwynda hopes to pursue her training as a sage. She's very anxious to study at Oxford. You will have room for one more?"

"For your daughter? Of course. I can still exert some gentle influence. There is much less prejudice than there used to be against female sages. Lovise set a fine example. She never had trouble mixing wisdom and motherhood."

After a pause, Eadig said, "So what happens now? Lord—I mean King—Richard is sworn to go on crusade, to drive the heathens out of Jerusalem. When will he do that?"

"He's not the sort of man to be deflected from his preferred course of action," I said. "It will depend on Philip of France. He's a man not to be trusted."

"Perhaps Richard will send Lord John in his stead?" The question was ambiguous.

I glanced around to make certain that no one was within earshot. "How much will you wager?"

Old friends—we both grinned. Lord John was nobody's idea of a martial hero.

Eadig snorted. "Every time that billy goat comes to Winchester, we lock up our wives and daughters. Women seem to find him absolutely irresistible."

I knew Eadig well enough to know that he was hinting that the new king's brother used black magic. I pulled a face and said, "Are you sure?"

"No. Just suspicious."

"I'll look into it," I promised.

29

"I expect you'll be busy, with a new king and all."

"I'm always busy." Which reminded me that I must return to the castle and wait upon Queen Eleanor. She had called me Merlin Redux, which suddenly seemed truer than I had known at the time. We broke up the other tete-a-tete, and I dragged my cantor away, not quite literally.

"Nice girl?" I said as we stalked along the street.

"All right," Lars said with a shrug. "I was trying to talk her into coming to Oxford. Why are girls always so stubborn?"

Back at the castle, we found well-wishers swarming like bees. Ranulf de Glanville had remained at his post, for he was still chief justiciar, but he must have spread the word to his friends. No doubt the worst of them were already packing, planning to flee from the new king's vengeance, while the optimists among them rushed to Winchester in the hope of currying favor after years of treating their queen as a leper.

I saw many that I knew, and was greeted exuberantly by many who yesterday would have rather thrown me in their moats. Some of the glory of my news had stuck to me, and the queen added to it by sending for me before all the other supplicants.

I expressed a desire to return to Oxford at once, but she bade me remain in Winchester for a few days. She then sat me down on her right and Glanville on her left, and proceeded to keep us there for hours, while she received all the fawning toadies and accepted their oaths of loyalty in her son's name. Those who saw me as an upstart Saxon turd smiled and bowed and kept their contempt warm on the hob for another day. Seemingly oblivious of how she might be storing up trouble for me, Eleanor was in the seventh heaven of delight at being a queen again, being in touch with the world, wielding power. She invited a few of her especial favorites to stay on for a small celebration.

Far into the night the party continued. Required to play the gittern and sing, Lars acquitted himself well. A page brought him a gratuity which popped his eyes, so Eleanor had acquired money from somewhere.

One of my own troubles arrived that evening as Lars and I were saying our prayers before climbing into our squeaky bed again. The door flew open without a knock, and in strode a young man, not tall but heavyset, extravagantly dressed in silks and satins and glowing with the confidence of high rank. He carried a lantern, which he set down on the table as if he intended to stay awhile.

We both sprang to our feet. Perhaps we should have completed our orisons first, but for all we had known the intruder was armed and dangerous. We both wore only our small clothes, meaning next to nothing in summer.

Lars opened his mouth to roar, but I sank to my knees again, reflecting that this time I was more honoring the Devil than God. Puzzled, Lars followed my example.

"So sorry to interrupt your perversions," Lord John said mockingly. "You," he told Lars, "out!" He jerked a thumb at the still-open door.

Both startled and furious, Lars looked to me.

"Do as His Grace says, Son."

So then Lars guessed who this newcomer was, with curly hair of Plantagenet red, distinctive even in the uncertain lantern light, so he jumped up and bowed, using the flowery contortions of a full court bow, which were absurd in his near-nudity. He scooped up his clothes and left, closing the door softly.

By his family's standards, Lord John was short, a foot shorter than the new king. Once he had been King John, but only briefly, because when he was eleven years old, his father had given him Ireland. Only three people truly believed that Ireland was

Henry's to give, the third one being the Pope. As soon as he reached eighteen and was knighted, John had been sent off to claim his inheritance. His efforts to convince the Irish that he was their God-given ruler failed so abysmally that he managed to alienate every man on the island, natives and Norman squatters both. It was after he fled back to the safety of England that his father named him John Lackland. It was unwise for anyone else to address him as such. I must be careful; he did not seem to be armed, but he was certainly dangerous.

He took the only stool, leaving me on my knees.

"Truly your son?"

"Yes, my lord."

"Such a relief! I thought I would have to denounce you. They castrate sodomists, you know. You have told my mother that my father died on Thursday. How did you, in Oxford, learn of this so quickly?"

I was very tempted to ask him how he had done the same thing, because I knew he had been in Nottingham on Wednesday evening. He did not know that I knew that, of course. How had he arrived in Winchester in three days? I would have guessed that to be impossible, even for a twenty-two-year-old renowned for a fanatical love of hunting. His fancy clothes showed that he had changed on arriving, but he had brought a strong odor of horse with him and his face was still filthy with road dust. He could not have set out any earlier than Lars and I left Oxford; he could not possibly have learned of his father's death by mundane means. He could not have made that ride without the aid of some sort of conjuration.

"By enchantment, my lord. That is my profession and my duty."

"You were spying on him? That's a hanging offense at least."

"My duties as enchanter general include advising the king of significant events. When His Grace is overseas, I report to

Regent de Glanville. I knew that both he and the queen were here, so I hastened here at once."

"That is no answer. Don't mince words with me, devil worshiper."

"My lord, I was not spying on the king, but I knew by the arts of my profession that he had died."

Lackland narrowed his eyes for a moment, aware that he was not intimidating me, at least not yet. "We only have your word for that. How do I know you're telling the truth?"

"Castration and hanging would be a pleasure compared to what your noble mother would do to me if she learned that I had lied to her."

His laugh sounded quite genuine. No one ever denied that John could be charming when he wished. "So true! And now my brother is king? He doesn't give a spit for England, you know. The only lands he cares about are Aquitaine, Poitou, Anjou, Normandy, and the other French ones." He shrugged. "Richard can't speak above a dozen words of English. I speak it well, don't I?" He had been doing so since he came in.

"Extremely well, my lord."

"So Richard will undoubtedly appoint me regent, to run England for him."

Hope and pray that he would not be so stupid!

"He has sworn the crusaders' oath, my lord, so he will have to make some such arrangement for all his possessions."

Pouting, John said, "Pah! Mother, you think? A woman ruling England? My grandmother tried that and made a total dung heap of it. Besides, the old bag can't last much longer. When she heads off to Hell, he'll have no other choice than me. I am, after all, his heir."

No mention of their nephew, Lord Arthur? Many people would think he had a stronger claim.

"Richard is a great butcher," John continued. "Massacres are his forte—peasants, towns, other peoples' troops, anyone who annoys him. He's never happy unless he's building himself a new castle or sacking someone else's. Yet he is as naive as a baby. King Philip plays him like a gittern. He convinced Richard that Father was planning to disinherit him and leave everything to me. That's what started this latest war."

This was fairly close to the truth as I knew it, and I wasn't inclined to argue. I was still waiting to find out what my visitor wanted of me. Almost certainly I would have to refuse him, and people who crossed any male Plantagenet were wise to wear their chain mail to bed.

He regarded me for a moment in silence, then said, "I hear you can smite castles with a wave of your hand."

"I did yesterday, but King Philip will surely hear of it. France has sages too, and they can put warding spells on all his castle gates."

"Then why haven't you been putting them on our castle gates, Enchanter General? Shouldn't that be part of your duties?"

"Because it would be an intolerable nuisance in peacetime. The guards would have to know the password to open them, so the secret would inevitably leak. Only when enemies approach is the time to ward them, my lord."

Another instant change of subject: "I have a small problem, Baron Durwin. You could help me with it."

"I should be glad to do so if it is possible."

"Quite possible. There is a certain fair young maiden whom I most grievously wish to mount. You could supply me with means to turn her icy refusal into feverish desire?"

Remembering Eadig's hints that morning I was startled, and must have looked it. Had Lackland been spying on us, just as I had spied on the kings' parley? If Eadig's suspicions were correct, why was Lord John asking me for help in his Satanic rapes? Fortunately he would have expected me to look surprised and shocked. I decided that he was just testing me.

"I could, my lord, but then I would have to denounce both you and myself for using black magic. Detecting and stamping out Satanism are my principle duties."

"And who decides what magic is black?" He was clever.

"Ultimately the Church does."

"And in the meantime Durwin of Pipewell will decide?" His pale eyes studied me for a very long moment. "I am the heir to England and sundry other domains. I am a very dangerous man to cross, Saxon."

"I do not doubt that, my lord, but I fear the Devil more. I will never dabble in black magic, not at any price."

He leaned forward so his eyes were close to, and level with, mine. "So you say, but you walk on the rim of Hell, Enchanter— day in and day out. You snatch your powers from Satan, like a mouse stealing crumbs beside a sleeping cat, but this cat knows you are there and one day the paw will strike. Then you will fall off that narrow edge, on the wrong side. When I was born, you cast my horoscope."

"I did."

"I want to see it."

"I do not have it. I gave it to your honored mother four days after your birth. I never keep copies of horoscopes." I still had my notes, of course, but saw no reason to say so.

My continuing defiance reddened his cheeks. "Then answer me one question, Saxon. Did the stars tell you that I will one day be king of England?"

Now I had to pause and think. "I'm sure you are aware, lord, that the stars do not make such specific prophecies. They merely warn of good times or dark times."

"But Thursday, for instance, must have seemed a very good time for Richard and a very bad time for Father?"

"I expect so," I said, seeing where this was going.

"You have cast both my horoscope and my brother's. Is there a similar match in our future, a very bad time for him and a very good one for me?"

I decided that lying to him would do more harm than good in the long run. With a sigh, I said, "Yes, my lord, they did. You will have to be patient, but it does seem that one day you will wear the crown of St. Edward." *And may God have mercy on us then.*

The following morning, I went back to the chantry, leaving Lars still safely asleep. The sick were already lining up at the door, but my green cape gained me immediate entry, and I asked for Dean Eadig. Seeing no sign of Gwynda, I wondered if her absence had anything to do with Lord John's presence in town.

Eadig received me in a small consultation room—a couch, a stool, and a solid soundproof door. Neither of us sat down. "You have new worries?" he asked right away.

"Possibly. You must know some workers in the castle stables?"

He nodded. Winchester is not huge and impersonal, like London.

"Lord John rode in last night. I should dearly like to know who came with him."

Eadig looked at me as if I were moon-howling crazy. "All two or three hundred of them? He is rarely discreet about his state, Enchanter!"

"In this case I'll bet he came with a very small train. I'm especially thinking about anyone who might be an enchanter."

"Ah!" Now I made sense, yet still Eadig looked puzzled. "There isn't a landowner of any worth in England who doesn't employ a house sage or two. I've always suspected that you kept a pretty close tally of them."

"I do," I admitted. "And I know most of them personally, because all but a few old-timers studied in Oxford. But I cannot recall any who work for Lord John—which is odd, because the high and mighty usually ask me to refer sages to them. He probably employs some Frenchman, or Frenchmen. If I knew their names, I could ask Couché about them." Armand Couché was the king's enchanter general for his French domains.

"I'll see what we can do," Eadig promised. "So you think Lackland is dabbling in something he shouldn't?"

"As you said, the notches in his bedposts certainly suggest that—he makes his late father look like a nervous nun. That, and the fact that he seems to travel faster than a stooping peregrine. Don't quote me on that, please."

"I never heard of a conjuration for traveling fast, Enchanter."

"Neither have I." That was partly what was rankling. I thought I knew every valid spell in the kingdom, certainly all the white magic, and I had copies of most of the black locked away in the crypt in Oxford. A go-like-the-wind conjuration would be enormously valuable. I could finance the entire college by marketing that to major landowners, whose estates are often scattered all over the realm. My other worry was that if John Lackland was using such lore, what else did he have that I didn't?

Back at the castle, I learned that he had already left, bound for France to do homage to his brother. I suspected from Queen Eleanor's icy demeanor when she told me this, that he had not asked her permission. That raised—but did not answer—an interesting question about who had precedence: the king's mother or his heir presumptive? And when Richard named an heir designate, who would it be? John or baby Arthur of Brittany?

The traditions of inheritance in England were not necessarily the same as those in his French domains.

I spent most of that day witnessing oaths of loyalty, as I had the day before. That evening, Lars mentioned that he had a message for me from his Honorary-Uncle Eadig.

"Been back to the chantry, have you?" I asked.

Baby blue eyes are wonderful for expressing innocence. "Well, I have nothing to do here, and I thought they might need an extra cantor, what with all these people jamming into the town just now."

"Quite. Did they? Or was one of their cantors able to take some time off?"

"We went for a walk together. You want the message, Father?"

"Tell me."

"Dean Eadig said that the man you were asking about arrived with a single attendant, a squire named Bran of Tara. He says Bran's often been here before, but no one seems to know anything more about him."

A king's brother traveling with a single attendant was a bizarre notion in itself, almost enough to confirm my suspicions—mere abbots have been known to lead armies of fifty. Bran was neither a French name nor an English one, and where in the world was Tara?

Although the messenger had made wondrous speed from Chinon, it was Thursday before King Richard's letters arrived, brought by a man I knew and respected, William Marshal. I was much surprised by this, because Sir William had been one of King Henry's closest confidants—the aides known as *familiares*, a group to which I had been honored to belong for many years. I had expected King Richard to send one of his own cronies. The fact that the new king had accepted William Marshal's oath of fealty so quickly showed the very high respect in which he was held. But William was also a shrewd judge of which side to butter his bread.

I was anxious to speak with him, but Queen Eleanor received him at once, wanting to hear details of her husband's passing and the current situation in France. It was a long time before she gave William his leave, and night had fallen when he won free of all the fawning courtiers wanting news.

Lars and I were standing on the battlements, enjoying the evening's coolness and studying summer stars in a moonless sky: Deneb and Vega, Aquila and Capricornis. Despite his size, William could move quietly, and we both jumped when the familiar voice came out of the darkness near my right shoulder.

"God be with you, Enchanter."

"And with you, Sir William."

"And . . . Lars, is it? Gods's knuckles, lad, you've grown! I gather that your sorcery worked well, Enchanter. My trip was barely necessary." There was a sliver of threat in his voice. William had always upheld his reputation with ferocity and I had just upstaged him.

"I am certain that you have brought much more news than I could convey. I congratulate you on gaining the new king's trust so soon. That speaks volumes for your abilities."

Like all knights of the slash-and-slice type, William was extremely touchy about his honor, which made him susceptible to flattery. He laughed. "Especially when I almost slew him outside Le Mans last month. I had him at the point of my lance, and he not armored! I killed his horse instead."

"Thank God!" And quick thinking, William.

"Could you chant another spell for me tonight, just a small one?"

"Of course we can. If we didn't bring the right enchantment with us, the city chantry will certainly have whatever you need."

His chuckle in the darkness sounded embarrassed. "It's a minor wound, and not earned in honorable battle. King Richard enjoined Gilbert Pipart and me to deliver his letters. We rode through Anjou, Maine, and Normandy. When we reached Dieppe, we jumped aboard a boat, and a plank in the deck burst under us. Pipart broke his arm and had to stay there. I scraped my leg a bit. And tomorrow I must ride to London."

I said, "Saints, man! After a journey like that can't you rest a day or two here?"

William's hand thumping my shoulder felt like a falling chimney pot. "I have to collect a bride, my friend. The old king promised her to me, and the new one has confirmed it—Isabel of Striguil, no less!"

I whistled, for even I had heard of the fair maid of Striguil. Was that how Richard had bought William the incorruptible?

William was sprung from minor gentry. His grandfather had been Henry I's marshal, meaning keeper of the king's horses, and had been succeeded by his son, so that the title had become their family name. The current marshal was William's older brother. By tradition and need, second sons become warriors, with third sons entering the clergy.

As a natural-born fighter, William had won acceptance into the retinue of the young king and been knighted. He had rapidly acquired a reputation in the lists, which were much more rough-and-tumble deadly in those days than they became later. When the young king rebelled against his father, William stayed loyal to his lord and was included in the pardon that followed. Taking William with him, the young king went off for some dozen years of knight-erranting and jousting. William became the most famous and admired knight in Christendom, so that no man dare meet him in the lists. After Henry died, William fulfilled his deceased lord's deathbed request and went on pilgrimage in his stead to Jerusalem, where he could slaughter Saracens instead of de-horsing Christians. On returning to England, he swore fealty to King Henry. And now that he had outlived another liege, he had been coaxed into Richard's service, and granted the honor and riches of Striguil.

William was in his middle forties, like me, and by then most knights must seek less strenuous employment, because their joints creak, their bones are crooked from badly-set breaks, and too many dents in their helms have jellied their wits. He was still in better shape than most, because he had ever been the best, always doing more damage than taking it. He had made immense fortunes in prize money and doubtless had spent every penny of all of them. His problem was a common one, and the solution to it must always be land, the source of all wealth.

In England—but not France—whenever any of the king's vassals die without adult male issue, his widow and orphans become wards of the king. He uses them as prizes to reward his older fighting men, who will breed another generation of staunch warriors. Isabel had been waiting for years to learn her fate, for her inheritance was huge and her beauty legendary. Striguil Castle was strategically located on the Welsh border, so Henry had perhaps been saving her for the greatest of his warriors; much more surprising was the fact that Richard had at once agreed to honor his father's promise—that was an even greater tribute to William's reputation. Or possibly to his nego-tiating skill, which was considerable.

Although we were the same age, William and I, any pair less alike would be hard to imagine. He lived a life of blood and steel, I one of fusty old books and music. He was universally honored, I was largely despised and distrusted as a worker in dark arts. He was a huge and ferocious man, I was a cripple. And yet we had become friends! We had met first when he followed the

Young Henry, and from time to time since, whenever he came to England or on my rare trips to France; we had met in council or just sitting around waiting on our betters, as courtiers always do. I like to think we hit it off because we recognized each other as basically honest, which is a rare attribute in the corridors of kings.

Down in our chamber, Lars and I discovered that what William dismissed as a scrape would have put most men in bed for a week. The healing enchantment I had in my baggage was not the one I would have chosen, but I knew it would work, so we sang it, and it did.

"All it needs now is some good English ale," our patient declared, adjusting the pillows so he could lean back comfortably on the bed. "That pissy French wine muddles a man's head too fast."

I took that as a hint to dispose of the witness, so I bade Lars go and find what was needed. Confident that he would know not to be too fast about it, I then settled on the stool and returned William's businesslike stare.

"I'm told Lord John got here just a day after you did," he said.

Aha! So we scented the same quarry, William and I. I nodded.

"He was in France a month or so ago. Then he vanished. His father was worried about him. I can guess how you learned the news, but how did he?"

"I don't know. I know for a fact—but I pray you not to spread this around—that he was in Nottingham on Wednesday evening, and here on Saturday night."

"Godamercy! How did he find out so soon, then?"

How indeed? "That is something I intend to discover," I said. "Of course, most men of high station keep a house sage. When you take up your honor of Striguil, I'll recommend some good men to you. I have a fair idea of most of England's enchanters, because they were trained in the Oxford College, but I don't know of any in John's service."

"Why did he come here, to Winchester?" William mused. "Just to check up on Dear Mommy? Or did he know you had forestalled him, so it was no use heading straight to the Tower of London and trying to claim the throne?"

"I don't know that either." The thought that John might be spying on me as easily as I could spy on him was enough to make a turtle itch. "What I do know is that I intend to keep an eye on what he is up to in future. King Richard will not prohibit that, will he?"

"Not as long as you are discreet. He killed his father, you know."

That *he* did not mean Richard. *"He did?"*

Sir William sighed. "Henry's last few days were terrible. He went to another parley with Richard and King Philip, but he couldn't even dismount for it, and we had to hold him upright on his horse. They dictated the terms, everything they could think of, and he just agreed to them all. He had to, he was in agony."

I had witnessed that meeting and had watched the dying man whisper something about being revenged on his son. William must have overheard that, but he didn't mention it.

"A month ago, when Le Mans fell, we put him on a litter and carried him north, dodging the patrols out looking for him, and heading for Normandy where he would be safe. Just think of it—the lord of the Angevin Empire being transported like a woman and scuttling from nook to cranny like a hunted outlaw! But when we were almost there, he sent his escort on ahead, and told us to turn around and go back to Chinon. We argued but he insisted."

Going home to die, as his wife had said.

"Every day he was worse. He insisted on attending that final parley. We made it back to the castle and put him to bed. But then he demanded to hear the list of traitors he had agreed to pardon. Again we argued; again he insisted. The list was long, but the first name—"

I had guessed what was coming. "Was John's?"

William nodded. "He didn't listen to the rest. He just turned his face to the wall, and soon after that he became delirious."

Five legitimate sons. Three dead and the other two both traitors, not one of them worthy to be his heir.

"But why John? The whole cause of the war was Henry's constant refusal to name Richard his heir. He kept hinting that he was going to leave everything to John. Surely John should have remained loyal this time?"

William's killer eyes narrowed. "You are implying that my liege, King Richard, would stoop to such foulness?"

"No," I said hastily. "Richard never would, but I wouldn't put it past Philip to sneak John's name onto the list, just to twist the knife more."

And I realized that I wouldn't put it past Lackland to play on both teams, pretending to join in the conspiracy to stay on his brother's good side when it seemed likely that he was going to win. Once he had curried favor with both sides, he might have then sneaked away, back to England, to await the outcome.

"We sent for Richard," William said, "but he suspected a trap and didn't come. Henry died early on Thursday, and we reported that, and he turned up on Friday, by which time we had moved the body to Fontevrault Abbey, where he wanted to be buried."

Then Lars returned, leading a burly footman carrying a small cask and a page bringing drinking horns. The conversation turned to merrier subjects.

I had overlooked the most incredible thing that William had told me.

Early the next day Queen Eleanor rode forth in procession, freed from her long penance at last and now, by royal decree, ruler of England until her son returned. Every town and hamlet turned out to cheer her. A strangely humbled Ranulf de Glanville accompanied her. The king's warrant had given her the power to punish him, but she had not done so.

I did not try to claim the role of queen's favorite, which could only increase my unpopularity in that company, so I found myself astride a scrawny, rawboned mare that no other baron in Christendom would have tolerated. I saw many smirks aimed in my direction. Those did not trouble me, because in the last week I had been sitting beside the queen while every one of those toadies knelt before us to swear loyalty to her son. There would be much jostling for status in the new reign, and I wanted no part of that. I had my own place in the government. If the Lionheart wanted me gone, then I would retire to Pipewell quite happily, and someone else could be enchanter general.

Lars fared even worse than I did in the horse stakes, and had to settle for a mule, trailing along at the end of the line, among servants and riffraff. I fretted, for I dearly wanted to return to Oxford and investigate the mysterious Bran of Tara. Even if he was not mentioned in any of my records, that absence would tell me something. I had done my best duty to the queen, I thought resentfully, and she did not need me now.

After a couple of hours, though, word was passed back that Her Grace required Baron Durwin, which gave me a lot of hard work to make my grudging mare move faster than all the mounts ahead of us. Eventually I arrived at the front, and Eleanor evicted a veteran bishop to make room for me on her right, which was the side she was then facing. Not that she couldn't ride astride when she chose to.

"Ah, Lord Merlin!" she said. "I want your advice."

"For what it is worth, it is yours to command, Lady Queen."

"My son was born here, but he is a southerner at heart. You know that for years he has ruled my ancestral Aquitaine for me.

Why he has hardly set foot in England since he was a child! The people barely know his name. The nobility do, but he is a stranger to the rest. I want to rouse them to joy over his accession. I want . . . where in the world did you find that wreck of a horse?"

"Just outside the glue factory door, my lady. I fear it has taken holy orders recently."

The queen's eyes glinted like dagger points. "Just because the first Merlin was allowed to speak in riddles doesn't give you that right."

I described how every holy house was required to maintain some of the king's horses, and how this was resented as an effective tax on the church that many orders could ill-afford. Such animals were often very poorly fed and badly cared for.

She beamed. "Then if I abolish that law in my son's name, it would be popular among the clergy?"

"Their tonsures would glow with joy."

"Splendid! I shall, of course, open the jails and free all prisoners. What other ideas can your nimble mind provide?"

By then I had thought up a few more, and our conversation prospered. Eleanor knew as well as I did that the nobility were aware of Richard's record in Aquitaine, where he had raised taxes until the nobles rebelled, and had then brutally suppressed their rebellions. He was both a brilliant warrior and a very effective ruler, but not a lovable one.

Eventually the queen gave me the sort of opening I needed.

"My son mentioned that he hopes to fulfill his crusaders' oath soon. Can you predict whether he will manage to retrieve the holy city from the Saracens?"

"I could update his horoscope, ma'am, if such be your orders to me. That should advise him of his best times for making the effort."

She guessed what I wanted, of course, and reluctantly gave me leave to go home, although she warned that she might send for me soon. I collected Lars, and we headed northward on the first available trail. Once we had changed our mounts at a handy monastery, we made better progress. I was ruefully aware that my advice to the queen about horses had probably made travel much harder for me in future.

We took our time, but the weather continued fair and in due course we returned safely to Oxford and the college. Lovise made us welcome, complaining how empty the house had seemed with both of us away, and only the servants for company.

I had kept profuse notes on Richard's horoscope, and I gave them to Lovise so she could update it, she being the only person I would trust with that very sensitive—and potentially treasonous—procedure. Similarly, I gave Lars the task of updating Lord John's.

In recent years I had shed all my direct oversight of the college in order to concentrate on my own studies and my occasional work for the king's council. I was therefore able to concentrate on our Irish lore, such as it was. I soon learned that the country was a political pigsty with innumerable petty kings squabbling like wild boars, unable to cooperate against the Norman intruders who had been staking claims to their trough at intervals for almost a century.

I learned that Tara was a hill, and whoever could claim the title of King of Tara was overall king of Ireland, except that there were usually several claimants. Of more interest to me was that the hill had ancient druidic connections. If Bran of Tara were a genuine sage, then he might be in possession of some lore that I had no access to. That made my metaphorical mouth water.

If I had imagined that I was going to return to my life of quiet scholarship, I was soon disabused. Queen Eleanor's summons to Westminster arrived within a week. This time I took a larger train, although extremely modest for my rank: Lovise, my trusty Sage Wilbur of London, a couple of cantors, four servants, and two packhorses. One of the cantors was Lars, because I would not entirely trust any adolescent of his age when left alone with time on his hands, and especially not an adolescent with training in enchantment. I put him in charge of our baggage, which included several dozen incantations that I thought we might need.

I discovered that when Queen Eleanor ruled, all England jumped. The importance of Westminster was that the coronation was to be held in the cathedral there, and it was near to London, England's greatest city and the center of its law and finance. If King Richard were really going on crusade, he would need money by the wagonload.

Eleanor had already issued a blizzard of edicts on a multitude of topics—pardoning criminals, relaxing the tyrannical forest laws, clamping down on corrupt officials. If her purpose was to make the people eager to accept King Richard, she failed. They wanted her to stay right where she was, on the throne.

I was granted an audience the day after we arrived. In less than two weeks, Eleanor had established a court, so that the throne room was packed with nobles and senior officials. The throne itself stood empty, waiting for its rightful occupant, but the queen sat in a canopied chair of state beside it, glowing with joy, and apparently thriving on a pace that would have exhausted men or women half her age. Her gown was sumptuous, far grander than the workaday garb she had been reduced to wearing during her captivity. She had gotten her hands on the crown jewels, too, so that she sparkled, from her coronet to her slippers.

She greeted me with calculated warmth—which of course was carefully noted by the audience—adding, "You and dear

Lovise will sup with me this evening." That was to tell me that she knew I had brought my wife.

I presented her with the updated version of the king's horoscope, which was all Lovise's work. I had not needed to change a thing, only copy it out myself, since both queen and king knew my handwriting. Eleanor scanned it briefly. It showed that current year as being exceedingly favorable for him, as any fool could have guessed, but in 1190 the stars began to turn against him. By 1191 the prospects were mixed and his fortune darkened dramatically in the latter half of that year. From then until 1194, the outlook was black indeed.

"It would seem that he had better move quickly," his mother said, giving me an angry look, as if I ran the heavens personally. She did know better, of course. "My son has little favor for enchantment. I sometimes think he even distrusts the stars. Take it to Francois, over there, and seal it. Tell him the red wax."

Next!

I bowed out. Francois's table stood nearby. I told him the red wax. He neatly tied the scroll with ribbon, dribbled the hot wax on the knot, and I sealed it with my ring, designed by Eleanor herself, many years ago now, a crown within a pentagram. I noted that red-wax scrolls went in the smallest of three bags.

A herald quietly informed me that the council would meet right after the private dinner, and I was expected at both. For "expected" read "commanded" of course. The frantic time had begun.

I did get a few minutes with William Marshal the following day, catching him in the middle of his wedding preparations. He admitted that he had heard Bran of Tara's name, but thought he was merely Lord John's chief ostler. When I asked if he had ever noticed John traveling at unnatural speed, he thought for a while and then nodded. "Since you mention it, he has seemed oddly nimble at times." I could hardly claim that lukewarm testimony as support for my suspicions, but it didn't deny them either.

Some of Eleanor's old favorites were back, but many of the leading men of the realm were new to her, so one reason she was relying on me was that she had known me for so long. She also knew that I belonged to none of the baronial cliques. Since most of the nobility regarded me as an upstart heathen, they were secretly hoping that the new king would put me back in my place, cleaning out stables somewhere. I had met Lord Richard so rarely, that I had no idea of his opinion of me, my art, or my usefulness. Perhaps I was fortunate in that I was given little time to brood over my own future.

During the next month, the queen engaged in a long series of progresses throughout southern England, and I was included in all of them. Yes, she had me sit in on the meetings and often asked for my opinion, but I confess that my main value to her was as a healer. Even I found formal receptions and endless days in the saddle exhausting, and she was half again as old as I was. Her back hurt. I knew an incantation that would soothe it and let her sleep. I was always careful that two or three of her ladies of the chamber were present, because I knew how easily rumors could be started and then used to destroy men.

Lord John remained in France with his brother. People chuckled and whispered that the king liked to keep him under his eye.

Eadig came on a brief visit, escorting Gwynda to enroll in her advanced studies. Lars eagerly appointed himself her guide and mentor, an offer she accepted graciously. As senior students were required to live in residence, Lovise and I had to start adjusting to a house quieter than it had been in twenty years.

The next time Lars dropped in for what he termed "edible fodder," I took a second look at him.

"What's wrong with your eye?"

"Nothing."

"Nothing isn't black."

A sad tale emerged. Gwynda's competent and trustworthy mentor had been preempted by a tall, dark young sage of Angevin descent, with a pedigree as long as a pikestaff and undoubted nefarious intentions. Lars had decided that eyelashes were the problem—his being very nearly as long as the interloper's, but too blond to be visible. He had attempted to dye them with ink, which had made his eye sting. He had not assaulted his other eye.

Which I said I thought was wise of him. Alas, my sympathy did no good. The Angevin pedigree triumphed over true worth, honest Anglo-Saxon descent, and undoubted musical talent. I never heard Lars mention Gwynda's name again.

On the 13th day of August, in the year of Our Lord 1189, Richard the Lionheart entered into his kingdom, disembarking at Portsmouth. His reception was tumultuous, having been organized by his mother. From there he went to Winchester, no doubt to secure the royal treasury, and then on to Westminster. Every property owner of consequence in the country had already sworn fealty to him at the hands of Eleanor, but now we all had to swear to him in person for our lands, and this took days.

The main hall of the palace was packed with the great of the nation. He must have felt cooked in the formal state robes—which looked short on him—but he had the sense to wear only a simple coronet, not a weighty crown. With eyes of wintery blue, hair between red and gold, and his truly outstanding height, he was every inch a king. He began, of course with his mother and brother, then the nobility in order of rank, which meant that he ended with me, the most junior baron. When my name was called, everyone present must have heaved a sigh of relief that at least that part of the program was completed, but it wasn't. I knelt, raised my hands for him to enclose in his—and he didn't.

I looked up in alarm, into those icy killer eyes. Since he was standing and I was kneeling they were a long way up, which made them no less scary.

"Your Latin is much improved of late, Enchanter General."

The nearer onlookers must have been puzzled, but I knew exactly what he meant. When he was seven years old, and an unwilling student, his mother had instructed me to cast his horoscope, but she had also made it plain that I was to make the text very un-plain, so I had written it in the most convoluted prose I could contrive. What boy could resist reading about his own future? Although renowned as a warrior, the adult Richard was also admired as a classical scholar, and I might claim some small part—or bear some blame—in having encouraged his studies.

"I am greatly honored that Your Grace remembers my humble work."

"I will never forget your Satanic pluperfect passive subjunctives."

I assumed he was joking. "Your honored mother did stress the importance of ablative absolutes, Lord King."

"Oh, if I thought you'd dreamed up all that gerundive shit by yourself, you'd be in the Tower by now." He had not smiled once during this exchange, and worse followed. "I understand that you informed my mother of my accession some days before my courier arrived in Winchester."

Now I knew what he thought of my art. I wondered if I might be heading to the Tower. Suddenly my mouth was so dry I could barely speak. "This is true, Lord King."

"Who told you the news?"

"No one *told* me, Lord King. Using those self-same powers that Merlin used to prophesy for Arthur, I *saw* your father on his bier." Since Eadig had told me that Myrddin was Merlin, I could say that with a clear conscience, and my mention of Arthur stopped Richard in his tracks. Anything his great predecessor had done must be permissible for him.

He pursed his lips, but nodded grudgingly, then clasped my hands in his much larger ones, I pledged my loyalty, and he accepted it. Then I could rise and bow myself away, out of immediate danger. I had been publicly scorned, but it seemed that I was going to remain in royal favor, if only just. I learned the price later.

If we had all considered Eleanor a whirlwind, we found her son to be a tempest. He had already settled his French dominions, and he now proceeded to hammer England into shape also. In addition to some French properties that he had given his brother, he added six English counties, making Lord John the second wealthiest man in the country, after himself. He kept the castles in his own hands, though—he loved his little sibling, but he did not trust him. Before the end of the month, he had John safely married off to Isabella of Gloucester, to whom he had been betrothed for some thirteen years. It was typical of King Henry that he would hold a man's loyalty by promising him some rich heiress as a wife, and then keep him unmarried for an age, while continuing to siphon the girl's income into the royal treasury. Now that John had an undeniable, if unofficial, prospect of inheriting the English throne, he must be safely married, before foreign rulers started dangling delectable daughters in front of his eyes.

Richard dealt with his half-brother, Geoffrey the Bastard, by promoting him to archbishop of York and insisting that he enter holy orders, which disbarred him from ever making a bid for the throne. He had already positioned William Marshal in Striguil, on the Welsh border, to keep the Welsh barbarians in line. He bought off the Scottish king, William the Lion, by selling him a formal admission that Scotland was a truly independent country. It was a masterful demonstration of onshore piracy.

On September 3rd came the coronation, and London had never seen anything like it. The whole city was garlanded. To the great annoyance of Lovise and about 999 other ladies in the realm, wives were not admitted to either the ceremony in the cathedral or the incredible banquet that followed. Queen Eleanor was the only woman present. This was not her doing, or Richard's—it was ancient tradition.

The food was plentiful, but cold, the conversation guarded.

Lovise and I would have been more than happy to head straight home to Oxford after that, but Queen Eleanor was organizing musical soirees, perhaps in the hope of illuminating this dark northern wilderness with some of the gaiety and zest of her native Aquitaine, and we had received an invitation to one about three days later.

It was a very grand affair, with the cream of the kingdom packed into the reception hall of Westminster Palace like fish in a barrel. Queen Eleanor was there, but one who should have been was not—Aalis of France, King Philip's half-sister. Richard had been betrothed to her for over twenty years, and her absence was scandalous but unmentionable.

Entertainment was provided by two of Richard's favorite *trouvères*: Gace Brulé and Blondel de Nesle. England had little experience of the songs of Aquitaine and other southern lands, so the audience's cheers and applause were probably more designed to please the king and his mother than to show appreciation of an art so unfamiliar.

And then, to my horror, Richard stood up and looked over the hall until his gaze settled on me like a hard frost.

"Baron Durwin of Pipewell! You are reputed to sing a fine tune. Come forward and let us hear some of England's songs. Blondel, lend him your gittern."

Being commanded without any warning to follow two of Christendom's most renowned performers, felt bitterly unfair. Lovise told me later that the queen frowned and seemed about to intervene, but then changed her mind and didn't. I was too furious to notice what anyone else thought, although I did hear some tittering. I slowly worked my way through the throng to the throne, leaving my cane behind to emphasize my limp and give me a little extra time to review what I might be going to sing. I accepted the gittern, and quickly checked the tuning. It was already perfect, so I could not steal any extra time to tune it while I gathered my thoughts. Then I bowed to the king and began.

I chose a love song that I had sung to Lovise on the evening we were betrothed—and many a time since. It seemed to me to go well, but the king's applause at the end was brief and lackluster, so everyone else's was too. Again, Richard had demonstrated in public that he disapproved of enchanters, and especially a baronial Saxon enchanter. My pride was not totally destroyed, though. As I returned the gittern to Blondel, he said quietly, "A most moving performance! Will you teach me that ballad, if it please you, Lord Durwin?"

His accent was hard for me to make out—he was from Picardy, north of Paris, but his courtesy was worth more to me than hours of cheering from the crowd.

"Me teach you, sir? I had sooner teach my horse to eat hay."

Thus are friendships born.

Then, as if just to show me up again, Richard called upon Sir Conon de Béthune, another famed troubadour, and he sang his celebrated lament over the loss of Jerusalem.

At last Lovise and I were free to go back to Oxford to try to restore order to our lives. I felt supremely certain that I need fear no more summonses to attend meetings of the privy council. I should have been careful what I wished for. The following morning, when Lovise returned from making her calls, she was informed that I wanted to see her the moment she came in. She found me in my workroom, scribbling furiously, and in a truly toxic mood.

She sat down on the edge of the couch and regarded me quizzically. "Now what? You frightened Ælfweard to death." Ælfweard was our doorman.

"The king has called a meeting of the great council!"

"I don't see how that is the Ælfweard's fault."

Whether it was a terrified child or a rambunctious horse or a vagrant husband, Lovise's tone always had a magically calming effect. I stood my quill in the inkpot and turned to face her.

"Probably not. I will apologize to him and tip him."

"And besides, what is unexpected? A new king always summons the great council as soon as he is crowned. He needs it to vote him taxes."

The privy council comprises whosoever the king chooses. The great council is a vastly larger affair, made up of all the bishops and archbishops and barons and earls in the kingdom, plus a few major abbots. Would-be wits call it *un parlement*, meaning a talking place.

"He is summoning it to meet in Pipewell Abbey."

Lovise said, "Oh!" and at once understood my rage. Pipewell Abbey, where I had learned my letters and thus begun my climb to scholarship, might be physically capable of holding the great council itself, but every lord and bishop attending would bring scores of servants, other supporters, and horses. They would overrun the surrounding countryside like a Hunnish horde, and our estate of Pipewell Manor was the closest habitation of any size. It would be the first to suffer.

"I was in the process of writing to Harald to warn him," I added.

"Why ever would the king locate such a huge gathering in such a mouse hole of a location?"

"Because our dear friend Ranulf de Glanville told him that Pipewell is in the very center of England."

Lovise's tone changed ominously. "Durwin! How do you know this?"

I said, "I overheard them."

I liked to think that I had never told my wife a falsehood, but that time I was very close to doing so, because I had not overheard the king and the former justiciar while we were in Westminster. I had overheard them about ten minutes previously, while I was alone in my workroom. I had looked around in alarm, finding that I was completely alone. The voices had been unmistakable, and that was all I heard.

Lovise was suspicious. "You've been meddling with the *Myrddin Wyllt* incantation again! You had a vision?"

"I have not. I haven't glanced at that accursed thing in weeks." Like her, though, I was beginning to wonder if it might be meddling with me. Anxious to escape such a worrisome subject, I said, "I must finish this warning and send it off to Harald."

"What can he do? The whole place will be wasted. You'd need a private army to keep the scavengers out." But then, suddenly, my dear wife smiled like the sun breaking through storm clouds. "Baron Weldon will be going, won't he? There's your private army! Invite the Legiers to stay with us during the great council!"

I knew at once that she had found the solution, but what I said was, "Won't the cure be worse than the disease?"

William Legier, Baron Weldon, requires an explanatory note, although to do justice to his eccentricities would need a great tome. He is two or three years younger than I, and we met when he was a squire in Helmdon College—a totally unruly, unwilling, rebellious, disruptive, and recalcitrant student. His ambition was to enroll in warrior training, but his equally stubborn father had decreed that he was to be an enchanter.

To William, I was a crippled Saxon serf with ideas above my station, and he would happily have smashed me to pieces with his fists and boots, except that I would not dare defend myself against a Norman, so it could not be a fair fight. The Fates, however, threw us together and he had to help me in my hunt for a murderer in Barton Castle. He then revealed all sorts of unexpected abilities—in Latin, penmanship, chanting, and playing the role of faithful assistant, although he only did that when someone else was watching. By the end of our quest, mutual respect had developed into friendship, and he seemed reconciled to taking up serious studies at Helmdon. I am certain that he would have made an outstanding sage. Alas, he was unexpectedly reunited with his father, and went off to help him instead.

And the Fates continued to favor him. Although he was the fourth son, in short order he inherited his father's baronetcy of Weldon, wooed and won the very beautiful Millisende of Huntingdon, whose dowry made him a rich man. He distinguished himself at jousting and fought for King Henry, both during the royal sons' revolt and later against the Welsh. Millisende bore him seven sons in ten years. And just to prove that he recognized no rules or traditions, he named them all after strangers instead of relatives, and in alphabetical order. How he ever talked his priest into doing this I cannot imagine. Every son took after his father, so a Legier family gathering was a permanent civil war, which William did nothing to discourage.

I wrote to William, and discarded my letter to Harald. Instead, Lovise and I mounted up and rode off to Pipewell Manor to warn him and help him prepare for the invasion.

The first Legier to arrive, only a day after we did, was Son Number One, Sir Absolon Legier, accompanied by Number Four, Squire Dominique. Absolon was his father *in excelsis*—taller, wiry, and sporting a mustache that implied that he was more arrogant than King Richard, were that humanly possible. In truth, he was a thoroughly likeable young man. He wore the cross of a crusader, which was to carry a lot of weight over the next few days. Squire Dominique was going to be his knight's exact double in five or six years.

William and Millisende arrived the next day, herding the rest of their private army. Millisende and Lovise fell into each other's arms as always. The years had thickened William, giving him the bull chest and shoulders of a warrior and a head to match. He greeted me with an embrace that made my ribs creak, lifting me off the ground as he always did. Nor could he quite hide his contempt as he was welcomed by Harald, for our eldest was a farmer born, with absolutely no martial inclinations.

"So it's to be a siege is it?" William declared, surveying the landscape. "How much of this scenery do you own, anyway?"

"Twelve-and-a bit hides."

"You're going to lose every blade of grass on it. You'd better start by buying up enough hay to keep your livestock over the winter, because the horde will strip every field within a day's ride of the abbey. Withdraw into the house and outbuildings. . . . And we'll have to guard everything on four legs, or they'll get eaten too. Pity you don't have a small castle here, Durwin."

I could not argue with that. Pipewell Manor was a humble seat for a baron, although it suited us. Even imagining a future where all four of our children gathered with children of their own, it might suffice. A dozen Legiers and their retainers it could manage, but only just. Servants would be sleeping on the floor, so we would not be lying when we turned away would-be boarders with the claim that we had no room.

"When is this invasion due to start anyway?" William demanded. "How did you get advance warning, humble baron?"

"Professional secret."

He gave me one of the looks he had used twenty-five years earlier when he was promising to pound me into gravel, but this time he followed it with a resigned smile and went off to start planning the siege with Absolon, Baudouin, and an audience of younger Legiers. He also warned Lovise and Millisende to work on provisions for the duration of the great council and the local famine that would follow.

I soon learned that the current bone of contention in the Legier turmoil was that only Absolon and Baudouin were old enough to have sworn the crusader oath without William's permission, and he forbade any of the others to do so, at least for now. They all wanted to go and slaughter Saracens, of course. Even five-foot-high Guiscard did.

Three days later, the first members of the council began arriving. They would all be supplied with accommodation in the Abbey itself—adequate, if not up to their customary standard. Their numerous attendants and horses would not be boarded there, and the nearest worthy house in sight was Pipewell Manor. There they found the entrance barred. Most of the apparent men-at-arms on guard were shepherds and footmen dressed up with armor and weapons supplied by William, but always at least one, and sometimes two, of the men on duty wore the cross of a crusader. They were sacrosanct and no one dare use violence against them.

Our two genuine crusaders, Absolon and Baudouin, had the youth and enthusiasm to cope with dawn-to dusk vigilance, but they did need breaks, and at times César borrowed one of the crusader surcoats and helped out, for he was tall enough to convince. This fraud was a serious offense, of course. He bragged later that he had refused admittance to the Archbishop of Canterbury.

When the king arrived at the Abbey and called the council to order, of course William and I were present, the two most junior barons. Probably no one in the kingdom knew what the crusade was going to cost, even Richard himself, and he didn't care. The previous year, after Jerusalem fell and the idea of a crusade was born, King Henry of England and King Philips of France had agreed to impose a special tax on their respective realms. This was to comprise one tenth of every man's income and the value of his movable property; it soon became known as the Saladin tithe. In England most of it had duly been collected, although a few dioceses were laggard. No domain in France possessed the mechanism to handle a universal levy, so the results had been poorer.

Possibly the clerics and nobles assembled in Pipewell thought that they had already paid their share. If so, Richard rapidly undeceived them. At times King Henry had seemed avaricious, but his greed was as nothing compared to his son's. There were twenty-seven shires in England, and the office of sheriff was always regarded as a personal gold mine. Richard charged twenty-two sheriffs with malfeasance, fined them large sums of money, dismissed them, and then sold their offices to other men for even larger sums—which they would attempt to recoup with even greater malfeasance, of course.

He levied heavy fines against the men who had kept his mother in jail, although they had been obeying their king at the time, and he even fined men who had joined him in his rebellion against his father. He sold castles, titles, and appointments; he let men who had taken the crusader oath buy their way out of it. It was a dazzling display of rapacity. He reportedly said he would sell London if he could find a buyer.

On the final afternoon, the king gave audience to the great council, one man at a time, and extorted—I use the word advisedly—money from any them who had not taken the crusaders' oath. Since he proceeded in order of rank, I again had the honor of being the last, long after candles had been lit and everyone of importance had been given leave to go and seek his lodgings, however damp, cold, and humble they might be.

William was second last. The king did not know him.

"Well, Baron? Are you not prepared to join the holy cause?"

"I am past it, Lord King, but I have seven sons, and I will send four."

"Why not all seven?" The king, I think, was joking.

"The other three aren't shaving yet, sire."

Only then did the king smile and nod approval. "You are making a noble contribution. May they triumph in the Lord's name. You have our leave."

The smile vanished as he watched me hobble forward and kneel. "Ah, the minstrel baron? Why have you not taken the oath and sworn to rescue Jerusalem from under the heels of the infidels?"

"I am no warrior, Lord King."

"No? I recall being told that you did once venture to tilt at an honest knight and contrive to unhorse him to his undoing by means of black magic."

If he believed all that, then it was no wonder that he disliked me.

"With respect, Lord King, he had accused me of murder, and I demanded that I be judged by wager of battle. I was innocent of the charge, so God Himself settled our dispute."

I won't say that the king snorted, lest I be suspected of lese majesty, but the royal noise did sound snort-like. He did not dispute the divine verdict, though.

"Well, those who will not serve can still help. Clerk, put Baron Durwin down for a mere one thousand marks."

"Your Grace! That is many years' income."

"Faugh! You can make it by boiling frogs' eyes in a cauldron."

End of audience.

But that was also the end of the great council, and the following morning we bade farewell to the Legiers, thanking them for saving us from our betters. William and I embraced, and then I turned away to speak to Millisende—

"What did you just say?"

Unaware of having said anything out of the ordinary, I looked back to William in surprise. "I said farewell."

He was staring very hard at me. "No, you didn't! You said, *'See you in Ascalon.'*"

I couldn't have done, because I had never heard that name before, but I saw that Lovise had caught William's protest and was watching. "I don't recall saying that, friend. It was probably just one of those stray prophecies that float around in summer. Best ignore it. Pay no attention."

William looked ready to punch me on the nose. "You were always odd, Durwin of Pipewell. But these days you're positively weird."

One week later a spotty youth in a colorful tabard turned up in Oxford to inform me that, while I had contributed as a baron, the cost of my continuing in the office of enchanter general would be another one thousand marks.

When I told Lovise, she bounced off the rafters. "We don't *have* that much!"

I sighed. "But we can raise it."

"Or we could make it," she said, in a softer voice.

I looked at her. She turned away to hide a blush.

"Yes, we could, but that would be forgery and therefore black magic, which would imperil our souls."

The church forbade Christians to lend money, but they could borrow it, so I donned my cloak and went off to speak to the Jews.

Richard's greed fell mainly on the rich landowners, for only they had wealth to appropriate, but the wild popularity that had greeted him in August shriveled like a raisin. On December 12th, he sailed away to France, and the country relaxed with an almost audible sigh. It was to be a long time before he and England saw each other again.

1190

Life returned to normal, although the formerly rich were left licking their financial wounds, while the poor licked their platters to collect every last trace of grease. Queen Eleanor spent the winter at various places in southern England, but I remained in Oxford and she never sent for me. In February of 1190, she crossed over to France.

The king had put England in the hands of his trusted William Longchamp, who had been his chancellor in Aquitaine. Longchamp was first appointed Bishop of Ely, then chancellor and justiciar, which meant that he was regent when the king left the country. Somehow Richard also persuaded the Pope to make him a papal legate, which gave him authority over the church as well as the state.

This low-born autocrat was a very unprepossessing little man, with a beard that started at his eyes. He walked with a limp and spoke with a stammer. His southern French was almost incomprehensible to the English nobility, who used the northern dialect of their Norman ancestors. He turned out to be quite as grasping as his master, importing a herd of his own relatives, all of whom he appointed to profitable offices, turfing out native-born gentlefolk, many of whom had just bought their appointments from the king. The clergy soon detested him as much as the nobility did.

He sent for me early in the new year. I rode to Westminster with Sage Wilbur, whom I had recently appointed master of the College, but the justiciar called for me only, and I entered alone. The justiciar, regent, chancellor, papal legate, and bishop of Ely were all seated at a desk half buried in parchment, but only the two of us were present. Although his chair was higher than standard, he still looked small. He raised a bushy eyebrow when he saw my cane, and waved me to a stool.

He leaned back and studied me. My conscience was clear, so I waited unblinkingly. I could match his stare, but leaning back on a stool is never advisable.

"I am told that you are Merlin reborn."

"Our Lady Queen, may the saints preserve her, is very fond of Arthurian allusions, Your Grace."

"You cannot tell the future for us?"

"Alas, no. Only Merlin could do that, Your Grace."

"But you have great occult powers. And you have been enchanter general for many years."

"Since 1166."

"A Saxon appointed to so high an office at so young an age? Your father must have had great influence."

"My father was an ostler in Pipewell Abbey. He died when I was a child."

That produced a smile, a rare one from this tyrant. "I have risen higher than you, but my father was a knight. I started higher."

"I had much good fortune to aid me, Your Grace. I foiled a Satanic plot to murder King Henry. He knighted me on the spot."

"And you must have served him well since. You will serve me in his absence?"

"Anything I can do, short of black magic."

"But you cannot foresee future events?"

"I can cast horoscopes to determine what the stars hold in store for a person, but no more than that."

"Lord John." It was a question.

I pulled a face, which was an answer.

Longchamp leaned forward. "King Richard has forbidden him to enter England without my permission."

I was tempted to wish him luck with that, but I just waited for more.

"Can you use your skills to warn me if he makes the attempt?"

At least I was not being asked to actively prevent John from crossing the channel, which I could not have done without dabbling in black arts.

"Very few enchantments reach across the sea, my lord, but if he remains in northern France, then I believe I can place him. Were I to advise you, say once a month, of his whereabouts, would that suffice?"

The justiciar shook his head. "Once a week!"

"You do not appreciate the effort you are asking, Your Grace. Every two weeks, and sometimes I may have to admit that I don't know. And I will need free use of the royal couriers to report to you."

Another intimidating stare. "You are of lowly birth, you hobble around on a cane, and you bargain like the Pope. We have much in common, Enchanter."

"You honor me, Lord Bishop."

There was a pause, but then he said, "Every ten days, then. Anything I can do for you?"

I guessed that absolutely nobody entered his office without begging for something, and he was nonplussed that I had not brought a list of my own requirements.

"Not for myself. Lord John has a retainer, an Irishman named Bran of Tara. I suspect he may be an enchanter of some power. I have had little success in learning more about him, but it might be to both our advantages if you did."

Longchamp gave me a second smile and made a note. It seemed that the two low-born upstart cripples were going to get along famously.

I returned to Oxford and my continuing efforts to improve the *Myrddin Wyllt* enchantment, which I would need to keep watch on Lord John for the justiciar. Any text that imposes cramps and headaches on the chanter usually lacks style. "The spirits dislike bad grammar," was what I told students, but rhythm and vocabulary were important, too. I went through the incantation word by word several times. I did manage to cure it of its more sadistic habits, but it insisted on imparting a raging thirst.

Because the *Myrddin Wyllt* was a single-voice enchantment, I needed no cantor to assist me, and even Lovise was unaware that I was spying on the king's brother for Bishop Longchamp. I reassured my conscience by reminding it that I had my own reasons for distrusting the man and a duty to suppress the use of black magic in the king's realm. I had no admissible evidence that Lord John and his Irish accomplice were dabbling in such evil. Even if I found any, it would have to be truly heinous before I would dare report it to the king.

Noontime worked best for my snooping because that was when John ate dinner, and the language he used to the servants told me which country he was in. If I saw him out of doors, the landscape served the same purpose— the style of the cottages or the presence of vineyards.

Longchamp never kept his side of our bargain by sending me information on the mysterious Bran of Tara, but I soon learned what the man looked like. Whenever John was having a private one-on-one with someone, it was either a girl he was seducing, or a certain swarthy, shortish, heavy-set man of around forty with a forked black beard. He kept the front of his scalp shaved from ear to ear, a style I have not seen anywhere else. Since I never witnessed the two men together with others, I could assume that this man must be a very confidential aide, so who else but Bran of Tara?

One day near the end of February, I viewed John on the move with banners flying and a train of a hundred or more. Clearly, this was no hunting trip. The countryside looked much like Norman *bocage*, but I wanted to know where he was heading, so the next morning I checked on him again.

I was astonished to find myself viewing a hall where at least a dozen men were seated around a very large table, actually several tables pushed together, all littered with thick law books. John was there, and so were the king and Archbishop Baldwin of Canterbury. I recognized Archbishop Geoffrey of York and several bishops I had seen at the coronation. Some of these men seemed oddly blurred, as if my eyes were malfunctioning. Such people rarely assemble so early in the day.

King Richard was glowering, clearly displeased. John seemed quietly amused, enjoying his brother's displeasure, no matter what its cause. I was most surprised to see Justiciar Longchamp in this assembly, looking attentive and obedient, waiting to learn where the royal anger would strike. I had not been aware that he had left England.

The king was tapping his fingers on the table and staring at the door, so he was being kept waiting by someone. Waiting *for* someone, I guessed when I noticed two empty chairs directly opposite him. At last two footmen on duty by the door opened it to admit the absentees. The first was Queen Eleanor, robed in splendor and wearing both a gold coronet and a triumphant expression which would have dropped me groveling on the floor in terror had it been directed at me.

Behind her crept in Aalis of France, Countess Vexin, half-sister of King Philip. Aalis was close to thirty years old, but her looks were fading and she seemed older. Her position two paces behind Eleanor gave her the status of servant, which her attire did not deny—I could tell at a glance that it had not been made by the same expert seamstresses as the queen's, nor of the same fine fabrics. Her hair was unbound and in need of better grooming. She was taller than Eleanor, although her stoop hid that.

Richard rose to honor his mother, and most of the other men followed his lead. Some, like the two archbishops, did not. The women curtseyed and Eleanor swept around to one of the empty chairs, which another footman had already pulled out for her. The instant she was seated, so was everyone else except poor Lady Aalis. The footman did move her chair for her, but reluctantly, as if he had been instructed not to hurry for that one.

Aalis, obviously aware that she was the agenda of the meeting, cowered in her seat like a guilty child.

"Begin," the king said. The three clerks dipped their quills in inkwells.

Archbishop Baldwin signified the opening of proceedings by thumping his crozier on the floor three times. "Aalis, Countess of Vexin, these noble lords are gathered here today to examine the condition of your betrothal to His Grace, Richard of England. Do you swear to tell the truth, the whole truth, and nothing but the truth, so help you God?"

Aalis made a visible effort and sat up straight. "Do you?"

That anybody, and especially a woman, should talk back to an archbishop in that way produced a roar of anger from every man present. Queen Eleanor just pulled a face to register contempt.

Baldwin hammered on the floor for order, and repeated the question.

Sullenly, Aalis muttered something inaudible.

"Louder!"

"I so swear."

"You are a daughter of the late King Louis VII of France and his second wife, Constance of Castile?"

"So I have been told, although it is a long time since I was treated as—"

Thump! "Just answer my questions, without comments. You were betrothed to Lord Richard, as he then was? When was that?"

"1169—January." She was sinking lower on her chair, like a snail retreating into its shell.

"And how old were you then?"

"Eight."

A quick calculation told me that Richard would have been eleven.

"At that date, what was his station?"

"Duke of Aquitaine."

"So you then went to live at his court in Aquitaine?"

Aalis shook her head. She had lost her brief defiance, and was now keeping her gaze on the floor.

"Answer! The clerks can only write words, not gestures."

"No."

For the first time the archbishop had received a reply that some of his audience had not expected. He ignored the murmurs of surprise and looked to the king for a nod to continue. To my astonishment, Richard was seated on his left. I was certain they had been arranged the other way around just moments ago.

"So where did you live during your betrothal?"

"At the court of King Henry."

71

"In England?"

"Or France, wherever he happened to be."

"And when did you first go to his bed?"

Silence. Everyone seemed to stop breathing.

Aalis managed to raise her head once more, but there were tears running down her cheeks. "Never! I never submitted voluntarily to him, but he did drag me to his chamber sometimes when he was drunk." Baldwin hammered the floor for order. ". . . often came to my bed. I asked and asked for a door with a lock, but was never allowed one."

Granted that kings collect mistresses like peasants collect fleas, their lemans are not usually royal princesses, and wards under their protection ought to be entirely off-limits, even for them. The idea of a young lady seducing Henry II was as ludicrous as a mouse challenging a cat to a wrestling match.

"And how old were you when you first copulated with King Henry?"

"He took my maidenhead when I was twelve. I fought and—"

Thump! went the crozier.

"And did you give him a child?"

Aalis showed her teeth in another brief flicker of defiance. "I *gave* him nothing! But he took *four* whelps off me!"

This time the archbishop let the howls continue until they died out by themselves. Most of the outage was pretense, because there had long been rumors around court that Henry was trespassing on his son's territory, but an issue of four offspring was a genuine surprise. I was not alone in finding it appalling. I noticed that Eleanor was enjoying every bitter syllable of this savage exchange, but she had always detested her husband's sweethearts.

"And where are these royal children now?"

Aalis made them wait for her answer, but at last she murmured, "They are all dead, Your Grace."

Baldwin glanced at the clerks to make sure that they were recording all this. There were actually two clerks, although earlier I had thought there were three.

"Their names?"

"They were never baptized."

"That is indeed sad," the Archbishop said. "And most strange."

His hint at infanticide seemed to chill the room, but he did not follow up, possibly because that would have created a scandal throughout all Christendom. Instead he went straight to the heart of the matter, the reason this conference, or trial, had been called at all.

"Are you aware that the Church forbids a man to marry a woman who has had carnal relations with his father?"

"Really? How interesting!" For the first time, Aalis turned her head to study the venomous jailer beside her, Dowager Queen Eleanor.

I saw not a few faces at the table struggling to suppress smiles, for there had long been rumors of a brief but torrid affair between the juvenile Eleanor and Geoffrey IV, Count of Anjou, Henry II's father. If that were taken seriously, then Richard himself was illegitimate, and should never have been crowned.

I did not witness the outcome, because I was awakened by banging and shouting. The voice was Lovise's, naturally, because no one else would dare disturb me. I lurched to my feet and staggered over to unbolt the door, while the room swayed all around me.

I croaked, "What?"

"The justiciar is coming! He's in Oxford and heading this way. He sent a harbinger to tell you that he will be inspecting the College."

"Justiciar?" I mumbled. "Longchamp? Is impossible." I had just seen him in Normandy.

But then, at last, the truth flashed like sudden lightning, and I understood.

Our new ruler, Bishop Longchamp, had taken to making royal progresses, and I should not have been surprised that he had chosen Oxford as one of his first destinations, for it was not far from Westminster, and Beaumont Palace was one of the most comfortable of the king's residences. He stayed two days there, peering over shoulders and being a thoroughgoing nuisance. He disrupted work in the College and expected me to act as his guide, although I had long ago managed to separate my duties as enchanter general from the day-to-day responsibilities of running the library and school.

He even demanded to see where I worked, so he came limping into my workroom with a herd of lackeys at his heels. I loudly warned them not to touch any of the scrolls racked along one wall, but of course one young idiot had to test me by reaching out a daring finger. He hit the floor with a scream of agony, and everyone left very soon after that.

As Longchamp was preparing to depart the next morning—with me holding his stirrup for him to mount—he remarked that he would be crossing to Normandy next week. I was sorely tempted to tell him that I already knew that, but I didn't, because I had assured him back in January that only Merlin had ever been able to see the future. That, as they say, had been then.

Once I was certain that the pest had left town, I went down to the crypt and brought up the chest in which I kept the original fragments of the *Myrddin Wyllt* parchment.

I began to compare them with my transcription yet again, checking every word. Both Latin and French have past, present, and future forms for verbs, but the Old Tongue lacked a future tense. To express the future required compound wording, and I saw that I had missed some of the implications in the poetic language.

Although I had thought that the spell was merely for spying, now I saw that it had been prophesying for me—foreseeing as well as farseeing. Even on that day back in the summer, when I had been shown that tragic last parley between King Henry and his son, the sun had been high in the sky, yet in Oxford the morning had been young. Two days later, I had been shown Richard surveying his father's body in the chapel at Fontevrault Abbey, but that had not happened until the following day, as William Marshal had told me. I had assured Queen Eleanor that the king was dead, but if *Myrddin Wyllt* was capable of foretelling future events, I had better be more careful from now on.

I also understood the strange variances I had seen in the Aalis trial. While the nature of the main event was inevitable, many unimportant details, such as the seating plan and the number of recorders, had not been settled at the time of my viewing.

Eventually I gave up and called on Lovise for help, which I should have done much sooner, for while I had a better eye for syntax, she had a better ear for deliberate subtleties in the original. She made me wait while she finished writing up some medical notes, and then came down to the workroom. As I expected, she pulled a face when I told her I was spying for Longchamp.

"He is quite capable of putting on his bishop's miter and putting us all on trial as Satanists," I said in self-defense. "He could lock us up in the Tower. We must make sure that he always sees us as useful to him. But this changes everything. I told him I could keep watch on Lord John, but my information on *where* I see him is useless unless I know *when* that is. I think I can tell foreseeing from farseeing by looking at the details, which are blurred and jiggle around in the prophecies. But I need to know how to direct the vision in time. I can't see it in the text."

Lovise pulled the parchment closer and read it over for a while in silence. At length she said, "You can't do that. You would be giving Carnonos orders, which gods don't like. Look here." She pointed to one brief verse:

Where fish swim low and birds nest high,
Where berries grow and great trees huddle,
Show me the path, the better way.

"This isn't a spying tool at all, it's for foretelling, an appeal to this horned deity to guide you to the best hunting. It gives you information you need to know, not what you think you ought to know."

I could see that, up to a point, and mentally kicked myself for not seeing it sooner. For instance, it had told me what Bran of Tara looked like.

"But it asks whom I wish to observe. Here, at the end: *Who must I seek to guide me?* That's when I tell it the name of—"

"Then you shouldn't. The god isn't asking you. You are asking the god. It means, *Who else?*"

I digested that lesson in silence for a moment, then said, "But what conceivable use can it be for me to know that Richard is not going to marry Lady Aalis?"

Any wife, I suspect, has a way at looking at her husband that warns him he is being as thick as a brick. Mine certainly did.

"He is jilting his betrothed after she has spent twenty years of her life waiting for him in his father's court while being royally raped and bearing four bastard children? How do you feel about that?"

"I am appalled. Revolted. I admired Henry greatly. I never thought he could sink to such depravity."

"Her brother is King Philip of France?"

"Half-brother, yes."

"How do you think he must feel? And he will certainly find out, somehow. Richard and Philip are going off together on crusade? Joint leaders? Just whom are they going to be fighting? Saracens? Do you still believe that?"

Saracens—or each other? "You may have a point, dearest."

Lovise stood up. "And this Carnonos? If the Church hears that you are worshiping a horned god, what name will they put on him?"

She was a sage too, so she should know better than to think along those lines. "I am not aware," I said coldly, "that the Gospels anywhere describe Satan himself as having antlers, although some of his beasts may. Horns possibly. Even that is just an artists' conceit, nothing more."

"I do hope so," my wife said sweetly, "because you know what happens to people who follow that one's advice, don't you?"

I kissed her cheek. "You are right, as always, darling. Prophecy is far too dangerous. I shall lock the devilish incantation in the crypt. No more *Myrddin Wyllt!*"

The following morning I locked all my texts and notes of the *Myrddin Wyllt* in a stout oaken chest in the cellar, and secured the chest with a fearsome warding. From then on, Lovise and I together kept track of Lord John with the *Loc hwær*. If it failed to report where he was, we would assume that he was not in England, and report this to Justiciar Longchamp.

King Richard's crusade would have been much more successful had he heeded the counsel given him by his horoscope. He dillydallied in France, meeting with innumerable barons, taking forever to organize his army. He even made a side trip south into Spain to woo Berengaria, daughter of King Sancho of Navarre. His interest in her as a future wife had been rumored for years.

No doubt the Berengaria match would be very advantageous for securing his southern borders, but the delay was another loss of crusading time.

There was very little official news. Rumors and gossip flourished, but even members of the king's council must rely on snatches and snippets. The whole story had to be put together months after the events actually happened. Personally, I was ambivalent about the great cause. As a good Christian I hoped that Richard would succeed in rescuing Jerusalem from the heathens. I dreaded hearing that he had died and left the empire to John. To be honest, I deeply resented the personal cost, which had completely swallowed money destined for our daughters' dowries. I was wounded by the king's distrust and dislike.

In Lyons Richard met yet again with Philip, and from there went on to Marseilles, where he encountered further delays. It was not until August that he set sail for Italy. He visited every port along the way, for that was the custom, and at Ostia declined to go upstream to Rome to hobnob with the Pope. Indeed, his reply to the invitation was said to be an exceedingly insulting message, describing the Vatican as a "snake pit of corruption," no better than the moneylenders Christ had driven out of the temple.

He arrived in Sicily on September 23rd. He had expected a triumphal greeting, because his sister, Joan, was married to King William there. Unfortunately, William had just died and Tancred, his successor, tried to be difficult. The ever-duplicitous Philip had arrived earlier, and was actively hostile, poisoning Tancred's mind against the English king. Richard settled the negotiations by betrothing his nephew, Arthur of Brittany, to one of Tancred's daughters. In order to sweeten this arrangement, he named Arthur as his heir. Until then he had declined to name a successor, playing the same game on John that their father had played on him.

This astonishing declaration was supposed to be kept secret. Either because he had spies in his brother's court, or by occult means, Lord John soon heard that he had been disinherited. John, being John, was not willing to put up with that.

It was about the time of Richard's dealings with Tancred that Queen Eleanor began an astonishing journey for a woman of her age. She went south to Aquitaine, her homeland and hereditary domain, and then crossed the Pyrenees Mountains to Pamplona to collect Queen-designate Berengaria. From there she returned to France and eventually crossed the Alps into northern Italy, arriving in late November. That land had been stripped of food by Philip's army, and was roamed by dangerous bands of outlaws. Somehow the queen and princess survived, but they did not meet up with Richard until March 30th 1191, in the extreme south of Italy.

Fifteen months since he had left England, the king was still a long way from the Holy Land, and his most notable achievement so far had been to insult and alienate his most powerful ally, Philip of France. He had also supported the Sicilian usurper, Tancred, which was to be yet another problem that would return to haunt him in the future.

Meantime, in England things were going from bad to terrible. The avaricious Longchamp kept acting like an emperor, making royal progresses around the country, and bringing in foreign mercenaries to seize castles. He even tried to take the great fortress of Striguil away from William Marshal by force, one of his stupidest notions.

I kept my head down in Oxford, mainly helping out at the college, because half the healers in England had gone on the crusade, so we were frantically training more. News of the war drifted back unevenly, usually two months old, even older in winter. Rumors flew, of course, as they always do. The country waited and prayed. The death rate among crusaders was brutal, and we all knew that King Richard had earned the name of Lionheart by his indifference to personal danger.

Lord John knew that also, and was confident that news of his brother's death would gallop up to his door any day. I would not have been surprised to hear that he kept a crown tucked away in his sock box.

As an omen that things could still become worse, just after Christmas, Longchamp sent for me. The weather was ghastly, and I had a long, wet ride to Westminster.

The-regent-justiciar-papal-legate-bishop had moved to a far grander office than the one I seen before, but he did let me sit in his omnipotent presence, an honor granted to few.

"I have news for you," he said sourly, and then proceeded to make me swear an oath of secrecy on what he claimed were holy relics. "The king has declared that the duke of Brittany is to be his heir."

"*Arthur!?* A three-year-old boy?" What craziness was that? Brittany was part of France, so Duchess Constance, Arthur's mother and regent, must be firmly under the thumb of King Philip. "Is this certain, Your Grace?"

"Quite certain. The king made the decision back in October and sent a special messenger to tell me. Of course, the declaration is only valid until Queen Berengaria gives him a son, but it is now that we must worry about. I have reason to believe that Lord John has heard of this, which could present problems. I need you to tell me where the infant is, and who is in charge of him."

"I regret to say, Your Grace, that I cannot do that." I had promised my wife that I would not use the *Myrddin Wyllt*, which was the only enchantment I knew that could work across the sea. "I have never met the baby duke or his mother."

He scowled. "What has that to do with it?"

"Quite a lot in the occult arts, I'm afraid. I will try, of course, and will let you know if I meet with any success." With that, I was curtly dismissed to ride back to Oxford.

Without mentioning Arthur, I asked Lovise if I might bring Merlin out of the crypt, and she said no. So that was that.

1191

When the sailing season opened again in April, Richard left Sicily and sailed on to Cyprus, where more complications ensued. He ended by conquering the entire island, although he did find time there to marry Berengaria. Cyprus would make a convenient staging post and food supply for the crusaders in the Holy Land, so his time was not entirely wasted, but the stars were turning against him.

The current fighting in Outremer, as the French call the Holy Land, was located around the port of Acre, which Sultan Saladin and his Saracens had taken from the Christians back in 1187. Crusader attempts to retake it had persisted ever since, fed by a continuing dribble of supplies and reinforcements from Europe. The Saracens had surrounded the Christian army, but had been unable to defeat it, so there was now a siege within a siege.

March of 1191 saw the arrival of reenforcements under Duke Leopold of Austria, who was to play a key part in Richard's later troubles. Philip and the French army arrived in April, but achieved nothing—Philip later claimed that he had been waiting for Richard so as not to deprive him of his share of the honor and loot. Some people might have believed him.

That was all I knew in early July, when the *Myrddin Wyllt* interfered once more. I did not call it; it called me, or possibly the ghost of Merlin himself sent it. I was relaxing under an elm tree in the Beaumont Palace park that surrounded our house, enjoying a summer afternoon, reading and re-reading letters from our daughters. Lovise was beside me, embroidering.

Then a tremendous crash had me on my feet, looking around in bewilderment. The park had vanished, and I was marooned in a tumultuous battle, under sunshine glaring hotter than a blacksmith's forge. The air was full of dust, and noise, and missiles. The noise that had startled me was that of a great rock striking a city wall about three hundred yards away, and shattering into a hail of rubble. At least six great trebuchets were working, with sweating teams of men hauling the throwing arms down, loading projectiles into the slings, backing clear as the arms were released, the counterweights fell, and the arms soared up to hurl the projectiles. Then they would rush in to repeat the process. I was amazed by both their rate of fire and their accuracy, because every shot was battering almost the same spot.

Up on the battlements, the Saracen defenders were far from idle—frantically spanning and loading their crossbows, then dodging out from behind the merlons to shoot through the crenels at the teams working the trebuchets. Those hardy souls were shielded by wooden bulwarks, but not completely, and every few minutes a man would fall and another come forward to take his place.

The ground behind the artillery, where I seemed to be standing, was even more chaotic. Hundreds of crossbowmen were keeping up a counter barrage, but their work was much harder than the defenders', because they were shooting upward, not downward, and they had only split seconds to aim and loose at a target. Horse-drawn wagons were bringing in ammunition and barrel after barrel of drinking water, and also carrying away the dead and wounded.

Some men wore chain mail and helmets; most did not, while some were close to naked in the overpowering heat. A great majority of the Christians wore the white crusader cross of the English army, and most of the rest were French, bearing red crosses. I saw few of the green ones that denoted men from Flanders. So I knew that Richard had arrived at last, and the convincing detail of the scene told me that this was no prophecy, but a true vision of the hell on earth that was the siege of Acre. I thanked God that I was not present in the flesh. And yet, watching the screaming wounded being carried off the field, I wished I were, so as I could help the healers and save some brave lives.

But why had the *Myrddin Wyllt* brought me here? Was I missing something?

Perhaps that knight striding purposefully across the battlefield in approximately my direction? He certainly did not seem to be playing any sort of role in the battle. He wore a chain mail hauberk and carried a large shield emblazoned with heraldry I did not recognize. It concealed his face from me, because he was holding it high, between him and the Saracen crossbowmen on the walls.

His destination, I decided, was a curious grouping of two men holding shields to protect what seemed to be a litter. Both shields were bristled like hedgehogs with spent arrows, and even as I watched one of the guardians raised his to catch yet another incoming. *Clunk!* All I could see of the litter's occupant was his feet.

But then there came the sharp crack of a crossbow being fired from behind the protective shields. The guardians watched its flight, then both cried out in triumph at the same time: "Got him!" "Well shot, sire!"

Sire? I moved in closer until I could see this invalid archer. At first, I did not know him. He was old, and obviously deathly ill. Much of his hair and beard had fallen out; his feet and many of his fingers were bandaged; sunken cheeks showed that he had lost some teeth. He leered at his success, and passed his crossbow to a youth kneeling at his side, who gave him a spanned and loaded one in exchange. He muttered, "Water!" and the youth held a flask to the invalid's lips.

I recognized the voice of my king. He had aged at least ten years in the last two. Even without a proper examination I thought I could recognize the symptoms of the sailors' disease—loss of hair and teeth, possibly even finger and toe nails. Probably no fever, for he would be unable to hold his crossbow steady enough to shoot straight if his hands were shaking. There were enchantments to treat the sailors' malady, so where were all the healers? Richard was renowned as a crack shot with a crossbow, but surely he had plenty of marksmen in his army who could do what he was doing and let him retire to bed to recuperate?

"The merlon between the third and fourth trebuchets, Lord King," said one of the shield bearers. "He usually shoots through the right crenel, but sometimes the left. Ah! There he is . . ."

For an instant a Saracen bowman in a black turban appeared in the battlements and shot his bolt, then quickly backed into safety again to reload. To hit so transient a target at that range would be marksmanship indeed, but before Richard could try, the shadow of the French knight fell over him.

The newcomer saluted. "My Lord King! I bring sad news from His Grace, Philip, king of France, your overlord."

"He's not my overlord here." Richard spoke with difficulty, as if his mouth hurt. "What does he want now, more money?"

"No, Your Grace. He deeply regrets to inform you that, on the insistence of his doctors, he will have to return in haste to France to recuperate from the sickness that has smitten both him and your noble self."

"I thought you said you came with sad news? Tell him I wish him God speed. Tell him also this: that I know some Frenchmen can fight, and I hope he will leave those men behind to fulfill the oaths that we all have sworn. He is welcome to take the rest of the cowards with him."

If the unfortunate knight blushed, his helmet concealed the fact. He started to protest, but I was lying on the warm grass and Lovise was fussing over me.

"You swore you wouldn't sing the *Myrddin Wyllt* again!"

"And I haven't," I mumbled with a familiarly dry mouth. "I haven't even been down to the crypt."

"So it's happened again. What did it tell you this time?"

I sat up and paused a moment to think. "I'm not sure. . . . Perhaps two things. Philip is going to head home very shortly, and if he doesn't drown on the way, he will be Longchamp's problem, not Richard's. And secondly, I learned that if there's a man in Christendom who can take Jerusalem back from the Saracens, his name is Lionheart."

Many weeks later I learned that Acre resisted even Richard's expertise in the siege craft until July 12th, when it finally surrendered and the banners of England, France, and Austria were raised on the battlements. Duke Leopold had some claim to this honor, in that his contingent was the last remnant of the German army that had set out the previous year—led by Emperor Barbarossa, who had died on the journey—but Leopold was not a king, and his flag implied that he was entitled to a share of the plunder. Richard had Leopold's banner removed and thrown into the moat, leaving only his own and Philip's.

After Acre fell, King Philip did sail away as he had said he would, although many of the French nobility remained, from a sense of honor and duty. Richard had brought the largest contingent to the Crusade and Phillip's departure left him the undisputed leader of the Crusade.

When negotiations with Saladin dragged on endlessly, Richard threatened to slaughter his 2,700 prisoners. Saladin still failed to come to terms—likely because he knew that Richard could not proceed with his mission until he had disposed of the captives somehow, and feeding them had to be a serious strain on his resources. So Richard carried out his threat, a day-long butchery that shocked all Christendom, even his own battle-hardened troops. Saladin promptly killed all his prisoners.

Richard had established firm control of much of the coast, where he could be supplied by sea, but he resisted pleas to march on Jerusalem right away. Seeing the prior need to take Jaffa, which would be a vital coastal supply base, he left his sister, Joan, and queen, Berengaria, in Acre Castle and marched the army south. Saladin tried with little success to harry the crusaders' march, but Richard's fleet had already driven the Egyptian navy from the seas, so the crusaders could safely keep their right flank on the shore, and use their armored infantry to protect their left. The Saracens' mounted archers were much faster and more nimble than the heavily-laden crusader horsemen, but they could do little harm as long as the crusaders stayed in formation. Day after day the great column kept creeping along, past Haifa and Caesarea, through a countryside already razed by Saladin's forces. Day after day the Saracens pestered it like mosquitoes, racing in on their smaller, more nimble horses, to shoot arrows at the Christians and then retire.

On September 6th, the Christians passed unmolested through the Forest of Arsuf and on the other side found the entire Saracen army lined up in battle order. Saladin had decided to risk a head-to-head clash. At first the harassing continued, but in mid-morning, he gave the signal and the huge host charged. Yet still Richard managed to keep his forces in formation, despite frantic pleas, especially from his rearguard, who were suffering the brunt of the onslaught. His strategy, I was later told by men close to him, was to wait until the Saracens had exhausted their horses.

To digress for a moment: battles are rare. Forget Alexander the Great and his Greek phalanx. Forget the Roman legions. Head-to-head clashes are unpredictable and dangerous. Henry II never fought a battle. Modern European warfare is based on castles. Whoever holds a castle controls the surrounding countryside, and his enemies must seize it before they can displace him. It was when the Knights Templar, the Knights Hospitaller, and other Christians holding Jerusalem marched out of their strongholds to do battle with Saladin's Saracens on July 4th, 1187, that they rediscovered this truth. In the ensuing disaster at the Horns of Hattin, the Christians were massacred. The Holy City fell in October of that year, to the horror of all Christendom.

At Arsuf, Richard revenged the defeat at Hattin. Before he was ready, two knights in his rearguard, tormented beyond endurance, broke ranks and charged the Saracen horde. The people I spoke to all insisted that under most commanders this would have brought disaster, and the enemy would probably have rolled up the Crusader army like a rug. But Richard was up to the challenge. He raced back through the column, bellowing orders, and the Crusader host turned face and charged. And won a bloody victory.

I am no tactician or strategist, but I later spoke with many who were there and who knew enough to judge, and they all insisted that his victory at Arsuf proved that he was the greatest warrior of his age. He had brought a huge army by sea, recovered Acre, and now had beaten Saladin at his own type of war as well. In siege warfare or battle, in tactics, logistics, or strategy, the Lionheart was simply the best.

But now his luck had run out, exactly as the stars had foretold.

1191

early in January, the *Loc hwær* told us that John was back in
England. I sent a warning to Longchamp, but he probably
knew from other sources before my note arrived. John was
still bound by Richard's ban against entering England without
Longchamp's permission, but if Longchamp wanted to enforce
this edict, he would have to chain the king's brother in a dungeon, and even he did not dare try that.

The justiciar's new problem was entirely his own fault, because
his tyrannical rule had gained John many friends in the land.
Richard's generosity had given his brother enormous financial
resources, and few problems cannot be solved by gold. Soon he
was parading around England, collecting castles like a ferreter net-
ting rabbits. If Richard died on crusade, then John was going to
seize the throne and baby Arthur could scream all he wanted. And
if the rightful king survived and tried to claim his kingdom . . .

Plantagenet family squabbles kill a lot of bystanders.

One chilly evening in March, Lovise and I were sitting by a
dwindling fire, reluctant to leave the warmth and withdraw to a
cold bed. Lars had left home to live in residence, and the servants

had all retired, so there were only the two of us old fogies in our empty nest. We were discussing those dark times and cursing Richard for neglecting his realm. In theory the Church's Truce of God defended the lands of all crusaders during their absence and to molest them in any way was a major sin, but now John was stealing England, bite by bite.

And my dear wife said, "So what are you going to do about it?"

"Me?"

"Yes, you. Obviously, the Church is not going to do anything, and you are still enchanter general. I thought you swore loyalty to King Richard?"

At first, I thought she was joking. "So tell me what I can do."

"I am not the one you should ask."

"I thought you did not like me invoking that incantation."

"I am more worried when it invokes you without being asked, but if you can think of anything better to do, then I think you should do it."

She was not joking! I should have known her better, although she ought to have warned me when she expanded my responsibilities to include the political future of the empire. I rose, went down to my work room, and hurried back, shivering, with the *Myrddin Wyllt* scroll.

"It's cold down there," I explained, and made myself comfortable on the hearth rug, leaning back against a pile of cushions. The floor was one place I couldn't fall off of when I went into my trance. I began the chant, but soon regretted my choice of position so close to the fire. I pressed on, ignoring the heat. Before I reached the end I heard singing and smelled a curious medley of scents, of which I was only sure of two—roasted meat, and the odor of a large number of unwashed men. I was hotter than ever in my winter clothing.

My eyes and ears seemed to be in a castle hall, filled with a large assemblage of warriors, many of them sporting crusaders' crosses, red or white. Daylight, but not direct sunlight, was streaming in through wide unglazed windows, bringing a midsummer heat that England never knew, especially in March. I was almost certainly looking at a crusader force, part of the English and French army led by King Richard, although I saw some unfamiliar surcoats and headgear that suggested other nations, possibly German. This host of two or three hundred had finished eating, but not yet drinking. A few brown-skinned slaves were moving among them, distributing wine or ale.

Some notables adorned a high table, but they were vague to my sight, as unimportant details always were in *Myrddin Wyllt* prophecies. What mattered was that this packed hall was strangely still, intent on a couple of minstrels, who were strolling around between the tables, as minstrels do. They were singing a Provençal ballad together and each carried a gittern, although only the younger one was playing at that moment. Obviously they were very skilled if they could hold that normally rowdy audience in thrall. They were both blond. The younger, larger one was Lars of Pipewell, and the old one with the limp was me.

If there was more to come I missed it, because the shock of seeing myself from the outside jerked me out of the trance. I probably cried out, because Lovise lowered her embroidery and demanded to know what was wrong.

I collected my wits. "I seem to be destined to go on crusade."

"You? You're not that sort of knight, Durwin. Don't be ridiculous."

"It is prophesied," I insisted.

"You're far too old."

"I wasn't a warrior in armor. I saw myself as a minstrel, entertaining the troops." I was not about to tell her that Lars was with me, or not until I had spoken with him, anyway. I was face-to-face with the basic paradox in prophesy: could I block one of the *Myrddin Wyllt*'s predictions? It was to be a long time before I plucked up enough courage to try.

"I suppose if the king sends for you . . . ." Lovise glared at me as if this trance session had been my idea, not hers. "But he'd want you as a sage, not a minstrel."

"No chance. Richard will never send for me unless he needs someone to clean up after his horse."

"What nonsense! Why in the world do you say that?" Even a wife as skilled as mine must still depend on her husband's status to establish her own place in society, and so must needs defend it.

"Because I forced him to study Latin when he was a child. Because I stole his thunder when his father died—Queen Eleanor heard the news from me a week before his letters arrived, so he suspects me of spying on him. I am right at the bottom of his list of approved people."

"The queen, then, perhaps? Can you think of any reason why she might want to smuggle an enchanter in somewhere by passing him off as a minstrel?" When anyone in England said, "the queen," they still meant Eleanor. If Berengaria ever made it back to the west and bothered to visit England, we might have to change.

"No, dear wife," I said. "I cannot imagine that, but I can imagine a disgraced sage losing everything and having to sing for his supper."

The next day I went out and bought a gittern. I began taking lessons from a hungry-looking youngster who scraped out a living in the taverns and brothels of the town. With my experience in singing, I progressed well, although I often wished my fingers were younger.

What Lovise and I had not known that evening was that help would soon be on the way. Queen Eleanor was already in Italy, and close to meeting up with her absentee son. Without doubt, she gave him a lambasting for putting that avaricious, overween-ing, despotic, idiotic, et cetera, Longchamp in charge of England.

After delivering Queen-designate Berengaria to Sicily, Eleanor waited only four days before starting her return journey, and this time she traveled with Walter Coutances, who carried royal war-rants intended to settle the English dispute. They traveled slowly, dallying in Rome to witness the enthroning of Pope Celestine III, and it was not until June that Walter landed in England, Eleanor having remained in Rouen, the capital of Normandy. Heaven knows, she deserved a rest after such a journey.

I knew Walter well, for he had served as Archdeacon in Oxford for years. Although born in England, he was now arch-bishop of Rouen, and one of Richard's most trusted *familiares*. He arrived just as Longchamp completed his siege of Lincoln Castle, whose constable—husband of my old friend Nicholaa de la Haye—was a fervent John supporter. Longchamp had imported mercenaries to besiege one of the royal castles. England was very close to civil war.

Walter came with a royal warrant naming him as co-justiciar. He promptly called a parley, to meet in Winchester on July 28th. He negotiated a settlement between John and Longchamp. He could rein in the latter because he had brought another, secret, warrant from the king, allowing him to depose Longchamp. He did not reveal this publicly at that time, although I am confident he showed it to Longchamp, and the threat was enough to bring him to heel. Controlling John was harder, because everyone knew that the crusade was going badly, and the king was repeatedly reported to be at death's door with fever. More than once this was actually true. More than likely, Richard never would return.

I had begun some serious research into foreseeing. Merlin had left many prophecies, most of which made no sense until the predicted events had occurred. Or, as disbelievers would say, until something happening that could be twisted to fit the words. We had several prophetic incantations in our archives, but I had always discouraged students from dabbling with them. For one thing, foreseeing can be dangerous and has been known to drive users insane. For another, the Church regards it as blasphemous, an attempt to bind God. Only astrology was grudgingly approved, perhaps because it was never specific enough to make much difference.

Time is like a mountain torrent, one commentator had written in the margin of one of my grimoires, *and we stand on a boulder in it, trying to see what the flow will bring down next*. Another hand had added, *Until we fall off the boulder*.

The ancient Greeks relied on the oracle at Delphi, which is no longer in business, or on the entrails of animals, especially the liver, which has a mysterious appearance for a few minutes after being exposed. They, and the Romans also, relied heavily on viewing the flight of birds. Crystal balls and fire gazing, inhaling the smoke of burning herbs, prayer and fasting—there seemed to be no limit to the means, and very little to the ends.

What I could not find was any guidance on what happened if you tried to circumvent a prophecy.

In July Lars received his green cape as a qualified sage, having graduated from the College with the highest commendations on record—which outsiders might think was just sycophantic flattery because he was my son, but I knew had been well earned. We had a splendid family reunion to celebrate. Harald and his wife, Hilda, came from Pipewell; Iseut and Royse were brought by their respective future in-laws.

A year earlier Lars would have been clamoring to go off and help the brave crusaders. Now, like everyone else, he had lost enthusiasm for the cause, and the subject was not mentioned. But on the day after everyone had gone home again, as soon as his mother had left to visit patients, he accosted me in my workroom. He sat down and eyed me quizzically.

"My lord Father?"

"I am not God, Lars."

"Of course you are, to me, anyway. You always have been."

"Gramercy! I never noticed. You want someone smitten with a plague?"

"I'd rather you'd find me some generous and benevolent lord anxious to employ an eager, witty, hardworking, and incredibly sapient young sage."

"Dear boy, such sages are even rarer than are generous, benevolent lords and I don't know any of either." I gestured to the couch. "I do think I have a serious job for you, if you want it. It will drive your mother into hysterics, but it will be lot more interesting than mixing laxative potions in some damp and gloomy castle. Move over there. Now see if this agrees with me."

I handed him the *Myrddin Wyllt* scroll. He unrolled the first part and scanned it with a glance.

"What does 'Myrddin Wyllt' mean?"

"I'll tell you later. Chant it, and it will surprise you, I promise. I'll bring you back in a few minutes."

He lowered the scroll and regarded me with suspicion. "You're telling me that *my* chanting will put *me* into trance?"

I nodded, unable to resist a smile, because this was against everything he had been taught in the College. It was the cantor who should be entranced, not the enchanter.

"Carnonos? That's the horned god? What's the melody?"

"I find *All My Days* works well."

Faced with a completely unfamiliar lyric, Lars set a slow pace, but he sang without a fault. I was fascinated to watch the spell in action. I knew roughly where it usually put me into a trance, but he continued without a break, all the way to the end. Even then, while his arms gradually sank down with his hands still clutching the scroll, his eyes stayed wide open, and mobile. The rest of him lay corpse-like, his breathing barely visible, but he was watching something. I allowed him a few moments before I called his name and shook him.

He blinked a few times before focusing on me. "Where are we going?"

"You tell me."

He peered around, steadying his wits. "We were on a ship. You were vomiting over the rail."

"And you, I suppose, were finding that funny?"

"Um . . . I looked sort of greenish, too. I was taught that magic couldn't work over the sea."

"I'm a little ahead of the College there, son, but this is still a big secret."

"I'm thirsty . . ."

I fetched the wine and two beakers. Then I told him the story—Myrddin Wyllt, who was Merlin of the Wilds, the scroll, and the visions I had seen. He listened with amazement.

"Now you can see why I have kept this a secret," I said. "This ship you saw—did you notice any details, how many masts it had, or if it was a galley? Any scenery, landmarks? Members of the crew?"

Lars shook his head. "Just you and me and the sea . . . and what you were doing."

"That means a prophecy. It must, since we are not at sea right now, and never have been so far. When the details are not yet determined, then they cannot be prophesied. It was telling us that you and I will go on a voyage and you will be a better sailor than I am. Everything else is still undecided."

"But you saw us as troubadours in the Holy Land?"

"The Holy Land, possibly. Somewhere hot and sunny, yes, so not England. Troubadours yes, performing on a hot day, somewhere. And an appreciative audience. We were both singing. You were playing, I was just carrying my gittern . . . and maybe a hat, for gratuities. I'm not sure."

"It would be hard to tune two gitterns perfectly together and keep them that way."

At that moment, Lovise swept in. "Durwin, we must remember—what are you two up to?"

"Drinking wine before noon," I said, as Lars and I stood up.

She eyed us as if she had just been appointed Senior Recording Angel for England. "No, you look too guilty for that."

"We were just planning a journey, Mother."

"A journey to where?"

Knowing that I would have to break the news to her sooner or later, I said, "To entertain our gallant fighting men in Outremer."

She lost color, looking from son to husband and back again. "Both of you?"

"It seems that way, dear. Tell me, where in Oxford can we buy silk?"

With the firm hand of Walter Coutances on the tiller, the country retreated from the brink of civil war. Indeed, the struggle degenerated into farce. Geoffrey the Bastard, who preferred to be known as Geoffrey Fitzhenry, now Archbishop of York, returned to England although, like John, he had been forbidden to do so by the king. He landed at Dover, where he was accosted by Longchamp's sister, wife of the constable of Dover Castle. She demanded that the archbishop swear an oath of loyalty to her brother. Geoffrey refused and sought sanctuary at the local priory, but the next day he was literally dragged from the altar and thrown into a dungeon.

This was far too reminiscent of the murder of Thomas Becket, and the entire country erupted in fury. Longchamp had to take refuge in Windsor Castle. With clerics on both sides, interdicts and excommunications began to fly to and fro like bats.

In September John took it upon himself to summon a great council at Reading, which I of course attended. The barons were all reluctant to offend John, because they knew that word of the Richard's death might arrive any day and no one seriously expected the infant Arthur to succeed. Offending a future king would be dangerous, but likely less dangerous than foreswearing the reigning one. In effect, everyone was sitting along the fence like swallows planning their migration. I guessed the part I would have to play, and it would put me right between those legendary crashing rocks of the Symplegades, so I had my answer ready. I sat and said nothing until the call came.

After several hours of bickering, cursing, and droning, it was John himself who jumped up and pointed straight at me.

"Your graces, my lords, why don't we consult the ultimate expert on all things, Baron Durwin? Arise, Merlin Reborn, and prophesy for us! Will our beloved King Richard ever return from the Holy Land?"

I waited for a moment in the silence, and then stood up. I bowed to Walter, who was in the chair. "Your graces, my lords, I have never claimed to be Merlin Redux. It was our Lady Queen Eleanor who dubbed me that, and she spoke in jest. I do not claim to prophesy—but . . ." I said quickly before another wave of tumult could break over us, "I can quote the great Merlin himself. In one of his prophecies, he proclaimed: '*When the lion returns to his den, the dogs go back in their kennels.*'"

The loyalist barons cheered uproariously as I sat down. Merlin had never said anything of the sort, so far as I knew, but he could have done. One thing I did know about prophecy is that it is much safer when attributed to somebody else.

I left it to the council to decide whether "Merlin's" reference to dogs included John, King Philip, and Longchamp, or just some of them. The majority settled on Longchamp and voted to depose him. Walter, revealing his authority as supreme justiciar, agreed, and that settled the matter. John, triumphant, marched into London and summoned a public assembly, which likewise agreed that the justiciar must go. The idea of letting the common mob determine state policy is not only crazy, it is extremely dangerous. The rabble are totally unpredictable.

According to numerous reports, probably too good to be true, poor little Longchamp attempted to escape from England disguised as a woman, until a raunchy sailor received an unexpected disappointment and shouted for his friends to come and look at this. The humiliated Longchamp did, in fact, go into exile. John proceeded to travel up and down the land, seeking to gather support, predicting his brother's death, and claiming to be his successor. I was continually pestered by people anxious to know if the king was still alive, so I had to keep insisting that I was not, and never could be, Merlin Reborn.

Once in a while Walter would come by Oxford, and from him I learned the true news, stripped of its usual bodyguard of rumor. By November, King Philip was back home in France, spreading lies about Richard—that he had accepted bribes from Saladin to stay away from Jerusalem, had tried to poison Philip, had sent assassins to kill him, and so on.

Philip wanted his sister Aalis returned to him—with her dowry of Vexin County—but Eleanor refused to release her. Two cardinals, sent by the Pope to interfere, tried to enter Normandy and Eleanor would not allow them into the duchy. The war in the Holy Land had become a stalemate, with little fighting, much negotiating, and both armies in winter quarters. King Richard had been within twelve miles of Jerusalem and hoped to leave the Holy Land by Easter, 1192—so Walter told me.

"God send him good speed!" I said, and we drank to that.

1192 (part 1)

hat fateful year began with a January attack by King Philip on Gisors, the greatest of the border castles defending Normandy. Eleanor's forces held out, and Philip had to withdraw, because most of his barons refused to violate the Truce of God. He rode off back to Paris to lick his wounded pride and plot other deviltries.

". . . and consequently," he declaimed, "it is our will and decision . . ."

He was striding to and fro, dictating to a team of secretaries. His tunic and mantle were of finest silk, trimmed with ermine, but all his finery and jeweled orders failed to make him anything but a weedy young man with a devious manner and shifty eyes. Even his voice failed to impress.

". . . that for all these demonstrated atrocities and iniquities, we do declare the aforesaid knight, Richard of England, to be a most treasonous and perfidious vassal . . ."

Three or four witnesses stood in the background, and at least one of them was a cleric of high rank, a bishop or an archbishop, but I could see none of them clearly. The secretaries were also misty and indistinct, even varying in number as I watched, but there was absolutely no doubt that the speaker was Philip II of France, spewing his spite. Every hair of his fur collar was as clearly displayed as the way his breath smoked in the cold palace air, and so was the gleam of hate in his eyes.

". . . and do therefore command you, our dearly beloved cousin, as heir to the said lands, to hasten here to our capital and do homage for them, *videlicet* the Duchy of Normandy, the Duchy of Brittany . . ."

I turned to peer through the snow swirling past the window, and I could indeed see the mighty Seine River below us. When King Philip added the hand of the Lady Aalis to the bribes he was offering, I had learned enough. I pulled myself out of the trance.

I was not on my couch, but I was in my workroom, sprawled over my desk. I had not chanted the *Myrddin Wyllt*—it had summoned me, yet again. The vision had been a dramatic warning, giving me more urgent matters to worry about than the mechanics of foreseeing.

King Philip had been as clear and solid as the fingernails I was driving into my palms, but the scribes and witnesses had been blurred, so what I had seen was a prophecy, not a current event. Philip knew what he was going to do, but the rest of the cast had not been selected yet. So when would this revelation become event? Outside my window, there in Oxford, I could not see as far as the palace wall, as snow added to a heavy overnight fall. Soon, before spring.

And why had I been shown this now, today, early? Because the justiciar, Archbishop Walter, had spent the night in Beaumont Palace, not thirty yards from my door. He had been planning to depart this morning, but he wouldn't go in this weather. I must tell him my news at once. Before I reached the door of the workroom, I realized that I must first find Lars or Lovise to chant the *Loc hwær* with me.

Dealing with Bishop Longchamp had always been a strain, a reminder to keep one's will up to date. Calling on my old friend Walter was a pleasure in itself. He had obviously decided that the blizzard that had blown in last night justified a few hours' extra sleep, which he had certainly earned during his strenuous months of ruling a bitterly divided country. I sent up word that I needed to see him on a matter of urgency, and in moments was ushered into his dressing room, where I found him wrapped in a fur robe, having his scalp shaved by his valet.

He was a tall, bony man of my own age or a few years older—scholarly, amusing, good company. It was rumored that he had absolved Richard for rebelling against his father, but what else could he have done?

He waved the razor aside long enough to say, "Baron Durwin, good morrow! Is this problem so urgent that I must send Jacques away immediately and wear my miter all day?"

"Not quite," I said. "It does concern the king of France, but I think it will wait long enough for you to be made symmetrical."

He chuckled and told his valet to be quick but not so quick as to bleed him. As soon as his head was dried he dismissed the man, told me to talk, and set to work to dress himself.

"King Philip," I said, "is going to offer to accept Lord John's homage for all King Richard's domains in France, and marry him to Lady Aalis."

Clutching his hose, the archbishop sat down heavily on his chair and stared at me as if hoping that I was making a joke. "*Is going to?* How come you by this knowledge, friend?"

"In performance of my duties as enchanter general, Your Grace."

"You mean that you are being Merlin now, and I have to play the part of King Arthur?"

Nicely put—but he was an archbishop and prophecy was blasphemous.

"Aye, Your Grace. I fear I mean exactly that. Philip has not yet sent the letter, but he will do so soon. Within the next week, or possibly two, I think. Will John refuse such a bribe?"

"He already has a wife."

"There were some doubts about that marriage, as I recall. The Pope was reluctant to sanction it." Wives could be discarded.

Walter thought for a few minutes and then nodded. "It isn't a case of, '*Will* John refuse such a bribe?' but rather, '*Can* John refuse such a bribe?' and the answer is no. He can't possibly, because if you disregard loyalty, honor, and duty, and are ruled solely by greed, then acceptance makes sense. So, what can we do to stop him? I feel strangely reluctant to cut off the king's brother's head. Richard is fond of his brother and wouldn't like it."

"Lock him up in the Tower of London until the king returns?" The moment I said that, I knew that this was not feasible either. Supposing the king does not return? Then you unlock the cell door and run like the Devil?

"Can you provide a copy of this letter, Durwin?"

"No, sir. I can only offer my word. And my head, I suppose."

"Well then." Walter sighed. "No one can possibly stop him except the queen." He meant Dowager Queen Eleanor, not the real queen, Berengaria. "You will have to make all speed to Normandy and tell her what you foresee."

Thoughts of racing over through drifts and over waterlogged countryside, of crossing the storm-wracked seas of January held no appeal. "Sir, let me write a letter. You have many younger men, skilled couriers, who can reach Rouen long before I could."

There I was speaking common sense as well as cowardice, and he nodded. "I wonder where Lord John is now?"

"Lincoln."

Even Walter flinched at that brazen display of sorcery, but he did not question my knowledge or ask how I knew. Belatedly, he resumed dressing. "Then go at once and write your report to Her Grace. I will write one of my own. I just hope that her response arrives in time. I will go to Winchester to wait for it. And you will come with me."

Back at my house, I wrote my letter and sent it over to the justiciar. Soon afterward, at dinner with Lars and Lovise, I faced an unexpected family rebellion.

"I am deeply concerned at the way you keep falling into trances without meaning to," my wife declaimed. "Suppose you do that when you are riding a horse?"

"Obviously the horse will have to stop and pick me up."

Humor was not appropriate, as I was quickly informed. I was arguing with two qualified sages, both of whom could quote dangers and precedents.

"That *Myrddin Wyllt* incantation is Satanic!" Lovise said. "It is taking control of you, and you must stop using it. Stop now!"

"She's right, Father. You know that it is questionable, and therefore a downward step." Reaching into his fabulous memory, Lars began to roll off a long list of initially well-meaning sages who had slid unwittingly into darker and darker magic. My ability to argue was limited by the fact that he was quoting instructors I had trained myself with the same examples.

I eventually had to bend my councillor's oath and reveal a little of what was happening. "The test is not the method but the purpose, correct? The end justifies the means?"

Two heads nodded, but reluctantly.

"I am not doing this for my own benefit. Today I was shown the most serious move yet by King Philip of France against our liege lord, King Richard. His treachery and deceit are appalling. He is violating not only his personal oath of loyalty but also the Truce of God that protects crusaders. If the Pope will not stop him, then we must try. Do you disagree with that?"

Lars said, "Father, let us help you. You must stop invoking the *Myrddin Wyllt!*"

"I haven't done so in months. It sends me visions when it wants to."

"Then let me use it instead and perhaps it will leave you alone for a while. I am convinced that it is leading up to something big, which may not be as innocent as you hope."

Lars was not a boy any longer; he was a skilled sage, and his opinions must carry weight.

"I will have to ask the justiciar's permission," I said. "He can swear you in as my deputy, I suppose. As soon as the roads clear, he is going to Winchester, and he wants me to go with him."

Lars flashed his old grin. "That will make a change from copying incantations, day in and day out."

Lovise said softly, "I too will enjoy a change of scenery."

So I was going to Winchester with two babysitters.

Later that day the snow turned to rain, and two days after that the justiciar and his train left Oxford, bound for Winchester, which was still the official capital of England, as it had been in the days of King Alfred the Great. We followed the next day. After a cold and unpleasant journey, we found the castle full, so Eadig made us welcome in the chantry. We settled in to wait upon events.

There was a race in progress, although we were the only people who knew it. On one hand, Philip had to dictate and dispatch his letter to John. It had then to be delivered to him, which was no small feat in the middle of winter, and John had to rush to Paris to do homage, an egregious betrayal of his brother.

On our side, my warning had to reach Queen Eleanor in Rouen, the capital of Normandy, and her reply had to reach us in Winchester. Richard had given her authority over John, so she could even order Walter to arrest him—provided she believed in my prophetic powers. My neck was definitely on the block. I told no one, but I had fears that the race was also a contest between me and Bran of Tara. King Philip, too, must have enchanters in his service.

Early the next morning, the three of us gathered in the room Lovise and I shared, and she chanted the *Myrddin Wyllt* incantation. Nothing happened, nothing at all. My wife was definitely displeased. Lars took her place on the bed and tried his luck. The incantation had worked for him once before, but this time he saw nothing. We had to assume that this was good news. The *Loc hwær* reported that John was still in Lincoln.

On our second morning, we gathered in Lars's room, which was as cramped as a monk's cell, and he stretched out on his bed to chant the *Myrddin Wyllt*. After he reached the end and just lay there with nothing happening, my attention wandered.

"Durwin! Durwin, wake up!" That was Lovise shouting, far away. I came back with a start. Had I nodded off? No. Thirsty, I reached for the beaker that we had set ready for Lars. It seemed that old Myrddin's ghost had chosen me as his disciple and voice, me and no others.

"What did you see this time?" my wife demanded furiously. Anger often masks worry.

"You barely gave me time to see anything!" I thought back... ."Queen Eleanor has received the letters!"

Lovise and Lars snapped, "And?" in unison.

"And oh, saints! That lady has a vocabulary like a veteran Brabancon!" I laughed at their expressions. "She is coming. She was shouting for her litter. If I understood her Occitan correctly, she plans to hang a ball and chain on Lord John's scrotum."

(For those of you fortunate enough not to have heard of them, the Brabancons are the most vicious and feared of all mercenaries, monsters who kill men, women, children, and old folk without distinction, except that they rape the women before killing them.)

But to cross the Channel in February, a woman of almost seventy? If her ship went down, the traitors would win.

Either Carnonos was an obstinate god or the *Myrddin Wyllt* was a stubborn incantation. It refused now to respond to anyone but me. If Lovise invoked it, it ignored her. If Lars did, it might or might not respond, but only through me, depending on how far away I was. The other two grew very worried about this, but I just accepted that it worked. As long as we could trust its predictions, it was an incredibly powerful weapon against the two renegades.

A few days later I headed over to the castle to make my regular report to the justiciar. As usual, Walter received me alone, although rumors of Merlin Redux prophesying for him were already circulating.

"The queen has not yet reached Dieppe," I told him. "If the weather continues to hold, she ought to be here in a less than a week."

He nodded, frowning. "The sooner the better. A troop of mercenaries turned up in Southampton yesterday, claiming that they were hired by Lord John."

"Lord John was at Warwick last night."

Now Walter scowled furiously. "Durwin, you told me yesterday he was still at Lincoln! He could not have ridden to Warwick in one day, not with the roads in the shape they're in."

"I think he could, Your Grace. I've caught him doing this before. He travels with one attendant, an Irishman named Bran of Tara. I assume that he is a sage. How they do it, I don't know." But would very much like to.

"Then he could be in Southampton tonight or sometime tomorrow. He'll be gone over to France before the queen gets here."

"Unless we stop him," I said. "How soon can we get there and start making arrangements?"

The rain had let up the following morning when Lord John rode into Southampton town, possibly the busiest port in England. He headed straight for the castle, followed by a single companion, as I had predicted. The castle officially belonged to the king, but by then most of the constables in the country were in John's pocket. They might not obey him against direct royal orders, but they would cooperate so far as they could, anticipating a fat bag of gold as a farewell gift, and preferment if Richard failed to return. John rode in unchallenged, dismounted, and ran up the stairs to the keep without a hint that he had covered two hundred miles in a couple of days.

Stable hands had come to hold the horses. John's attendant, a stocky man with a forked black beard, had just unfastened a fat and obviously weighty saddle bag, when he realized that armed men had closed in around him. Lars was with them, wearing his green cape.

"You are Bran of Tara?" he said.

"What of it?"

"In my office as deputy enchanter general, I arrest you on suspicion of practicing black magic. Come with me and bring that bag with you."

Glaring, Bran dropped the bag and raised a hand as if about to cast a spell. Lovise, who had come in close behind him, jabbed a finger in his back and put him to sleep with a single word. It was safer to keep things in the family.

By then Lord John had cheerfully walked straight into the constable's office and found himself in the presence of the justiciar and me—no constable. We were both seated in the most comfortable chairs I had ever met. I had promised myself some like them.

"Greetings, my son." Walter extended his archbishop's ring, so that John had to kiss it, dropping on one knee to do so. "Did you have a good journey?"

"Until now I did." John rose, glanced around, then slammed the door shut behind him. There was a third seat present, but it was a simple three-legged stool, nothing like the two richly padded seats that Walter and I occupied. That was not my idea. I thought it petty.

John snarled and said, "On your feet, Saxon!"

"Stay where you are, Durwin," Walter said. "Please be seated, John. The enchanter general and I have some questions to put to you. At the moment this is just an informal inquiry, you understand. It probably won't have to proceed any farther."

In the two years since I had seen the king's brother, he had changed very little—just as dapper, just as arrogant, perhaps a little thicker in the belly and jowls. He put his hands on his hips. "I am sure it won't, Your Grace. Ask your questions, and I will decide whether or not I will answer them."

"How is your dear wife, the lovely Lady Isabella?"

John shrugged. "Haven't seen her in months, and she was never lovely."

"We have reason to believe that you have been in communication with King Philip of France."

"Have you really?"

"Have you been?"

"What if I have? We're on friendly terms, the king and I."

"He has been spreading vicious lies about your brother, accusing him of terrible crimes. How can you be on friendly terms with a man like that?"

"Richard can be very trying at times."

We were treading water here, waiting on evidence. If matters were proceeding as planned, my wife and son down in the yard were hastily rummaging through Lord John's baggage, hunting for incriminating evidence. Unless they brought us some soon, the archbishop and I were going to be in deep trouble. All we had against John was his bizarre ability to travel like a bird, and the only evidence for that was my word against his.

Walter said, "Durwin?"

I took a turn in the lists. "Tell us where you slept last night, my lord."

John's contempt flamed into scarlet rage. "What business is that of yours?"

"Black magic anywhere is my business, my lord. I am charged to find it and report it to either the king or the church. I admire your riding raiment. It is very finely styled, and the leather is clearly of excellent quality. Doe skin, is it? Yet it is remarkably splattered with mud and dust for such an early hour. A nobleman on the road would normally have his servants clean it for him overnight. If he lacked servants, his host would provide some. So I am curious to know how far you have come this morning."

"And you can remain so." John was starting to display the beginnings of a Plantagenet temper tantrum. His father had been known to chew a mattress in his fury.

"Yes, but to arrive here at Southampton so early? All the way from Warwick!"

He showed his teeth in an animal snarl. "You've been spying on me, you lopsided Saxon slug?"

"I know you were in Lincoln until two days ago. Just convince me that your journey here wasn't aided by Satan."

He had a hand on his sword hilt. "No, first you convince me that your spying wasn't."

Walter intervened. "So, John, you don't deny that you were in Lincoln two days ago?"

"I refuse to answer lies thrown about by a Saxon witch. I—"

Lars strode in, detoured around Lord John, and handed me a vellum scroll. He nodded respectfully to the archbishop and went out again. I unrolled the parchment. It was fine, soft calfskin, and the surface was totally blank. Why should a man travel with a saddlebag full of blank vellums? I could feel the warding spell on it. Whatever was written there could not be read without the antiphon. I turned it toward Walter, so he could see that we had failed.

Knowing that he had won, John was smirking. "What have you done to my ostler?"

"He has not been harmed," I said.

"I warned you years ago not to annoy me, witch. I will deal with you later."

Walter frowned at him. "We'll have no threats here. Baron Durwin was only doing his duty, and we will find out when you left Lincoln. You will be staying here for a few days, I trust?"

"I have not decided."

"I do hope that you tarry until your honored mother arrives. We expect her here very soon."

John guessed my part in this right away, for his anger flipped back to me again, flaring up like oil on a fire. "You are a meddling pest! Stay out of my affairs from now on, for I shan't warn you again." He faked a smile at Walter. "I am waiting for the rest of my escort to arrive, *Your Grace*, and then I am heading over to France to inspect some of my lands there. This is none of your business." He wheeled around and was gone, slamming the door behind him.

So our plot failed. I hung on to the scroll that Lars had brought me, and later that day I managed to remove the warding on it, revealing a long text written in a language unknown to me. I ran the Algazelus test for evil on it and the entire parchment turned black. That convinced me, but it would not have brought the wrath of civil law down on Bran of Tara, and it was certainly not enough to clip Lord John's wings.

More of Lord John's mercenaries arrived over the next few days, but Walter had interdicted all the ships large enough to carry them, at least for a short while. John was still there when Queen Eleanor arrived. She moved at once into the castle and sent for him. Their interview was brief and private, with no one else present except her faithful Amaria. I had foreseen it the previous evening.

Eleanor was seated, while Amaria brushed her hair for her. Her hair, I saw, was white and cut quite short, for she kept it hidden inside her French hood when she was in public. When the knock came, Amaria answered the door and reported, "Lord John, Your Grace."

"Admit him."

In he strode. He blinked at seeing his mother *déshabille*, then bowed low and started to say something.

"Shut up!" she snapped. "I don't need any of your buttery words. I am ashamed that my womb could ever have spat out such a faithless slug as you. All the oaths that you have sworn, and all the riches your brother has poured out to you, and you stab him in the back at every chance you get!"

John displayed amusement. "Had a rough crossing, did you?"

For a long moment they stared at each other, furious mother and insolent son. Then—"Just tell me why you are here," she said quietly.

"I am on my way to inspect my French lands, Mother. The best fertilizer is the owner's shoe on the soil, you know."

"Then listen carefully, Farmer John. If you leave here on a ship, I will confiscate every acre you own in England, every hide of land, every inch! And don't doubt my power to do so."

John did not, for he lost color.

"Now get out," she said, and he went without a word.

I had written to my long-time friend Nicholaa de la Haye in Lincoln Castle, and her reply was waiting for me when I returned to Oxford. She confirmed my spying—John truly had journeyed from there to Southampton in less than two days. I hoped that he would be more careful in future, as long as I was around to watch him. He might well try to arrange that I wasn't, of course, and I warded our house to repel curses.

In the following weeks Eleanor summoned four successive meetings of the great council and had every member swear a new oath of fealty to Richard. The peace could not last, however, and the news from the Holy Land was not good.

One morning I looked out the window and saw summer. By the calendar it was April, but the showers had done, the blossom had fallen, and swallows were frantically snapping up insects to take home to feed their broods. I trotted downstairs and found Lars already at work. We exchanged blessings.

For many months he had been copying incantations onto rolls of silk. I helped him with the proofreading, but it was tedious work for both of us, especially him. The advantage of silk was that a couple of bags could hold spells that would weigh a ton if written on vellum.

"The time has come," I announced. "We must go."

He looked at me darkly. "Another vision?"

"No, just a hunch, but it will take us at least two months to reach the Holy Land, perhaps longer if we travel as minstrels. By then the war may be over."

Lars took up the rag and wiped his pen very carefully. "Father, you have never told me exactly why we are going there."

"Because I don't know. I have been shown the two of us serenading an audience of crusaders. You saw us on a ship. I suspect that our exact purpose has not yet been settled, just that we will be needed somehow."

He nodded solemnly and stood up. "Then we must go for the sake of our souls." He added innocently, "I must remember to collect some worthwhile sins, for which I will be absolved when I have completed my pilgrimage to Jerusalem."

The hard part was saying farewell to Lovise. In the early days of our marriage, I had often been absent for long periods. Sometimes she had accompanied me, riding fourscore miles or more in a week, but even when I had to leave her behind, she had never complained. This time she did, because she thoroughly distrusted absolutely anything to do with the *Myrddin Wyllt* enchantment.

I prevaricated. "We are going to Westminster to see the queen. If she sees no need for us to go farther, then we shall turn right around and come home. All right?"

"You have foreseen this meeting?"

"I swear that I have not touched that spell since we returned from Southampton."

Which was true, because I had discovered that I knew it by heart, and sometimes, in those hazy moments as one drifts off to sleep, I found the verses singing through my mind. And then I would dream. Who can chose to dream or not dream?

She embraced me. "I have spent more than half my life married to you. I want you to come back safely and make it two-thirds."

"I want it to be three quarters or more," I said. "It will never seem like too much."

A leisurely ride through two wonderful spring days brought us to Westminster. I had visitor privileges at the palace, so as soon as I made myself known there, we were assigned comfortable quarters, together with water and towels. I had barely finished drying my face and hands when there came a knock on the door, which Lars opened to reveal a page in Queen Eleanor's livery. He was no more than twelve, and looked absolutely terrified as he reported that Her Grace would receive Lord Durwin right away.

I felt a jolt of alarm myself, mingled with triumph. I tried to remain impassive as I looked at Lars.

"Just a hunch, mm?" he said coldly.

"We shall see." I turned back to the boy and tried a soothing smile. "Lead me. I won't eat you, you know."

That comfort didn't work. He did say, "No, my lord," yet he seemed to cringe away from me as he led me downstairs to the Queen's withdrawing room. A cleric I did not know, undoubtedly one of her secretaries, seemed just as apprehensive as he rose from his desk and went to announce me.

The queen dowager was alone, except for her faithful Lady Amaria, who sat quietly in a corner, embroidering a sleeve with only the rhythmic movements of her fingers to show that she was alive. Eleanor had no use for the gossipy chatter of palace women. Ever since she had inherited Aquitaine as duke in her own right, she had lived in a man's world of war, rebellions, and crusades. She considered men best employed in the roles of troubadours or the gentle make-believe knights of chivalry.

She jumped up from her desk and came to greet me with hands outstretched, just as I seen in my dream. She was showing her age now—the long years of imprisonment had preserved her like a flower pressed in a book, but the exhausting work of ruling her son's empire was making her pay for every minute twice over. Yet, while her face had more lines, the glitter of her eyes under the long lashes was as fierce as ever.

"Welcome, Lord Merlin!" She offered me fingers to kiss, which was a signal honor. "You are very prompt."

"Prompt, Lady Queen?"

The smile deepened. "I had just finished dictating a letter summoning you, when word came that you had arrived at the gate. The news sent poor Francois into a paroxysm of prayer. I thought he would need a long sustaining draft of ink to recover."

"It was purely by chance, Your Grace. No magic involved."

"No?" She registered disbelief, but then let her amusement fade as she led me over to chairs and bade me be seated. "Well, the timing is suspiciously fortuitous. I need your service."

"As healer, minstrel, or enchanter, Your Grace?"

"Probably all of them! Know you John of Alençon, archdeacon of Lisieau?"

I recalled a rather plump cleric with an amiable face whose constantly convivial expression masked a powerful, analytical mind. "I have never spoken with him, but have heard him address the council."

She nodded. "He knows you. My son values him highly. I am sending him to Outremer to beg the king to come home. Beg! That shameless recreant, Philip of France, not content with spreading vile lies about him to anyone else who will listen, is now plotting against him with the German Emperor."

I waited for her to mention her other son, but she did not.

She said, "Philip swore to observe the Truce of God. He swore a separate oath with my son that they would not move against the other's lands until both were safely home. Hah! Renegade! Perjurer!" She fell silent, biting her lip.

After a moment I ventured to ask, "Just what are you asking of me, Lady Queen?"

"You are Merlin Redux, Lord Durwin. Prophesy for me! Will my son be able to take Jerusalem?"

I drew a deep breath and said, "No." Twice now I had dreamed of King Richard standing on a ship—at the stern, facing back over the wake, under billowing sails filled by a joyfully blustery wind. He was staring at the brown landscape fading into evening, and there were tears on his cheeks.

She nodded, saddened but unsurprised. "It seems that the army is badly divided. The leaders, especially what are left of the French forces, oppose anything he wants to do. They squabble over who will be the king of Jerusalem. They disagree over what the army should do next. Go to him, Durwin, and tell him that his empire is falling apart without him. Outremer is a trap and a snare."

She fell silent, perhaps remembering her youth, when she went there with her first husband, Philip's father. She had been quite a hellion in those days, it was said. There had been rumors of an affair with her uncle.

"The king my liege puts no stock in my prophesies, Your Grace."

"Then convince him! Go with the archdeacon. Bring my son home, alive and well. Or swear to me a prophecy that he will return safely."

"I have no guidance to offer on that, Your Grace. But I do swear that I will do anything I can to help my king, according to my oaths."

She smiled wanly. "His obstinacy may not be the worst of your troubles. That will be to avoid King Philip's spite. It is said that Philip, on his way home, held a secret conference in Milan with the German emperor. If he has turned Henry into another enemy, then my son's future is dark indeed."

Now I could see why she had been desperate enough to send for me, but not how I could possibly help. Nevertheless, one cannot refuse frightened queens or sorely worried mothers.

"If there is a way, I will find it for him, Your Grace," I said—rashly, as it was to turn out.

Later that evening I was formally presented to John of Alençon and in turn presented Lars. As I expected, the archdeacon was affable enough on the surface but hard as horseshoes underneath. In the presence of the queen, we were all very gracious.

An archdeacon is a bishop's senior deputy. Clerics distrust enchanters, of course, suspecting them of dealing with the Devil, and they are almost as opposed to troubadours, who are given to singing bawdy songs mocking noble persons, or praising the allures of other men's wives. The following morning, when we all set out with a troop of guards, John of Alençon and I rode side by side, and then the mask was dropped.

"I trust that neither you nor Sage Lars will be casting spells and summoning spirits while you travel with me, Lord Durwin?"

I was a peer of the realm, a member of the king's council, and just as much an emissary of the queen as he was, so I was not about to submit to bullying. "We will sing and play joyfully upon our gitterns, Your Grace. You may then wish we were castling spells and summoning demons of the most horrible aspect."

He frowned. "If your talent be that threadbare, you had best stay clear of the king, for he is no mean troubadour himself."

"Indeed yes, my lord. I have heard him sing. And Queen Eleanor herself praised my rendition of one of his compositions."

We called it quits then, for the time being.

Only once on our two-month journey did anything out of the mundane occur to upset our divine. It was not by my design, but by then I had pretty much accepted that the *Myrddin Wyllt* had a mind of its own—and had taken charge of mine as well. We sailed from Portsmouth over to Dieppe, and from there we had a four-day ride to the archdeacon's house in Lisieau. I would have called it a palace. There we spent two nights, enjoying the greatest comfort and best food any of us were to experience in the next year or more. On the second afternoon, I reached for another pigeon stuffed with truffles, and the room faded. . . .

I was standing in a grossly overcrowded street, or perhaps market place, for open stalls defined the sides of it. Half the people filling it were struggling to go either this way or that, while being impeded by the other half's clamoring to sell them something—garments, snacks, jewelry, fruits, themselves, their sisters, or drinks of uncertain nature poured from wineskins into much-used cups. The inhabitants blurred into the architecture. No one noticed me, much less tried to sell me anything, so I knew I was not present in the flesh.

When? Where? Why? What was I supposed to see?

The noontime sun stood higher over the rooftops than it ever does in England. The constant tumult of voices was dizzying, as were the odors of spices, cooking, perfumes, people, and the dung that paved the roadway. A plague of flies made the air almost unbreathable. Heavily bearded men wore strange head cloths and long robes, some black, some brightly colored; the women were packaged until only their eyes showed. But there were also monks, priests, and armed crusaders proudly flaunting the cross on their surcoats.

I was somewhere in the Holy Land, without doubt. Jerusalem itself, or one of the coastal cities? The background details all seemed very sharp, which meant that I was being shown imminent events, possibly even happening at that very moment.

Then I heard shouting drawing nearer through the babble.

The words were mostly in French, being repeated in a harsh tongue I did not recognize. "Make way!" they proclaimed. "Make way for the king!"

I heard horses, saw armed riders advancing through a surf of angry protest from the displaced throng. What king? Richard himself? I felt a sickening presentiment that I had been brought there to witness something both epochal and horrible.

Indeed I had. As the vanguard passed me, I saw their principal following, a finely dressed man of around fifty, wearing the crusader cross, and mounted on a curiously nondescript horse. He alone in that mob had some space around him, although not much. He was smiling, acknowledging the cheers of the Christians, ignoring the sullen silence of the browner faces. He seemed every inch a king, but he wasn't Richard.

A couple of monks shouted to attract his attention, holding up a letter. He edged his horse closer and reached down to accept it. They grabbed his arm, pulling him out of his saddle. Knives flashed. There were screams, blood—

I recovered my wits lying on the floor, looking up at many worried faces. Apparently I had started shouting, "No! No! No!" and then fallen off my chair. Someone had thrust a knife handle into my mouth to prevent me from chewing my tongue, although the *Myrddin Wyllt* chant did not produce that sort of fit. They told me I had been unconscious for a very few minutes, however long it had seemed to me.

I managed to sit up, with Lars's help, and demanded a drink. In a few moments I was back on my chair at the table, and John of Alençon had dismissed the servants.

Our host disapproved strongly. "Does this happen often, my son? I mean, you are facing a long and strenuous pilgrimage, not a journey to be undertaken by anyone whose health is precarious."

"It is a very rare event, Your Grace. How many *kings* are there in the Holy Land at the moment?" I racked my memory for any clue to the victim's identity, but he had worn no armorial bearings, and his guards had been Templars.

John of Alençon's frown darkened. "To the best of my knowledge, only our own King Richard. The German emperor died on his way there, and his son and successor, Henry VI, has remained at home, struggling to hang onto his crumbling dominion. King Philip tucked his tail between his legs and fled after a couple of months. The king of Jerusalem, of course, but the last I heard there were still two rival claimants—Guy of Lusignan and Conrad of Montferrat. *Why?*"

"Because I just saw either Guy or Conrad murdered, Your Grace, struck down by two assassins dressed as monks."

The archdeacon stared hard at me for a long minute, then turned to look at Lars, who sprang to my defense.

"If my father says that this is so, Your Grace, then you should believe him. I have never known him be wrong. He told Queen Eleanor of King Henry's death a week before the official news arrived."

"So I have often been told." John of Alençon made the sign of the cross and then drained a beaker of the superb wine. "I cannot see that this makes any difference to our mission. If anything, it makes King Richard's departure even more urgent. When we reach Outremer, you will be able to issue warnings to whichever claimant was elected, Durwin."

I said, "Aye, Your Grace, but I doubt that there is still time to do that. I believe the deed was done while I was watching."

We followed much the same path to the Holy Land that King Richard had taken two years before. We had no trouble within his empire, all the way south to Gascony, or even after that, when we rode across Toulouse. The count of Toulouse was officially one of Richard's vassals, but not one he would trust very far. Fortunately, an archdeacon on pilgrimage was not to be hindered or impeded. In the port town of Marseilles, we were fortunate to obtain passage on a ship of the type called a *buss*, which had thirty oars and one mast with a square sail. It was cramped and foul-smelling, but we had been warned about that many times.

The master, whom I knew only as Onfroi, specialized in shipping pilgrims and crusaders to the Holy Land—and back again, although he grumbled that there were far more going than coming. He was waiting for a full load, but the archdeacon had royal money enough to change his mind, and we left the following day.

From Marseilles we followed the coast all the way to Sicily, touching in at Genoa, Pizza, Salerno, and finally at Messina—so many wonderful cities, but never did we have long enough to explore them properly. A couple of hours to stretch our legs in the docks or along the beach was all. Lars went half mad with frustration, and I was not much better. We played and sang every day the weather permitted to keep our hands in. Our repertoire was chosen more to amuse the sailors than the archdeacon, but when he celebrated mass on Sundays, we duly switched to holy songs.

We had two days at Messina, in Sicily. Lars went off with some of the younger sailors, John of Alençon disappeared on his own business, and I explored the city. I hated the local language, which sounded like Latin run through a flour mill, but our second day there was a Sunday and I was deeply impressed by the singing in the cathedral.

No sooner had we raised sail and continued on our journey, than John of Alençon beckoned me to where he was standing on the fo'c'sle, his gown writhing in the wind. He was wearing his archdeacon face.

"Good morrow, my son."

"Good morrow to you, Your Grace."

"I learned in Messina that the dispute between Guy de Lusignan and Conrad of Montferrat over which should be king of Jerusalem was settled in the latter's favor. A few days later, in Tyre, he was dragged off his horse by two infidels dressed as priests and stabbed to death. That happened on the 28th day of April."

I just nodded. It had been a farseeing, then.

"You receive these prophetic visions often?"

"More often than I would wish, Your Grace."

"You do not summon them? Then who is sending them?"

I was not about to mention horned gods, of course. "I have to believe that they come from Heaven, not Hell, my lord. I try to put them to good purpose, never evil."

John of Alençon pursed his lips in frustration. "Queen Eleanor told me she dictated a letter summoning you and you arrived at the palace before it could be copied and sealed. I assumed that this was a blessed coincidence, but your description of an event that was happening hundreds of leagues away has to be a sending from either God or Satan."

I shrugged. "Did you learn who ordered this devilish murder?"

His Reverence scowled at the way I had changed the subject. "Sinan. Or so one of the murderers confessed before dying."

I suppose I looked utterly blank, because he continued. "Known as the Old Man of the Mountain, Sinan lives in Alamut, a mountain fastness somewhere in Syria, controlling a sect of infidels who worship him and will reputedly do anything he tells them to, believing that they thus go directly to Paradise. They will leap off cliffs at his command—or kill people. Even other infidels fear him. Reputedly even Sultan Saladin himself does, because he has found some of Sinan's followers among his own bodyguards."

If the *Myrddin Wyllt* enchantment expected me to battle this Sinan, it was backing the wrong tortoise.

"So tell me, Lord Enchanter," the archdeacon said, "why were you vouchsafed this revelation? And how will you use it in Our Lord's service?"

"I don't know yet, Your Grace." That was a lie. The vision had been sent to convince my companion—a personal friend of King Richard—that my prophecies were reliable. He would so inform the king. The king would believe him and start to trust me. It would be up to me to nourish that trust and use it to good purpose.

From Sicily we headed eastward to Corfu, Rhodes, and Cyprus, then sailed as close to southeastward as the wind would let us, aiming for Outremer. Saracen pirates had been a problem there in the past, so the master told us, but King Richard's ships had cleaned the sea of them. By then the archdeacon had taken my measure—or succumbed to my irresistible charm, as my irreverent son put it—and our relationship had become less formal.

He demonstrated this as we were standing together in the prow, watching the coast of the Holy Land creep up over the horizon. "I am not entirely looking forward to this, Enchanter."

"What in particular, Your Grace?"

"Having to tell our king that his mother says it's time for him to stop playing and come home."

"If his temper is as bad as his father's was, then I certainly do not envy you."

"And I confess I do not envy you either, Durwin. Richard has always detested practitioners of the occult. He is convinced that you are all either frauds or devil-worshipers."

My lord king had made that very clear even before he left England.

We came, then, safely to Outremer, and specifically the city of Tyre. After the fall of Jerusalem, five years earlier, Tyre had been almost the only part of the Holy Land still in Christian hands. In the twelve months since King Richard arrived, he had recovered a narrow strip of coast, marked by a line of small ports like a string of beads—from north to south, Tyre, Acre, Jaffa, and Ascalon. I was to see all of these, but very little of the interior. Tyre is the largest, and was where Conrad of Montferrat had been murdered.

King Richard, we were informed, was presently in the far south of the Holy Land. As yet, he had made no attempt to take Jerusalem.

Master Onfroi had brought some cargo that he was anxious to unload now, but again Archdeacon John produced a large bribe and persuaded the master to take us south to where the army was encamped, at Ascalon. Reluctantly, Onfroi embarked a local pilot and set sail again.

We made a brief stop at Acre, so Lars and I disembarked for a hurried inspection of the battered little town. In my vision of the siege I had seen it only from landward, not inside the walls. The damage from the long battle was still very evident, with hardly a building not bearing scars inflicted by the diabolic blizzard of rocks hurled at it by the Christian catapults. When we returned to the inner harbor, we were hailed by a tallish, deeply tanned man in his forties.

"Lars!" followed by an even more surprised, "Baron Durwin!"

We turned and together exclaimed, "Maur!"

Maur son of Marc was the Oxford sage I had assigned to lead our crusader contingent. He was a brilliant healer and a fine organizer, but in two years he had acquired a shocking stoop and streaks of gray in his beard. He had the haggard look of a man who sleeps poorly. "What are you doing here, my lord?"

He was carrying a bedroll and he was at the dock, so what was he doing there, instead of tending the army? And I wasn't sure what I was doing anyway, so as we clasped hands, I countered with, "I might ask the same of you, Sage."

"I am going home, my lord. There is nothing to be done here. Men are dying like moths in a campfire, but we healers are not allowed to do anything at all now. Only priests and mundane doctors are allowed to treat the sick, and they are useless. Fever and dysentery kill five times what the infidels do, yet enchantment is strictly forbidden."

"God help us! It's that bad?"

"Remember Ranulf de Glanville, who used to be justiciar? They buried him just three weeks after he stepped off the boat at Acre."

Appalled, I said, "Well, we are on our way to see the king. You come with us and tell us all about it and we'll see what we can do to put things right." I took his arm. When he began to protest, Lars took his other arm, and we headed back to our ship with Maur between us.

The winds were so skittish that for the next two days we were rarely out of sight of the Holy Land, and it was not an attractive prospect. The coastal plains were generally fertile, but baked brown by the summer sun, not lush like England or France. The hills beyond were drab and dry, almost desert, although somewhere within them lay Jerusalem, sacred to Christians, Jews, and Muslims. Without that objective, Lars and I agreed, Outremer would hold no appeal at all.

Those two days were not wasted, though. Sage Maur was well informed on the war—after all, what else was news in the Holy Land?—so the Archdeacon and I, and even Lars, cross-examined him in great detail. The army, he said, was champing at the bit, frantic to head inland and free Jerusalem—that was what they had come for. Even the French barons were back in line, now that the squabble over who was to be king of Jerusalem had been settled. But Richard was intent on cutting the road to Egypt, or even invading that country, for it was Sultan Saladin's main source of supply. I was not hopeful that I would be able to carry out my mission from Queen Eleanor to see the king safely home that year. It was already the end of May, and the Middle Sea became impassable about the end of September. Next year he might have no kingdom left to return to.

Of course, we asked about the death of King Conrad, and Maur's account confirmed what the archdeacon had learned in Messina. News to us, though, was that the barons had later elected the young Count Henry of Champagne to be his successor. He had the virtue of being a nephew of King Richard as well as of King Philip, so he was acceptable to both factions in the Christian army.

"And who ordered the murder?" Lars asked, a question neither the archdeacon nor I had yet put.

Maur seemed strangely reluctant to answer, but eventually dropped his voice to a whisper and named the *Hashshashin*, followers of the Old Man of the Mountain. Killing with knives was their style. And why, Lars demanded, would this Old Man want the new king of Jerusalem killed? Nobody knew that, the sage insisted, and would not even name anyone who might have hired the killers. Two years in Outremer had wrought drastic changes in my old friend of Helmdon days.

The most troubling thing of all that we discussed during his long interrogation was the king's ban on enchantment and the resulting disastrous state of the army's health. I wondered if my main duty might be to see the army home, not just the king.

"It began when the kings arrived at Acre last year," Maur said. "Many newcomers, including both kings, came down with a strange disease, which made their hair and fingernails fall out.

King Richard had himself carried to the front on a litter and joined in the fighting by using a crossbow. He is reputed to be a crack shot with it. King Philip just stayed in bed. The doctors could find no cure except rest and patience. They prescribed fasting and bloodletting, of course, but those just weakened the patient, as usual. The king adamantly refused enchantment."

None of which was news to me. "It sounds like the sailors' sickness," I suggested. "Did you try any of the enchantments for that?"

Maur shook his head, avoiding my eye. "Nobody had thought to bring any of those. Not us, not the French, not the various baronial healers . . . we had come to help an army, not a navy."

"I brought one," Lars muttered angrily.

Because of the Church's ingrained suspicion that enchantment was unholy, the two kings had banned its use in the crusade. Some men accepted the sages' help in secret, and those efforts were often successful, but the ban had remained. If flux or fever felled you, the medics would bleed you, priests pray over you, and a chain gang of prisoners bury you.

Around noon on the 29th of May, we were towed into the harbor at Ascalon, whose name was oddly familiar to me, although I could not recall where I had heard it. Its tiny harbor was jammed like a herring barrel with ships of all descriptions. Even flying Queen Eleanor's banner, we had to wait while room was cleared for us. There was very little town to be seen, for Muslims and Christians had fought over Ascalon many times in the last hundred years. The army's tents had replaced it, spreading far off out of sight, but everything was dominated now by the walls that King Richard was rebuilding, sprouting like a giant cancer, stronger and greater than before. No wall that Richard built was likely to fall down in the next strong wind.

"Ascalon is the gateway to Egypt," Sage Maur had told us. "Saladin tore down the old battlements when he heard that a new crusade was coming. If the Templars, say, or the Knights Hospitaller, can hold Ascalon, they will split his realm in two, Egypt south and Syria north."

"And Jerusalem?" Lars asked.

Maur pointed at the barren, dead hills. "Go forty miles inland. Don't try it without an army."

A little later, as Lars and I were leaning on the rail together, he said, "This is where you meet William."

"William Who?"

"William Legier. My godfather. Don't you remember? Three years ago, right after the great council at Pipewell, you told him you would see him again at Ascalon."

"That may have been what William thought he heard, but I didn't say that. I couldn't have done. I'd never heard of Ascalon."

"I was there, Father," Lars said softly. "I heard it too."

"Oh." What else could I say? I looked back at the turmoil ashore and wondered why on earth William would have come to the Holy Land himself when he had promised the king he was going to send four sons in his stead.

The moment we docked, an earl and two deacons hurried up the gangplank to learn who aboard merited that flag. Archdeacon John was whisked off to meet with the king, but it took me a little longer to persuade a mere knight that I might indeed be a member of the English aristocracy, not just a minstrel. Lars and I were escorted to the barons' compound, where Earl Robert of Leicester, laughingly vouched for me. He ordered his chief squire to find us a tent—somewhere, anywhere, for space was at a premium.

The size of the crusaders' camp was amazing—tents, horses, oxen, camels, mules, weapons, kitchens, stonemasons, builders' yards, makeshift chapels, banners, bakeries, latrines, paddocks, armories, hospitals, wagons, stretched out in all directions, farther than the eye could see. Above all people, thousands of people. Even this enormous sprawl must have borders, though, which must be constantly patrolled and guarded against Saracen raids. All of this was the responsibility of one man! I marveled that even royal shoulders could carry such a burden.

"Durwin! I might have known! Durwin!"

I turned at the shout, but for a moment I did not recognize the crusader pushing his way through the crowd in our direction. It was William, of course, but his beard was more white than brown, and three years had aged him ten. I dropped my bag and gittern to accept his embrace.

"You foresaw this!" he muttered as we separated.

"Not truly. What brings you here, old friend?"

"Revenge."

I recoiled from the torment in his eyes. "Not Absolon? He was such a—"

"All of them: Absolon, Baudouin, César, Dominique. I came to collect some dead Saracens in return, so their souls can find peace. And also," he added fiercely, "so that their brothers do not come on the same mission. Their mother is close enough to insane already."

I mumbled something meaningless, as one does. What words could replace four stalwart sons? Then, "Where did it happen?"

"In Acre. They had barely set foot ashore when the fever got them. They never blooded a sword, not one of them. They lie in unmarked graves, but I swear I will see they are avenged."

I looked to Sage Maur, for this horror tale confirmed what he had told us, and then at Lars, who was as white as a sun-lit cloud. We are all aware of Death lurking in the far distance and we all pretend not to notice. He only becomes truly terrible when he comes close.

"Show us where you are billeted, William," I said. "We have only just disembarked and need to find our way around."

He laughed. "Come then. We'll clear some corpses out of the way to make room for you."

A little later I registered at the royal enclosure. I was informed that the king was in conference, which of course I could have guessed. I left word of where I could be found.

I did not try to spy on Alençon's meeting with the king, but the whispers that sped around the camp were consistent. The astonished Richard had embraced his old friend and then taken him into his tent for private talk. Outside that tent only Lars and I knew why the archdeacon had come, or the substance of Queen Eleanor's message, although many people could probably have made a shrewd guess. After the archdeacon had taken his leave, so it was said, the king sat alone in silence for a long while. That did not surprise me. He must now choose whether to stay in the Holy Land in fulfilment of his oath, or hurry home to defend his empire from the avarice and treachery of his brother and King Philip. Richard always trusted his mother's judgment, and if she said the danger was acute, then he would believe her.

Confident that the court secretariat would be able to find me when I was summoned, I spent the next two days inspecting the hospital situation with Maur and Lars. It was appalling. As Maur had warned me and William now confirmed, disease was killing far more Christians than Saladin was. I did not interfere, because Richard was quite capable of marching me onto a ship and sending me home. Or of chaining me to a rock and dropping me into the harbor, for that matter.

Just as troubling was the state of the army's morale. Less than half a year ago, the crusade had been within twelve miles of the Holy City it had come to rescue. Many men had ventured

to high ground and actually seen it in the distance. Now summer had come, and they were back on the coast, mainly in Jaffa
and Ascalon. The men wanted to head inland and finish what
they had started. Richard disagreed. He knew the strength of
Jerusalem's defenses, knew that Saladin was pouring men into
it, and knew that every man in his own army would consider his
oath fulfilled the moment he stepped into the Holy City. Then
they would all head for home like bees at sunset, and who would
then man the ramparts against the inevitable Saracen retalia-
tion? The king wanted to head south, invade Egypt, and thereby
drag Saladin to the negotiating table. Alas, high strategy was too
subtle for the rank and file. It was even beyond the understanding of most of the barons, and mutiny was brewing.

My summons came toward evening on the second day, as a
welcome breeze off the sea began to soften the unbearable desert
heat. The king's tent was an elaborate complex, and he was seated
on a plain chair in a sort of courtyard where he had only sky
above him and could not be observed by anyone, except God and
perhaps his own concealed guards. After what had happened to
King Conrad, I would have wagered a lot of money that those
concealed guards did exist, even if Richard had not ordered them
himself. The ground was covered with an uneven, muddy carpet.
Tables and more chairs stood around in no discernable order.

I bowed. He looked tired, and gaunt. My eyes told me what
I already knew by hearsay—that he had repeatedly been sick. I
wondered if he was managing to sleep.

He began without formal greeting. "Describe the murdered
man's horse."

I thought back . . . "An elderly bay gelding with a white blaze
and four white feet."

"A newly appointed king riding trash like that?"

"That was what I saw, Your Grace."

King Richard shrugged. "You are likely right; he was on a private visit to a friend. Why are you here?"

"Because your royal mother sent me."

"To do what?"

"To be useful in any way I can—and I do have some unusual skills."

"Like seeing what is happening hundreds of leagues away?" He truly hated the thought; he did *not* want to believe, and it is very hard for any of us to credit unwelcome news. Above all, Richard the Lionheart wanted to be known as a man of honor, never one who had dealings with the Devil. Yet he did keep corresponding with Saladin, which the fanatics considered worse.

"Sometimes I can, Lord King," I said cautiously. "I cannot do it to order. The visions just happen." Not quite true.

"When the Devil sends them? Will we take Jerusalem and drive out the heathens?"

"I have received no direct guidance on that matter, sire. I suspect that the answer is no. Of course, I cannot see a negative, but I have foreseen you leaving the Holy Land with tears running down your cheeks."

He glared at me in silence. I kept my eyes lowered and waited, not venturing to return the gaze.

He said, "Sit down." And when I obeyed, "You are not afraid to offer unwelcome news, Baron Pipewell."

"Such would be no true loyalty."

"My mother trusts you. My father did. So I will try to. How can your unnatural arts be useful to me, as you put it?"

"I will tell you of my visions when they come, if they do. More urgently right now, your army is wasting away. You must know that you have hundreds of men lying at death's door, yet you will not let people like me try to help them?" This time my anger won, and I did look straight at him, a breach of decorum. Kings should not be questioned.

The wintery eyes chilled even more. "I suppose I could let you prove it on a few victims."

After two days of silent rage, I found it difficult to control my temper. "About five years ago, gracious lord, I was summoned to treat a dying woman. I had two days' hard ride to reach her and by the time I arrived, she could not breathe, her lungs were full of phlegm, her fingernails were turning blue. Her physician had given up hope. My cantor and I chanted over her, and she recovered. Had she not done so, Archdeacon John would not be here now."

His face turned white, but whether from rage or shock I could not tell.

"Your mother," I added unnecessarily.

"Go then!" he barked. "See what your magic will do for the fluxes and the fevers of Outremer. But you must first warn your patients that your treatment may imperil their souls, and they must give their consent."

I stood up and bowed. "And one thing more, sire?"

"Ask."

"If I am granted a vision and it suggests immediate action—an enemy attack coming, say—I shall need access to your presence." No subordinate would dare interrupt him to say that a wizard wanted audience.

He showed me the royal teeth. "I am tempted to cut off your head and mount it on a bedpost. At least it would be handy."

"But not much use, even as decoration."

"I suppose not. *Fulk!*"

A leather flap billowed, and a young knight appeared. Noting that he held an already-spanned crossbow in one hand and a bolt in the other, I felt the hair on my neck stir.

"Lord King?"

"This is Baron Durwin of Pipewell. Some credulous folk call him Merlin Reborn. He is to be kept supplied with the passwords, all of them."

From then on, wherever I happened to be, every day just before the night watch came on duty, either Fulk Gourand or some other royal aide would appear at my elbow to whisper passwords in my ear. I was usually so busy that I barely heeded them. Fortunately the *Myrddin Wyllt* never distracted me with visions when I was healing.

As Richard had known, rumors about the man with the cane being Merlin Redux were already circulating in the camp. I wasn't happy about them, but I assumed that they would aid me rather than hinder, so I paid them no heed. I had a fairly imposing flaxen beard by then, which may have helped give me archaic status. I was also known as Three Legs, which I liked even less.

We soon discovered that there were more healers still around than Maur had known, mostly barons' personal sages. All of them had been healing in secret, but their patients had been mostly knights and lords, not the common archers, men-at-arms, or servants. When we passed the word of our new royal authority and set to work, it did not take us long to find the best incantations for the local plagues, and soon we were hauling men away from death's door by the wagon load. Those who were too far gone to give consent, as the king had required, we had to allow to die, but most of those had passed out of our reach anyway.

Soon I had organized teams, starting with cooperative priests or deacons, who began the process by explaining to each potential patient the Church's official view that enchantment was devil worship. Knowing the chances of dying from whatever disease they had contracted, very few of them decided to refuse treatment.

Next came a squire or page, who asked about symptoms, and thus was able to advise the enchanter and cantor of what they had to deal with—dysentery, typhoid, or tertiary fever. Those were by far the commonest, but there were a few others just as nasty.

One man I was happy to meet again was the king's favorite minstrel, Blondel de Nesle, and we soon renewed the brief friendship we had struck three years earlier, in England. He came and listened to my chanting one morning, and after a while asked if he could try. He sang like an angel, that man, and the spirits rewarded his patient with a very fast recovery. Tall, slender, blond as his name implied, and a wry observer of mankind, he made an excellent enchanter, or cantor. And when a sufferer declined enchantment as devils' work, Blondel would sing a psalm or two over him, which often seemed to help too.

I saw very little of William Legier. While I was busy healing, he was busy hunting Saracens. He went out daily with any scouting or foraging party he could find, but the enemy was rarely available for his murderous purpose. Lars had decided that my old friend had gone mad and I found that hard to deny with conviction. To avenge four deaths from fever by slaughtering other human beings hardly seemed rational. I think if his sons had died in battle he would have been happier. It was the very futility of their lives that drove him.

While I was working two thirds of every day at healing, the barons mutinied. Led by Duke Hugh of Burgundy, who had taken King Philip's place as leader of the French contingent, they voted to attack Jerusalem. Richard seemed to dither for a few days. I may have helped him decide, for I was able to report that I had just seen Lord John in Nottingham Castle, which I knew well, so he wasn't conspiring with Philip in France.

Early in June, the king announced that he would agree to make another try for Jerusalem, and would remain in Outremer until the following Easter. So the crusader army set out, unwinding across the plain like some gigantic hungry serpent.

Most of our patients were recuperating by then, so I left a small party of healers behind to tend the invalids who remained, while the rest of us went off with the vanguard. The Saracens increased their night raids, but lost more men than they slew. By June 10th, we had reached Beit Nuba, a small fortress at the base of the hills. It had been razed by Saladin and repaired by the crusaders, for this was where they had halted in January, a mere twelve miles from the Holy City, just one easy day's ride on a good road—had there been a good road and no resistance.

So near, and yet so far!

And there all progress ceased. The heat was much worse there than it had been in Ascalon, where breezes off the sea had brought us some relief. For a few days, we healers were less in demand, and it seemed that we had left the diseases behind, but they soon caught up with us. Probably it was just that the army had dug fresh latrine pits, which soon became as foul as usual. Even the Romans had known that fevers are caused by bad air.

Rumors abounded—that we were waiting for reinforcements, that the Saracens had poisoned every well between Beit Nuba and Jerusalem so the summer heat would dry us up like prunes, that the walls of the Holy City were so strong that a siege would take longer than the two-year struggle for Acre . . . and so on. I was not so much concerned with why we were going nowhere as I was about Lord John and King Philip conspiring back in France, but I had no more visions to guide me.

Then, on the 20th, or thereabouts, one came. It was while Lars and I and a group of similarly dog-tired healers were slumped around a fire in the evening, chewing some appallingly vile dried meat. It think it had previously been part of an elderly camel. The fire, I should mention, was minuscule, for there was almost no fuel to be had except dung. It barely warmed the meat laid on it, but it scattered sparks upward to the stars. There was no conversation. I suppose we were all dreaming of the loved ones we had left behind, so very far away. Somewhere much nearer, a group of crusaders were singing *Le Chanson de Roland*, in Burgundian accents.

According to what Lars told me later, my eyes rolled up and I began to mumble in some unknown tongue. He grabbed me lest I topple into the fire, while everyone else began to mutter about Merlin.

After a few moments I came to myself and looked around to see where I was. Then, "The king!" I said. "I must tell the king!" I scrambled up, almost forgetting my cane in my urgency. Ignoring warnings that there was no way I would be allowed in to see him at this time of night, I went stumbling off through the camp, with Lars at my side, steadying me every time I stumbled over tent ropes.

Passwords! Passwords? What in the name of Holy Peter were tonight's keys to Heaven?

Fortunately, I had remembered them by the time I reached the guards around the royal enclosure. Challenged by two pikes with a flashing sword right behind them, I said, "Blessed are the meek!" That got me inside, where a flaming torch demanded my name and the second password, but I had the third one ready: "Barleycorn." The third would win me immediate entry, even if King Richard was in bed with Queen Berengaria—except that she happened to still be far away in Acre.

That same young Sir Fulk Gourand I had met the first time I had been allowed in nervously raised a flap for me and announced, "Baron Durwin de Pipewell, Your Grace."

I limped into the lions' den. His Grace was not alone. He was in conference with at least a dozen nobles, all standing in a circle, meaning that they were talking business. At least thirteen pairs of eyes turned to glare at the intruder.

"Durwin!" Richard barked. "You have news for us?"

"Um, yes, Lord King." I glanced uneasily around the audience. Did he really want me to babble prophetic heresy about visions? I tried to convey with my eyebrows that the two of us ought to withdraw to somewhere private.

A voice said, "Merlin? . . ."

"It had better be from a reliable source!" the king snapped, and I caught the hint—he wasn't yet ready to receive reports of visions in public.

"One of our best sources, sire. He says that there is an enormous enemy caravan on its way north, guarded by a large escort. At least a thousand camels, he estimates, possibly twice that. He thinks it will be in our area right about the time of the full moon . . . sire."

Well! The mood brightened dramatically. The lions smelled antelope and smiles blossomed everywhere. The king, especially, looked delighted.

"Excellent! Do you know what route the infidels will take?"

"Alas, no, Your Grace." One rocky hill or sandy gulch looked like another in a vision. "It may not even have been decided yet."

"True, very true. My lords, I shall send out more scouts. This may be a chance to bring Saladin to his knees." The king gave me a nod of dismissal.

Sweating, I found my way out into the chill desert night. Lars was there to escort me back to the Leicester camp—his night sight was much better than mine. I fully expected an early morning summons, but it seemed to come one minute after I closed my eyes. Lars was fast asleep, so Fulk guided me back through the maze to the royal enclosure.

Richard looked almost as weary as I felt, but he was obviously well pleased with me. The strain of leading such a motley army was telling on him, making his moods unpredictable. I was granted a chair and a goblet of fine wine, then he demanded a proper report on my vision.

"I saw some place in the desert waste, Lord King, at first light. The moon was just setting, so it was at the full or one night past it. The caravan was assembling to move out. The vanguard had already left, and they were definitely heading north."

"Truly a thousand camels?"

"More, sire, many more. Plus horses, mules, dromedaries. A huge host."

"I already have spies out, you know. They haven't reported any signs of a great caravan leaving Egypt."

"It probably isn't within their range yet, Your Grace, and they have to come back here to report, which takes time."

"You are very confident, Baron."

"I stake my word on it, sire. And something I can tell you that your spies cannot—something I could not reveal earlier—is that you are going to intercept it. While I was watching, I watched the Christians' attack. I swear I saw you in the lead, sire, on a gray horse, with a full moon setting."

He laughed. "But you did not see yourself there? Because I am going to take you with me, Baron Durwin of Pipewell! And if your vision is not a Satanic trap, we shall deal the Saracens a deadly blow."

Which would be nothing compared to what he would deal me if it was.

That brief struggle was honored with the monstrous name of Tell al-Khuwialifia, after a pitiable oasis in an otherwise empty desert. On the 24th of June, the Christians attacked in force, charging out of the dawn. No one had suggested that I don armor or carry a lance. I stayed on the outskirts with a band of other healers, ready to treat our wounded, but few needed us. Although vicious, the fight was short, for most of the Saracens soon panicked and fled. Quite apart from the thousands of baggage animals we took, the loot was stupendous, and it was the first real booty the crusaders had seen, for Acre and other towns they had liberated had all been already stripped bare by the Saracens. Weapons and food, silks and jewels, silver and gold—it was a mythical hoard.

My name was made. The pretense that I was a spy-master running a secret troop was needed no more—not that anyone had ever believed in it anyway. There were no more jokes about devil worshiper or Lord Three Legs. From then on I was a hero, Lord Merlin Redux. Even bishops were sometimes polite to me.

And from then on, King Richard believed in my prophecies—usually.

Soon after that profitable raid, I had a vision of near-panic in a congested city that could only be Jerusalem. I stood atop David's Tower like an angel on a cathedral spire and watched fortifications still being strengthened. With the vision of a hawk I could make out dead animals being dropped into wells of sweet water far outside the city walls.

But then my view shifted to a street where a long string of camels ridden by armed men was wending in single file through a crowd of weeping and wailing spectators. Dreamlike, I went with them, although in the real world I would never have been able to keep up with them in the crush. I could tell from the riders' rich raiment and fine weapons that these were no ordinary troops. Eventually we reached a great city gate, which shadows told me faced north, and there foot soldiers were holding the spectators back and the camel riders were forming up in formation around one man. So richly clad he was, and so impressively attended, that he could only be Sultan Saladin himself. Who else would command an escort of hundreds? When the force was properly assembled in formation, the gate was swung open and he rode out.

I went and told King Richard, as soon as he dismissed yet another conference, that Saladin was fleeing Jerusalem. He just grunted that I must not tell anyone else, and dismissed me.

The barons' meeting had been noisy, and secrets spread like plague in the crusader camp, so I soon leaned the gist of the arguments. The barons still wanted to push on to Jerusalem. The army, almost to a man, agreed strongly. Some of then had been far from home for years, struggling to reach a city that was now a mere day's walk away. The French, under the Duke of Burgundy, were especially insistent. The Latins who resided in the Holy Land—mainly Templars and Hospitallers—all agreed with Richard, for it would be up to them to hold Jerusalem after it had been liberated from the Saracens' grip and the crusaders had departed.

Richard, of course, had the added problem of the renegades, his brother and King Philip. What were they up to, back in France? Now that John of Alençon had left to return home, only two other men in the camp knew about that problem—Lars and I—and Richard did not know that Lars did. That same night I was shaken awake and summoned back to the royal compound.

His field tent was almost as sparse as the one I shared with Lars, only slightly larger. Clearly the king had been unable to sleep. He was barefoot, wrapped in a silk gown, and pacing. He greeted me with a grim but apologetic smile.

"I need your advice, Lord Merlin. Pour yourself some wine, sit down somewhere and listen to my troubles." He took one seat, leaving me a choice of the other.

"I listen well, Lord King, but advise poorly." His wine was the best in the entire Holy Land, and if to lend a loyal ear was the best way I could serve him, then so I must.

"I apologize for mistrusting you in the past."

"No need, sire. I am overjoyed that you trust me now." But did he? I think even now that Richard never trusted any man completely. He knew men too well. And he was right, because I was later to learn that even my *Myrddin Wyllt* prophecies could be fallible.

"I must warn you, Lord King, that your honored father, may he rest in peace, would heed my counsel on almost any topic except warfare. I am no warrior."

"But I am," he said. "And every other man in this camp thinks he is. I want some common sense, that's all. If you have a vision or two to add, so much the better. Now listen!"

He rose to resume his pacing and began to stack his troubles on my shoulders like straw on a camel. If he lingered too long in the Holy Land, he might lose his kingdom. If he could not take Jerusalem, he would slink home a failure, and that would greatly aid Philip in his aggression, whereas if he could take Jerusalem, he would be a hero throughout Christendom, and no man would dare lift a finger against him. But could he take it, even with all those camels and other pack animals that the caravan raid had provided? His supply lines would be a flimsy thread winding forty miles from the coast through hostile terrain, and even water would have to come from Beit Nuba. Horses and camels drink rivers of water. The holy city itself was almost invincible, protected by rocky cliffs, vulnerable on only one side, where the defense could concentrate.

"Worse," he growled, still pacing and speaking more to history than to me, "even if it falls, who will hold it? The Hospitallers and Templars are spread too thin, and every other man in the army wants nothing more than to say a prayer at the Holy Sepulcher and then run home with all his sins forgiven. When the next fighting season opens in March, we shall be gone and Saladin will pluck the peach from the branch again."

The king refilled his goblet and at last sat down. "He is an honorable man."

For a moment my sleep-starved brain did not understand. Then I said, "The sultan, sire?"

"Aye, Saladin. We are negotiating, he and I. Not face to face, but through his brother, Safadin. If we can make a treaty, we can save thousands of lives on both sides."

That there had been talks was common knowledge, but I was astonished to hear that the war might end in a truce. Some men—especially Frenchmen—would certainly call these negotiations treason and betrayal. I confess that I was frightened as I glimpsed the full horror of the king's predicament. Was he seriously expecting me to advise him? Must I bear that cross?

Then my thoughts went otherwise. I looked up and saw that he was regarding me wryly. "You are nodding at something. What?"

"I have been wondering why, if you are so reluctant to attempt an assault on Jerusalem, you brought the army out of Ascalon and so far inland, back to Beit Nuba, where it was last Christmastide. But if you are negotiating a treaty, your voice must sound much louder here than it was when you were down on the coast. You are feinting? Twisting the sultan's arm, Lord King?"

Those cold pale eyes studied me. "I suspect that you are the only man in the army who has worked that out, Baron Durwin."

"Perhaps just the only one rash enough to say so, sire."

He smiled—faintly. "It helps me just to talk it out with someone, and especially with a clever man. If you have foreseen anything that would help, then I want to hear it. But also, I am curious to know what you suggest."

"Your Grace has already heard everything I have foreseen, and I do not know how any of that will help. I feel almost as if a curtain had been drawn across events, and I am not permitted to meddle further. But a question, if I may? Would you have caught that caravan at Tell al-Khuwialifia had I not foreseen its existence and prophesied that you would intercept it?"

Richard's eye narrowed, but that may have just been a reaction to the unusual experience of being questioned. "Possibly not. Our spies might not have detected it in time for us to prepare. Why?"

I hesitated, because I wasn't sure why I had asked. "I am puzzled that I was sent such a clear and helpful vision a few days ago, and now, when you need it, sire, I receive nothing."

Richard Lionhearted was many things, a very complex person, but stupid he never was. He frowned. "You are assuming that your visions come from God and that the wealth that fell into our laps at Tell al-Khuwialifia was a blessing, but I cannot be certain that it was. It boosted morale enormously, yes, but many men now find themselves much richer than they were, and this tempts them to forsake the cause and go home. It could be that your visions do come from the Devil, and now the Lord is blocking them. You cannot argue that the other way, can you?"

Sadly, I said, "No, sire." Satan could not block God.

His nod indicated that my audience was now over. "Take that lantern and my thanks, Baron," he said, and headed for the crucifix to pray.

I had failed him.

The stalemate dragged on. Richard announced that he would go with the army to Jerusalem if it went, and would fight with it, but he would not lead it there, for he was certain the assault would be a disaster. The French took him at his word and saddled up for the journey. No other contingent joined them, and by the end of the day they had returned to quarters.

That effectively ended the Third Crusade. On July 4th, that fateful anniversary of the disastrous Battle of the Horns of

Hattin, an unhappy and sulky army pulled up stakes and began its move back to the coast.

In Jaffa, Lars and I were assigned a very pleasant room—cramped for two, but with a fine view of the citadel and the harbor. The city had surrendered to Richard immediately after the battle of Arsuf, almost a year ago by then, so it had suffered none of the siege damage that had wrecked Acre. We inspected the hospitals and chanted healing spells for anyone who wanted them. We also performed as troubadours a few times, and after one concert, I recognized the hall and realized that we had just fulfilled the long-ago vision that told me we were going to go on crusade.

All too soon the king went north again to Acre. Lars and I followed, and there I was presented to the two queens—Berengaria, queen of England, and Joan, Richard's sister and widow of King William of Sicily. They were both very gracious and regal, although neither seemed a fabulous beauty to me, who so yearned to be reunited with Lovise.

Acre was still recovering from its long siege, much of it still in ruins. I was assigned a room because I was a baron; Lovise would have called it a closet. Lars had to make do with a blanket on the floor, which was narrowly better than sharing a tent with a gang of men-at-arms.

Richard allowed his negotiations with Saladin's brother to become public knowledge, because agreement seemed very close. The Christians would keep the coastal strip and the Saracens Jerusalem. The Holy Sepulcher itself would be a Christian church again, which pilgrims would have the right to visit. One indigestible problem was that otherwise insignificant town of Ascalon, south of Jaffa. Richard had invested many months in fortifying it again, because it was the throat between the two halves of Saladin's empire, Egypt and Syria. He insisted that it remain fortified. Saladin would not agree. Neither side would yield on this. Needless to say, Richard's enemies continued to spread more rumors of treachery and bribery.

Timing was becoming critical. The shipping season in the Middle Sea ends at the end of September, and many ports forbade departures much after that date. Richard had previously announced that he would stay in Outremer until Easter, but now he seemed so frantic to be off homeward that twice he summoned me and demanded a prophecy of when he would have a signed treaty in hand and could leave. Twice I had to confess that I had been sent no vision.

He scowled at this admission, as he did whenever his Merlin failed him. "Then you had better do what the rest of us do, Baron Durwin. Go away and pray for a miracle, because we surely need one."

I took that as a dismissal, and departed. I did remember to put a smile on my face as I limped across the crowded anteroom. It wouldn't do for the king's prophet to be seen delivering bad news.

A few days later, on 29th July, King Richard received his miracle. It was sent by Saladin.

I was no longer kept informed of the daily passwords, because Richard's Merlin was so well known that no one would deny me access to him. He had already retired to bed when I came hopping and skipping, banging my cane, in a fevered rush to tell him my news. This was the palace of Acre, not an army camp, and the king slept with the queen. There was a slight delay before Richard emerged from his bedchamber with a sheet wrapped around his nudity and a glare that would have panicked Hannibal's elephants.

"*Well?*" His roar might have been heard all the way to Jerusalem.

I did not flinch. "Lord King, the Saracens are attacking Jaffa."

His reaction was a surprise. His glare faded into a blank, faraway stare, and then into a delighted grin. Everyone else exchanged astonished glances.

Then the Lionheart said, "Well, that cunning old rogue!" It was exactly the response an expert chess player might make when his opponent makes an unexpected, but clever, move.

Again, I glanced around at the surrounding guards' faces, and saw that they were still as much at a loss as I was. The king barked one question at me: "When?"

"Now, sire." I knew that because the foreseeing could not have been clearer had I been standing on the Jaffa town wall.

Nobody got much sleep in the rest of that night. By dawn the king was aboard ship and ready to sail, with a band of about fifty knights and a couple of thousand archers. A small army under Henry of Champagne was preparing for a long march south to Jaffa. Lars and I were in that land party, and it gave us our only real experience of warfare. Of course, Saladin had foreseen this expedition, and had posted troops all along the way to harass and impede us.

As Richard had seen immediately, Saladin's attack was a masterstroke. If he could retake Jaffa, the port closest to Jerusalem, then the crusaders would be right back where they had been a year earlier, and the Third Crusade would have been an even greater failure than the Second. He very nearly did succeed.

Of course, I can only report what I learned later. Lars and I were busy riding southward while trying to stay alive under the Saracens' blizzard of arrows. On the second day Saladin's siege engines brought down a section of the Jaffa town wall and his troops swarmed in to begin the looting and other horrors that always follow such an event. Saladin ordered an immediate attack on the citadel, but was unable to stop the violence in the streets and houses. Thus the citadel was still holding out when

Richard's flotilla arrived. Faced with enemy flags flying in the town and a noisy army lined up on the beach, he assumed that the whole city had fallen until a young priest leaped down from the citadel wall into the sea and swam out to explain.

The king ordered an assault. A storm of bolts from his archers cleared the beach for him, sending the Saracens fleeing to the shelter of the town. As soon as the ships were in shallow water, Richard tore off some of his armor, jumped overboard, and waded ashore. His knights followed, and one of the fiercest struggles of the entire crusade followed on the beach. The giant Richard fought like a legend—Achilles, or Arthur—but so did the man beside him, Baron William of Weldon. Screaming, "For Absolon, for Baudouin, for César . . ." he even out-fought the king himself. That triviality may seem unimportant, but it had a strange influence on later events.

The citadel forces sallied to help. Despite their enormous advantage in manpower, the Saracens were driven off. A couple of days later Saladin ordered a counterattack and there was more ferocious fighting, in which Richard again fought like a one-man army. His utter disregard for his own safety was legendary and the source of his nickname. It was also madness in a king, especially one who ruled such a jumble of territories and had yet to sire an heir. Even Saladin himself is said to have criticized him for this. But again he triumphed. The Christians prevailed, and the Saracens withdrew with their proverbial tails between their legs. Henry of Champagne's relief force arrived just after that. Lars, Blondel and I set to work repairing the wounded.

William Legier had received an arrow in his left shoulder, which can be a very dangerous wound, but we managed to extract the head and it healed cleanly. He was a happy man at last.

"So, how many Saracens did you kill?" I asked him as I bandaged him.

"Lost count," he admitted. "Either seven or eleven, but I finished with César, so I need one more for Dominique, to make them all equal."

"No, you don't. I am quite certain that Dominique, wherever he may be, is quite satisfied with his memorial, and would be happiest if you just went home now to be a father to his surviving brothers. Won't that satisfy you?"

He thought for a moment and then shook his head sadly. "You'd never make a warrior, Ironfoot. You never understand."

The Battle of Jaffa was the end of the crusade. King Richard and Sultan Saladin had fought each other to a standstill. All that remained was to agree on a truce, and then the crusaders could all go home. For the Lionheart, going home was to be much easier said than done.

Jaffa before the battle had been far from a paradise. After the battle it was much less like one, and Richard chose to keep the army outside the city, in tents. This was little improvement, for there were hundreds or even thousands of dead Saracens and dead horses lying everywhere. No one was prepared to bury them, and the stench became indescribable in the August heat. Inevitably, it brought fever. One man badly smitten was the king of England.

As I well knew, this was far from the first time he had been sick since he arrived in the Holy Land, but it was the first time since we enchanters had been allowed to use our art to treat diseases. Alas, Richard was a stubborn man, and he refused to accept our help in his own case. Possibly he feared more accusations of devilry. He grew steadily sicker.

Meanwhile efforts to end the war continued. Saladin's brother, Safadin, was the main go-between, accompanied by various emirs, their equivalents of our barons. The sticking point was still the fortification of Ascalon, and eventually it was Richard who yielded—the walls would come down. On September 2nd the Treaty of Jaffa was signed, although the Lionheart was reputedly too weak to do more than offer a handshake.

My information on this came from his aide, Sir Fulk Gourand, who often came to visit Lars and me when we all happened to be off-duty. The three of us would drink wine in the dark, because lights brought such hordes of insects—not that we didn't get well bitten anyway. Poor Fulk was a fifth son, whose gift for languages had won him his post at the king's side. With the crusade ending, there would be plenty of able young knights wandering around Christendom looking for employment, and he had no prospects for a living if Richard died. He was appalled that the king was throwing his life away by refusing the healing that conjuration could bring. How could any healing possibly be evil? Had not Jesus healed the sick?

But one night soon after the signing, Fulk seemed more cheerful. "He's going back to Acre," he announced after his first swallow of wine. "Says he'll go in a litter, and he'll feel better when he gets there."

"Cleaner air will certainly help," I said. "Is he strong enough to bear the journey?"

Fulk groaned and said, "I hope so."

"Lars and I will tag along, just in case he changes his mind on the way." I could leave the rest of the army in the hands of all the other healers who were now free to serve.

Even with the war ended, a king must not travel without guards, and it was a large procession that wound its way back northward. Lars and I had no trouble attaching ourselves to it. By the middle of the month we had reached Haifa, a small settlement across the bay from Acre itself. The original crusader fort there had been destroyed by Saladin, but some pleasant buildings were still standing, and here Richard called a halt. I feared that he now felt too sick to travel and was preparing to die.

"This is ridiculous!" I told Lars. "I am going to heal him whether he wants it or not. Bring the whole bag. We may need all of them by now!"

In practice we both knew almost every healing chant by heart, but it never hurts to prepare for the worst, so Lars grabbed up the sack of enchantments, and we set off to beard the Lionheart in his den. I stooped out of our tent and almost butted into Fulk, who was puffing as if he had been running. It was, as usual, a very hot day.

"Lord Durwin! The queen wants you!"

"She's here?" Silly question, because Fulk couldn't have run all the way from Acre in that heat. "We are just on our way to see the king."

"I think you'd better hurry if you want to catch him alive."

We were ushered quickly into the presence of not one, but both queens. Joan, Richard's sister, was tall and fair-colored. Berengaria, his wife, was tall and dark. They were seated under an awning on the flat roof of a house, and a lady-in-waiting was standing by to interpret, for Berengaria's Latin was poor and her southern French baffled me completely. Translation is always an awkward arrangement, but that fact might come in handy if either of us ever had to plead that we had been misunderstood. The patient lay under another awning, distant enough that the sea breeze would carry away sounds, and prevent him hearing whatever we said.

"Baron Durwin," the attendant said, "Queen Berengaria wants to know if you can heal her husband's fever, as you have healed so many others."

Wasting no time, Lars had hurried straight from the top of the stairs, over to the dying man. He came back to me to report: "Maybe. Worth a try."

"Lady Queen," I said, "your royal husband, our liege, forbade us to chant over him. If we disobey him, he might cut off our heads. Only if you assure us that he has since changed his mind, and that he asked you to send for us, will we dare to do this now."

Before the attendant could even translate what I said, Joan said, "Yes, he did. I was here and I heard him." Her reactions were faster than the Spaniard's, although the language problem might have had a lot to do with that. I didn't believe what she said, and she did not expect me to, but now we had all the excuse we needed.

I bowed. "Then, by your leave, we will begin at once." And so we did.

As we strode over to the patient, I heard Lars mutter, "Pray God we are in time."

The king's breathing was a heartrending sound, even for me, who was hardened to that choking rattle.

I said, "Amen. Let's start with the *Vene*." We had no need for texts. I gave Lars a pitch and we began a long and desperate battle against the king's sickness. For the first hour or so, I thought we had come too late, and I would probably have given up had our patient been anyone else. At last he began to breathe more easily, and after that we progressed rapidly. His fever dropped, his pulse steadied, and eventually his eyelids flickered.

I raised his head and let him have some sips of wine.

When he had drunk, he whispered, "By what right?"

"Her Grace, our queen, passed on your orders, sire, saying that you wished us to treat you."

He frowned, then smiled faintly, and his beard moved in a nod. I was relieved to see that he understood. Patients who have sunk so close to death often recover their physical health but not their wits.

"It is wonderful to see you back, Lord King. The land will rejoice. Now I will send for fresh bedding, and a sponge bath for you. Drink as much as you can, and eat a little when you feel able. You have a lot of recovering to do."

So we left, spreading the good news to the queen and a whole crowd of courtiers waiting in suspense downstairs. Church bells were rung in Acre.

Three days later, when I paid my usual evening visit to see how the patient fared, I found him already sitting up, sipping broth. I inquired after his bowels and so on. He was still very weak, but I had done all I could for his flesh. His spirit, I judged, now needed help much more. His crusade—for it was his, more than anyone's—had failed. At best he could claim a draw, but the Holy City remained in the heathens' hands, and he must see that as a loss. He still had to find a way home, time was running out, and we did not know what John and Philip might be up to behind his back. I feared that his will to live was faltering, and I needed to boost it. I knew exactly how to do this.

"I was granted a vision, Lord King. It was very brief, but quite clear. Saladin is dying, sire! Not right away, but I have seen his death, and there were spring flowers and herbs beside his couch."

The king took his eyes off me and stared into the distance for a long minute, while I waited for an answer. When it came he spoke it to the scenery. "So all I have to do is stay here until Easter, as I promised, and when the Sultan dies, all his emirs will start scrapping like raunchy cats, and I can pick up Jerusalem like a fresh-laid goose egg?"

"I can only report what I have foreseen, Lord King," I said uneasily, wondering why he was not more pleased by my news.

The fighting season was almost over. The chances that King Philip would attack Touraine or Normandy before next Easter must be very slight. What was wrong?

His eyes, no longer bright with fever, turned to me again. "You swear this is the truth, Enchanter?"

"Aye, sire. Have I ever lied to you?"

"If you haven't, then you are the only one who hasn't." He smiled. "You had better spread the news. Tell my brother."

"Better to go home and show him," I retorted, which was extremely improper of me.

He raised an eyebrow, but did not comment, just waved away the two nurses. They scurried off, no doubt to whisper the exciting prophecy they had just overheard. I realized that he had some more personal matter on his mind.

"Bring that stool close," he commanded, and when I had done so, he continued quietly, not looking at me. "I am very grateful to you, Lord Enchanter, and I no longer doubt that your gifts are from God. I have another matter that troubles me. Can you cure . . ." He drew a deep breath. "Sterility?"

This was a king talking! All men want heirs, but kings especially need them.

"We are not talking about impotence, sire? You can perform the act itself? It is the lack of results that distresses you?"

He nodded, reluctant to put the problem in words. He had been married to Berengaria for a year and a half. Of course they had been far apart for much of that time, but even so, two strong and healthy lovers should have become a threesome by now. The most likely prevention was a curse, and for a moment I thought about Bran of Tara. It did not seem wholly out of character for Lord John to have a sterility curse laid on his brother.

"I have heard rumors to the contrary," I said.

He shook his head. "I have acknowledged two by-blows. It doesn't matter, because they cannot inherit, and kings are expected to keep mistresses. Just between us two . . . I doubt that the timing made it possible in either case."

"Babies do not count very well, Lord King. They can emerge at seven months or ten, whenever they choose. Their mothers have been known to tamper with the data, too. I do have an incantation for the condition you fear, but it is back in England. It requires a single voice, so only the subject and the enchanter need know its purpose."

I recalled that its marginal notes implied that the singer almost never detected acceptance, and therefore it might be no more effective than plain encouragement, so I continued: "The best treatment is a compound of love and persistence. It is the easiest medicine to take that I know of."

The Lionheart closed his eyes. "Go, then. And if you breathe one word of this discussion, I will personally cut out your tripes."

As soon as the king was strong enough to travel, the court moved back to Acre. When I went to see my patient there, I was informed that he was in conference. When next I had a vision I believed was urgent enough to report to him, I was again denied admittance. Finding myself persona non grata, I could only assume that he now so regretted his medical confessions that he could not bring himself to look me in the eye again. As it happened, I was wrong, and he had another reason for avoiding me, but there was nothing I could do. I could not even explain to Lars, who was sorely puzzled.

A few days later I was summoned by the Bishop of Salisbury, Hubert Walter, a close friend of the king, and a nephew of the late Ranulf de Glanville. If you expected a senior priest to be effete and emaciated, he would have disappointed you, for he was a tall and vigorous young man who looked as if he had been carved out of oak. There were a couple of dozen of us standing two-deep around the table, from earls to bishops to minstrels. I was not surprised to see William Legier there; ever since the battle of Jaffa he had been high in the king's favor. I wasn't sure in what capacity I had been included—prophet, healer, or minstrel?

Walter began by swearing us all to secrecy. That done, he said, "We are here to plan King Richard's departure. He has named us as his chosen companions. The two queens will be leaving imminently, but he still has matters to attend to, and must delay his own departure. Sailing so late in the year is always dangerous, and this voyage will be especially perilous. Do any of you wish to visit Jerusalem and wait until the sea lanes open again next year?"

All heads shook.

He smiled. "I expected nothing less. The danger we shall face is that our king has acquired a number of very powerful and unscrupulous foes. Chief among them, of course is Philip of France.

"Nor must we forget the freelance pirates—Moorish, Greek, Saracen, and others. One thing is certain: if anyone can catch King Richard on his way home, Philip will pay a huge price for him, and what will happen after that does not bear thinking about."

He looked around the glum faces. "Anyone want to change his mind? No? Well, then, you wonder how we will travel? The winds are westerly just now, and no ship ever built can sail through the Gut of Gibraltar against the winds and the current. Nor can any survive the rages of winter in the ocean beyond, so the sea route to England or Aquitaine is out of the question. I do not know which road the king will choose."

All eyes seemed to turn on me, the king's prophet, but I did not know either, and did not speak.

There was very little discussion. A sea voyage so late in the year was a daunting prospect in itself, and the political threat was worse.

The bishop dismissed us. "The password will be, *May St. Brendan be with you.* On the day you receive that, go down to the dock at sunset."

I lingered, indicating that I needed to speak with him when we were alone. He was obviously reluctant to grant me a private interview, either because he was a bishop and I was a devil-worshiper, or because he knew I was currently out of royal favor. But I persisted, and when the last witness had left, I said, "Your Grace, I have important counsel to offer the king regarding this journey he plans."

"Then you had better write it down. He does not wish to speak with you."

"I do not understand. Do you know why I have fallen out of favor?"

"No." Obviously this was not his fault, and I ought to be glad that I was included in the escort—assuming that I was not to be forgotten at the last minute. I bowed and departed.

On the way out I was accosted by one of Queen Berengaria's ladies and conducted into her presence. She made me welcome, and we had the usual struggle with dialect and translation. She again thanked me for saving Richard's life and presented me with a splendid ruby ring, which fitted on my pinkie.

I then begged a favor—that Lars be allowed to accompany her. I assured her that he was very good at curing sea sickness, and she readily granted my wish. My real motive, of course, was that I thought her chances of surviving the journey to England were much better than her husband's.

When I told Lars of this arrangement, he saw through me right away. "So that at least one of us will survive to comfort Mother in her old age?"

This heavily tanned young man with the sun-bleached hair was not the youth who had left England with me. Crusading had aged him, and me perhaps even more.

"That's part of it."

"What has *Myrddin Wyllt* been telling you now?"

The answer was dusk, a storm, and a ship driven ashore, men fighting for their lives in the surf, myself among them. "Nothing," I assured him.

"Father!"

"Nothing except this: I have foreseen you arriving at home and greeting your mother, but I am not there. If we leave here together, then the implication must be that I have died on the journey. If we go our separate ways, then perhaps I am merely delayed. You want my oath on this, Son?"

My logic was very shaky, and honor required that he resist, so we had a long argument. In the end I won, and he agreed to accompany the two queens. Thus I took one more step down the slippery slope. When I had implied to King Richard that I knew a cure for sterility, I had not mentioned that I believed it to be useless, so I had not quite told a lie, but what I told my son was outright falsehood. Thankfully, it worked anyway, and when the two queens sailed away on September 29th, Lars was aboard and my burdens felt lighter.

1192 (part 2)

Still the king dallied in Acre. Shipping grew scarce as vessels were beached for the winter, and I suspect that this was part of his plan, for the coasts of the Middle Sea swarm with pirates, all of whom must be salivating at the thought of the ransom they could collect if they could just capture the richest king in Christendom—he would not be traveling with a fleet of a hundred ships this time. If he dared wait until there were no other vessels at sea, then their spies could not report his departure.

It was not until October 9th that I received the password. That evening, no banners flew and no bugles sounded as the Lionheart tiptoed out of the Holy Land like a mouse leaving a house full of cats. The ship was another *buss*, this one having two masts bearing triangular sails, and twin rudders. The king had a small cabin at the stern, so I did not see him actually leaving, but I knew from earlier visions that he wept as Acre slid away into the darkness.

I had forgotten how much I hated sailing. Ships are never still and ever noisy—ropes and planks creaking, waves and sails slapping. The crew claimed that the vessel would carry a thousand men, but I cannot imagine how, for even our small party seemed too many for comfort. We also carried horses in the hold, so we preferred to stay on deck as much as the weather allowed. Even in the Middle Sea, which is usually calmer than the ocean waters around England, vessels rarely ventured far from land, and we ate and slept ashore as often as we could.

Our captain was a Genoese, whose French I could not understand at all, but the real commander was Robert de Turnham, Richard's admiral, who had done such magnificent work in sweeping Saladin's fleet off the seas and keeping the crusade supplied.

On the third day, we entered Limassol harbor in Cyprus. Richard had conquered the island on his outward trip, then sold it to the Templars. When they failed to pay him for it, he had given it to Guy of Lusignan as compensation for losing the throne of Jerusalem. Probably this visit involved money, because I noticed that the king was accompanied by a couple of heavy chests when he came back from wherever he had gone.

From Cyprus we pushed on to Rhodes, sailing against the wind as best we could. We had been fortunate with the weather so far, but autumn had been stormy and kept sending brief squalls to remind us of what it could do. I had no idea where we were heading, and I doubted that either king or captain knew either. God would decide.

We had two notable minstrels aboard, Blondel de Nesle and Sir Conon de Béthune, and in fair weather they would sing, with all the passengers and most of the crew listening eagerly. Sometimes they would invite me to perform, which I was honored to do, and rarely Richard himself would. But he never acknowledged my presence. I worried, but I had to assume that he had some reason for bringing me, and another for ignoring me.

Even from a distance, I saw great improvement in my former patient. Relieved of the stress of running the war, he rapidly reverted to regal form—abrupt, confident, inquisitive, unpredict-able, and autocratic. He had a fine musical ear and could compose masterful ballads, or even very humorous songs, as he did once at Beit Nuba in response to one the Duke of Burgundy composed to mock him. You could never be quite sure with Richard when he was being humorous, for he could also be deadly, like most kings.

We bypassed the Aegean Sea, although I had secretly hoped that we would turn north and head for Byzantium, no longer ruler of half the old Roman empire, but still the world's greatest city. We didn't, but early in November we arrived at Corfu, an island off the west coast of Greece that is officially ruled by the Byzantines. In practice its dock area was a boiling pot of every race and nationality from Spain to Outremer and England to Egypt. Richard went off with an armed escort and the rest of us pitched in to help unload the horses so the poor brutes could see the sun again. Passengers drew the line at helping with the mucking out the hold, though.

I never learned who Richard visited, probably several people, for it was almost dark when he returned. By then water casks had been refilled, victuals purchased, and the four-footed cargo had been reloaded—unhappily.

At dawn we set out again, heading roughly westward, as if bound for Italy, but the winds were erratic, so we made little progress. One evening, as I was hanging over the rail wondering whether I would feel better or worse if I did lose my dinner, who should set his arms alongside mine but William Legier. It was entirely in character that William never got seasick. He would regard that as unforgivable weakness.

"So what do you foresee, Merlin Red Duck?" he demanded with loathsome joviality.

"Too many things."

He gave me a quizzical glance. "Good or bad?"

"Bad, mostly."

"Where is the king headed?"

Perhaps it was the queasiness in my stomach, but I forgot discretion and snapped at him. "How should I know? I haven't spoken to him in weeks."

"What? Why not?"

"Because he refuses me audience. I am out of favor for some reason."

"But you could advise him?"

"I could certainly warn him of disaster if he stays on this course."

"Stay right here!" William told me, and marched off to beard the Lionheart in his den. I doubt if any other man aboard would have dared do what he did—or survived doing it, whatever it was. Nobody *confronts* kings! All I know is that he came skating over the rocking deck a few minutes later and careened into the rail beside me.

"The king will see you now."

When I tried to protest, he took me by the scruff of the neck and propelled me in the right direction.

"Don't try to kneel! Sit there." King Richard pointed to the bunk, where he would have been short of headroom, and settled himself on the solitary chair, which was lower. I had never seen inside the royal cabin before. It was tiny, especially for a man of Richard's size. He poured two beakers of wine and handed me one. I accepted it, although my belly roiled at the sight of it.

He said, "Sage Durwin," then took a moment to gather his thoughts. "Baron Weldon tells me that you have news for me. I admit that I have been neglecting you of late."

I muttered something as tactful as I could fashion. Royal apologies are so rare that there are no rules for dealing with them.

He smiled bitterly in the flickering lamplight. "At our last meeting, you told me I had won. You said that all I need do was wait until spring and Saladin would be gone, his empire crumbling into pieces. What you didn't know, but I did, was that I could not stay until Easter as I had originally planned. I was out of money, and the army was dwindling as men gave up and went home. The French refused to cooperate in any way, although they expected me to cover their expenses there—while they continued to spew out vicious lies about me, accusing me of taking bribes, betraying the cause by dealing with the heathens, having people stabbed or poisoned. They were even denouncing you as a devil-inspired witch. I absolutely had to leave before winter! Saladin was in much the same predicament. His emirs were tired of the war, threatening to take their men and go home. But I had to have an armistice to take away with me, so that in two or three years I can come back and try again."

Return! I had never imagined anything like that. He had bled England white to finance one crusade. He had showered money like rain to fight his campaign—kings never count costs. Now he intended to do it all over again? Nor had I ever been able to understand why my prophecy about Saladin's death should have made me so unwanted. Kings think in strange ways. I said nothing and tried not to watch the wine swilling back and forth in my beaker.

"So?" the king said. "What prophecies do you have for me tonight, Lord Merlin?"

I looked him straight in the eye, which is a breach of courtly etiquette, and asked him a direct question, which is another. "Where are you heading now?"

He frowned but answered civilly enough. "To the coast of France, west of Marseilles. There are many little ports I could land at. The shores of the Middle Sea are not far from my duchy of Aquitaine. Count Raymond is a vassal of mine. He has done homage to me for his county."

"Perchance he has, Lord King, but he is now in connivance with King Philip. I have seen them together, drinking toasts to your destruction. Count Raymond was boasting that he has set guards on every point at which you might land. And Philip swore that, once Raymond handed you over, you would never see the sun again."

Richard's glare chilled my blood. "You swear this?"

"I swear it as I swore to you of Jaffa, and Tell al-Khuwiali-fia! Toulouse means death for you, Lord King. Philip will lock you up until you die, an event that he may hasten by losing the key."

It is not unknown for kings to starve prisoners to death. Even Richard's father sometimes indulged in such an execution, although he did not normally favor barbarities. And Richard's great-grandfather, Henry I of England, locked up his own brother for 26 years, until he died—childless, of course, so that Henry could inherit his dukedom.

King Richard sighed. "We were good friends once, Philip and I."

Not now, though.

As though he had heard me thinking, the king said, "But not now. He has not merely broken his crusaders' oath, but another oath, which we swore together, not to molest each other's lands until we were both home again. His hatred of me has become a madness, a canker of the brain. He has attacked our dukedom of Normandy. He has been spreading lies all across Christendom: that I tried to poison him when he was in Outremer, that I paid the Old Man of the Mountain to have King Conrad assassinated, that I accepted a huge bribe from Saladin not to attack

Jerusalem, that at the end I poisoned the Duke of Burgundy, and so on. Worst of all is the bitter, bitter truth—that the huge effort and expense put into the crusade has failed to recover the Holy City, and I was its leader, the traitor who would not even lay siege to it."

He began to rise as if he wanted to pace, but then he remembered that he could not even straighten up in the cabin, and sat down again.

"If Toulouse is out, then I must sail to Italy. That is how my wife and sister were planning to go. They were to proceed to Rome and seek protection from the Pope. I shall follow. The Pope, certainly, must respect the Truce of God."

Ha! Although the current Pope was not the one Richard had so grossly insulted on his way out to Outremer, the Vatican has the longest memory in the world. Besides, Pope Celestine was close to ninety and well past his best.

"And where from there, Lord King? The northern half of Italy is ruled by the German Emperor. He is another who has sworn a treaty with Philip, your foe. They agreed that the Truce of God does not apply to you, that you must be put on trial for all those imaginary crimes you just mentioned—murder, treason, and so on—and that the Truce of God cannot shield a traitor. I have seen them shaking hands on it."

The Lionheart scowled, but he nodded. "Aye. Henry is another of my enemies, because he claims to rule the island of Sicily, and I befriended King Tancred when I was there."

There was a pause, while I wondered if I was about to be thrown overboard. When the king spoke again, his voice was louder and harsher.

"God's legs! Must you croak like a raven all night, Merlin Redux? Have you no good news for me at all? Where do you suggest I go?"

The air was icy. I wondered if the real reason he had denied me audience for so long was just that he feared what dismal future I might reveal.

"King Philip boasts that you cannot set foot anywhere between Spain and Byzantium without falling into his hands, Lord King, but if he is watching the ports and harbors, you may escape him, for I foresee a shipwreck in my own future, a vessel driven aground in shallow water by a mighty storm. Many men will make their way to the beach, so I do not believe that the death toll will be high. On such a night no one will be watching for a king's landing. I prophesy that you will wade into Christendom unseen, not stroll down a gangplank to be arrested."

He stared at me in silence for a long minute, his face expressionless. Then, "Is shipwreck the best comfort you can offer, Baron Durwin? Tell me some positives you foresee."

"I wish I could just pour good news out for you, sire, like ale from a barrel, but my skill does not work that way. I admit that I have one sure prophecy to give you, but it is not without its own shadows. I know where you will celebrate Christmas—feasting in a great hall with music and good cheer."

He smiled then, but his smile was wary. "Who hosts this wondrous Yuletide banquet, and where?"

"It is a mighty castle, sire, Dürnstein by name."

He frowned. "Sounds German. Whose arms does it bear?"

I braced myself for trouble. "The banner it flies shows one white bar between two red."

I had never seen those arms in real life, but it had not been hard to find someone aboard who could identify them for me, and Richard certainly knew.

"*Leopold?*" he roared. "The duke of Austria? That avaricious, pretentious, opportunistic weasel, who tried to claim a major share of the booty in the relief of Acre?" And whose banner had ended in the moat, thrown there by Richard's own men, or so I had heard. "You would have me fall into his greedy, grasping little hands?"

"Not by my choice, Lord King!"

Richard slumped back on his chair. "Besides, his liege is the German Emperor. I am so far above Leopold's rank that Henry will undoubtedly demand that Leopold turn me over to him, as the laws of chivalry require. And you tell me that Henry is in league with Philip!"

Here I must tread with care. "But did you not just describe Leopold as greedy, my liege? To King Philip you are a hated foe, to be butchered. To the Germans you will be a very valuable hostage."

Richard knew what I was thinking, and did not like it, but he nodded. "And of course you assume that the king of England can surely outbid the king of France?"

He took up the wine flask and offered me more until he saw that I had not touched what I already had. For a few minutes we listened to the creaking and splashing of the ship. Then—"There is another possibility," he said, "and that is Hungary. It has a seaport on the eastern coast of the Adriatic sea, and King Bela's wife, Margaret, who is King Philip's half-sister, is also the widow of my late brother Henry. I am on good terms with Bela, and he detests Duke Leopold, so I am sure he would aid me, and his lands abut Saxony in the north. And Saxony is also possible! My sister Matilda was married to Henry the Lion, duke of Saxony. She died three years ago, but that Henry would give me safe passage to the Baltic. I could sail to England from there. You follow?"

I said yes, but in fact I had not the slightest idea about all this geography he was throwing at me. In the end it did not matter, so I have never bothered to investigate it.

"So there we are, Latter-day Merlin. If ever a king of England needed a prophet to guide him, it is I. You have never failed me yet, so I must trust you now. Can you find the admiral for me?"

I found de Turnham for him, and he found the captain, who called out the watch. The sailors went aloft to do whatever it was that the sails required. Then the helmsman turned the ship, and soon we were running eastward, before the wind. I found a sheltered corner and went to sleep.

Driven by westerlies, we returned to Corfu much faster than we had left it. As we were entered the harbor, which was strangely empty now, with so many vessels taken out of service for the winter, I saw the king up on the aft castle, conferring with de Turnham. He was pointing and I could tell he was indicating a group of three galleys, rocking at anchor.

Galleys are faster than sailing ships, but their low freeboard cannot tolerate high winds and rough water. They could not carry our horses, nor even all the king's companions. To venture out to sea in them now, near the end of November, was insanely risky, but men can be bribed to do anything, and the Lionheart never skimped when he wanted something.

He sold off the horses. He made sure that the men he was leaving behind were supplied with money to pay their fare homeward in the spring. I was not asked if I wanted to stay or continue, I was simply told I would be in the king's boat. I felt it my duty to obey, although I admit I was heartily sick of the hardship. I was the oldest man in the party, and felt it.

We were well into December when we left Corfu for the second time. In the first two days we made excellent progress, but then the weather changed. A wicked storm began to churn the sea, making the rowers' work impossible. The galley had a sail, but it could do little except run before the wind, and as the tempest rose, we began to ship water. I remembered that I had foreseen a shipwreck.

The Adriatic Sea, as I now learned, is a northward-pointing arm of the Middle Sea, between Italy on the west and the Balkan lands on the east. Venice is at the north end, on the Italian side, although it is an independent state, and likes to think it rules the Adriatic. That claim is increasingly being challenged by the city of Ragusa, on the opposite side, but farther south, and it was toward Ragusa that we ran.

The other two galleys made it safely into the fine harbor there. The king's did not. Night was falling, the surf was fearsome, and we were up to our knees in icy water. Ahead of us was a rocky shore. We were all praying, but no man was louder than King Richard, and he swore a great oath that he would build a church worth 100,000 Venetian ducats if he were spared. Not all of us made it safely to shore, but he did.

The galley grounded in a gully between two great rocks. Waves rolled past us, then surged back, and the trick was to ride the surf inward and find something to hang onto to resist the backwash. I managed the first part, and then felt myself being swept seaward again. Someone caught my arm and held me until it was safe to struggle landward once more. I did not see who it was, but he must have been as strong as a bull. I still suspect that it was Richard himself, although he just laughed when I asked him later.

"You did warn me about a shipwreck, Merlin. You were right again!"

No. The shipwreck I had foreseen had not contained rocks. There was another still to come.

We scrambled into the woods in search of shelter. Two sailors were missing and three others had broken bones, but that was a small price to pay for such a landfall. Most of us had escaped with scrapes and bruises. Either our luck held or Richard's donation was accepted with a bonus, for we discovered a small priory. The monks greeted us fulsomely, although we outnumbered them many times over. They lit fires, prepared food, and generally could not have been kinder. Nor did the prior object when I asked him if I might chant over the casualties. It was fortunate that months of war duty had taught me the spells for healing wounds so well that I knew them by heart.

Morning brought a penance of aching bruises and a bright sunny day to mock our ordeal. We had eaten all the food on the island, and anxiously awaited information about the other two galleys. Boats were reported approaching from Ragusa, so it was a fair guess that at least some of our companions had survived. I and others had been billeted in the scriptorium, which reminded me that I had not written to Lovise since we left Acre, almost two months ago. How long a letter would take to go from Ragusa to Oxford in mid-winter I could not guess, but the shipwreck had been a reminder of mortality, so I asked one of the monks if I might buy a piece of vellum to write a brief letter. He pointed to a box and told me to help myself to anything in it that would serve.

I chose the most worthless scrap I could find. It had originally been quality goat skin, but it had been written on and scraped clean for re-use at least twice. Peering at the shadowy remains of letters, I decided that the earlier texts had been written in either Arabic or Hebrew. Only a genuine miser could grudge me this, so I found a quill and some ink and sat down to write to my dearest. A scriptorium, by definition, must have light, and large windows on a breezy winter morning mean that a scribe must spend more time blowing on his hands and chafing them than he does writing, but I scribbled away in a frenzy of loneliness and homesickness. When I had reached the bottom of the page, I signed it and sprinkled sand on it.

Then I read over what I had written, which was not at all what I had thought I was writing. I had not addressed it to my wife, and I had not signed my own name to it. The writing bore little resemblance to my usual hand. After staring at it in bewilderment for some time, I decided that the ghost of Myrddin Wyllt was directing me, and I must continue to trust in its benevolence.

A little later that morning, I found a chance to sidle up to the king and hand him the little scroll. "I think this must have slipped out of your portfolio, sire. It looks as if it may be important—some day."

He frowned, read it over, and lost color. "Where did you get this?"

"I, um, not sure where it came from. All I can say is—keep it safe."

He stared at me for a moment and then made the sign of the cross.

It was to be a long time yet before I learned what had happened to Lars, but this would be a good place to summarize his adventures. The two queens had a relatively uneventful voyage from Acre to Italy, disembarking in Naples, and then traveling by land to Rome. There they were made welcome by old Pope Celestine, and they were content to remain until in Rome they learned where Richard was and what he was doing. They would have received the latest news, which was that Queen Eleanor and Justiciar Coutances were managing to hold England together. Lord John had not yet managed to seize the crown, although he was poised to do so the moment word of his brother's death arrived.

Nor had King Philip annexed Richard's domains in France, but he had warrants out for his arrest in virtually every port from Spain to the Hungarian border. No one knew where the Lionheart was, or even when he had left Acre, if he even had.

Lars had no desire to waste months doing nothing in Rome. He offered to carry letters for the two queens, and they obtained a passport for him from the Pope. While his king and father were struggling to go anywhere, Lars made travel look easy. He managed to buy passage on one of the last boats to sail from Ostia, and landed in Marseilles. No one was much interested in a twenty-year-old minstrel, and anyone who thought to impress him as sailor or foot soldier was easily deflected by the papal passport.

He purchased a couple of horses and set out for Aquitaine. There he located Otto of Saxony, one of King Richard's many nephews, who was running the duchy in his uncle's absence. After that, Lars traveled royally, with an armed escort, all the way to Dieppe and the tricky crossing to England. Even there the sun shone on him—literally this time—and he played his gittern and sang to the sailors. He stepped ashore that same evening, refreshed and happy to be back in a country where people spoke his mother tongue and knew how ale ought to be brewed.

He reported to Queen Eleanor in Winchester, and then rode home to Oxford, where he found his mother chopping herbs in the dispensary. He claimed later that this was the first time he had ever seen her weep.

By then all Christendom knew that the Lionheart had left the Holy Land, but nobody knew where he was. His brother, of course, was already insisting that he must have drowned.

Which he very nearly did in our second shipwreck.

Ragusa was a bustling, thriving city, a port that served as a market place for Muslims, Christians, both Catholic and Orthodox, and even for folk from as far away as Barcelona and Damascus. After our wreck on Lokra, any sensible voyager would have settled down there for the winter and resumed his travels in the spring, but the Lionheart had an empire to lose and dared not tarry.

Ragusa was also awash with money, home to both banks of its own and representatives of the great Venetian and Tuscan houses. Because the king of England had unlimited credit, in two days he somehow formalized his impetuous donation of a church and arranged for the remaining two galleys to continue the voyage. How much he paid their owners for that death-defying contract I never learned. The two galleys could not carry us all, so he again provided some men with money to find their own way home. After a special mass in the cathedral, he herded the rest of us aboard, and off we went.

I assumed, although I hated the thought, that he had accepted my vision of him as a Yuletide guest of Duke Leopold, and was therefore heading to Austrian territory. I did not ask him, and nobody else seemed to know his intentions. He might have hoped to sneak all the way across Austria in disguise to seek the safety of Saxony and the Baltic, or he might have been on his way to Venice, which could have agreed to smuggle him across Europe disguised as merchant. I doubted that, because everyone knew that if you tried to buy a Venetian's mother, he wouldn't agree until he had asked around to see if he could get a better offer. Possibly Richard's hopes were still set on King Bela of Hungary. All of these prospective destinations were located at the northern end of the Adriatic.

Whatever his aim, the weather made the final decision. A storm blew up and the galleys were helpless, shipping water and driven helter-skelter by the wind. Waterlogged, they ran aground in the surf and at once began to break up. We had to wade and swim ashore in rain and darkness. I was struck on the head by a floating oar and almost drowned. I swallowed so much seawater that I had to be held upside down to drain. My memories of the rest of that night are fuzzy indeed.

We had made landfall, if the term can be stretched to serve, somewhere in the armpit of the Adriatic. The coast was low and marshy, but when morning came, one of the sailors could testify that we were not far from Aquileia, and that there was a monastery there.

I managed to walk some of the way and was carried the rest. I remember little of our visit, mostly just lying on a very hard, narrow bed in the sanitarium, and croaking to an angry monk that I did not want to be treated with leeches, thank you. It was a cold and narrow room, very dark because the shutters were closed against the storm. They rattled and whistled. A dying monk on one side of me never stopped croaking psalms in a mixture of Latin and a patois so garbled that only angels could have understood it. On the other hand lay one of our former oarsmen, writhing in pain. In my feverish condition, I simultaneously wished that Lars was there and thanked God that he wasn't.

Our stay there was brief, just long enough for Richard to acquire horses and less conspicuous clothing. He was facing a journey of weeks through country that was itself as hostile as its inhabitants and the current winter weather. His following had shrunk to around twenty, even if I was included—I, who counted as much less than one. He came in person to see how I fared, looming over my cot in the gloom like a red-bearded pine tree.

"Are you well enough to travel, Baron?"

The thought of standing up was terrifying, but I said, "When, Lord King?"

"Right now, and you are addressing the merchant Hugo, returning from pilgrimage to the Holy Land."

"You are still my liege, Master Hugo—if you could just give me a hand up." My head alone weighed more than a horse. He hauled me upright without trouble and steadied me as my wits flitted around like a flock of bats. Then he lowered me back down again.

"Your fever is worse than mine," he growled. "Stay here and live."

He turned away. I was too relieved to argue, but just then that accursed monk with the leeches appeared beside my cot again and I raged at him to go and do something anatomically impossible—German is a good language for cursing. The Lionheart whirled around and came back. "You can speak their tongue?"

I said, "No, Lord King!" but he didn't believe me. In no time I was dressed, outside, and being hoisted onto a horse.

In Roman times, Aquileia had been one of the world's great cities, but Attila and his Huns sacked it in 452, and the monastery was about all that remained. In as much as anyone held overall authority in that area, it was probably Duke Leopold, although others might dispute that. The monks could converse in Latin, and Richard and most of his company understood it, but they were at sea in the dialect of German that the local people spoke.

In truth I could not speak German either, but I had spent all my life working with documents written in what in England we called the Old Tongue, and some of those incantations, like the *Myrddin Wyllt*, dated back almost to the coming of the Anglo-Saxons. The Old Tongue and Old German had so many similar words that I could recognize much of what the locals said, likely much better than I could have understood the imperial nobility or even city-dwelling commoners.

And Fate or the Good Lord had put me in the next bed to that delirious monk with the psalms. He had a repertoire of four, which he sang in a mixture or Latin and German, and I knew three of them, so after a couple of days I could have sung along with him, had I been capable of singing anything. In short, I had picked up a working vocabulary. My grammar was hopeless, but given enough time, I could understand and make myself understood. In the next couple of weeks, I was to become almost proficient.

And so began what must surely be the worst journey that any king of England ever endured, and was certainly mine. Fortunately, my memories of it are very patchy. The sight of the great icy mountains ahead scared me so much that I closed my eyes. I did not ride, I just sat on the saddle and shivered, letting my mount go wherever the others went.

The sailors remained at the monastery, probably intending to make their way south to Venice. I knew all the rest of us, of course, those who had survived the latest shipwreck, although four of the Knights Templar who had joined us at Cyprus tended to keep very much to themselves. Some who had left Acre with us, almost two months ago now, had parted at Corfu or Rugosa. Some had drowned. More were to die shortly.

There were no roads, only trails and forest paths, plus cold and drizzly rain. That first night we came to a town below a big castle on a hill. King Henry had rid England of private strongholds, but I have often wondered if there is a single hill in the rest of Christendom that lacks a castle or the remains of one. We invaded the inn, a tiny cottage, which we overwhelmed. I found a corner not too far from the fire where I could sit on the floor, lean back in the angle, and doze. I refused food, drank what they called beer, and wakened only when people tripped over my feet. I think I was really hoping I would die soon, or that they would all just go away in the morning and leave me behind by mistake.

Richard summoned the innkeeper, who understood some French, and demanded to know the name and style of the lord who owned the castle. He was told that it was Count Engelbert of Gorz.

"Then summon a strong lad to carry this message to the noble count, and tell him that Hugo the merchant and his companions seek hospitality this night in the name of God." Whereupon he handed the man a purse.

"Aye, my lord, I shall send my son, who is both strong and honest."

After that everyone settled down to drink while the drink lasted and eat whatever the man's wife and daughters could cook as soon as they produced it.

I suppose it was near to an hour later that the fevered seer in the corner suddenly opened blank eyes and croaked, "My liege!" Whispered calls for silence spread out through the crowd like ripples on a pond. And again I croaked, "My liege!"

The king said, "What do you see?"

"It was too much! That ring was too rich a gift. He has guessed who sent it."

I vaguely remember farseeing the swarthy count with the shaven chin and thin moustache. I remember him frowning as he opened the purse and gazing in wonder at the ruby ring he took from it. In what language he spoke, I do not know, but old Myrddin Wyllt understood for me.

"No mere merchant sent this! Describe this man!"

The stammering, cringing youth described the red-bearded giant he had left back in the inn.

"Only a king would own such a treasure, and I know of only one king who might venture into these parts, and only because he is returning from the crusade. The emperor himself ordered me to arrest him, but I will not break the Truce of God. Give him back his gift and bid him God speed."

As soon as I had quoted Engelbert's reaction, I stopped talking and went back to sleep. To provide hospitality to travelers, especially pilgrims and crusaders, is any Christian's sacred duty, but Engelbert was being unusually devout in defying orders to the contrary from his liege. Every other landowner from there to Barcelona must have received such orders also, and few would have made the choice he had. On the other hand, given Richard's fearsome reputation as a warrior, Engelbert might reasonably have declined to rally his own small troop of knights and send them down to seize the royal fugitive by force. Would he clear his conscience by sending word of this encounter on ahead to higher authority, so that a larger force could be arrayed in ambush?

We did not tarry to find out. I was later told that nobody, not even our highly skeptical Father Anselm, suggested that my farseeing should be ignored. In a mad rush, everyone wrapped up again and went out to saddle the poor tired horses. Unfortunately, someone remembered to fetch me.

The rain had stopped, the sky was icily clear, and the moon was at, or very close to, the full, and eastward its light glittered on icy peaks. We rode off into the forest again, heading northwest. I remember even less of the ensuing day than of the one before. I do recall being fevered and very hungry, for that bleak land held few inhabitants, and those few had little spare food to sell. I remember cursing Myrddin Wyllt root and branch. Late in the day we reached another town, Udine, but news of our coming had preceded us.

A castle on a hill overlooked the town, of course, but Richard now knew better than to seek hospitality in castles.

We found an inn, a larger place than the previous night's, and the landlord was happy to board such a large company this late in the year. Our horses were in worse condition than their riders, for they had been given little time to graze, so the king distributed money and sent men off to acquire as many fresh mounts as possible before curfew sent everyone home to bed. They wanted to take me along as interpreter, but I refused and the king forbade me to go anyway. He, being of memorable stature, wanted to stay out of sight, and no doubt he also wanted to keep his eye on me in case I began raving again. I remember the two of us in a dim room, on either side of a crackling fire. We were both feverish and exhausted. I had the uneasy sensation that he was using me as a guard dog, relying on me to bark prophecies whenever danger threatened.

There were others present, of course, guarding their liege. I was the only one not armed, but I did not feel strong enough to lift a sword, let alone swing one. My head ached, my throat burned. I floated in and out of consciousness—yet once I roused myself slightly, forced my eyes to focus on Richard, and muttered, "Lord, where is Argentan?"

Richard's gaze flickered, for he never took well to being questioned. "A small town in Normandy. I remember family Christmases there, when I was a child." He probably then asked why I had asked, but I doubt if I replied.

Morning came, and a grubby, hungry rabble of fugitives roused themselves to gulp down a wine and rye bread snack. At best we faced more days of backbreaking travel, at worst early graves.

Suddenly the mood changed. The landlord appeared, bowing to Richard and presenting a well-dressed young man. "A gentleman wishing to speak with you, Goodman Hugo."

He withdrew, but the newcomer just stood there, staring in shock at the king as if he knew him. Hands slid to sword hilts. Even I roused myself from my stupor.

"What can I do for you, fine sir?" asked the fake Hugo.

"I . . . I was told to look for . . . if it please, you, sir, I am Sir Roger of Argentan."

The group of locals at the far end of the room were watching and listening, for they must sense the tension, although they probably could not understand the French being spoken—the unmistakable Norse-adulterated French of Normandy. The king glanced at me and then back to the intruder. "God be with you,

Sir Roger, but you have yet to tell me how I may serve you." He was a terrible actor, his tone completely lacking the humility of a merchant addressing a knight. He should be up and bowing, or else down and kneeling.

"I was told to inspect the inns in town to look for a man going by the name of Hugo, calling himself a merchant."

"Then you have found him."

Roger shook his head. He glanced at the angry glares surrounding him and whispered, "I think not, my lord. I was only a child, and you did not have that beard . . ."

"Who," asked the king, "told you to look for me?"

"My liege," Roger said, as if that must be obvious. "Count Meinhard, my wife's uncle. He is also the brother-in-law of Count Engelbert of Gorz, who sent word that . . ." Sensing the sudden upsurge of rage, he stopped.

I felt a stab of despair, but the Lionheart would not despair if his head were on an executioner's block. "You are mistaken, Sir Roger of Argentan!" No merchant would speak to a knight like that, clasping his sword hilt so menacingly.

Roger seemed close to tears. "I sang for you, Your Grace. In the choir . . . at Christmas."

Obviously, pretense was not going to work. Richard released his sword. "And now you will go back up to that castle and sing *about* me, instead of *for* me?"

"No, no! My lord I know who you are, and my family has served yours for untold generations, ever since Duke Robert. I will not betray you, but the word is out, Your Grace, the word that you are in town! I do beseech you not to tarry here."

Richard nodded and gave up the merchant pretense in favor of regal charm. "I must know of your family? Name some of them!"

Roger nodded eagerly and named two grandfathers and a great-uncle. Truthfully or not, Richard said he remembered them and named some of their campaigns. Greatly relieved, Roger even offered to give up his own horse, but the king declined the gift tactfully. Roger went on his way, swearing in the name of Our Lady of Rouen that he would not betray him.

The moment he was gone, the king turned to me. "Well?"

For once I just closed my eyes and summoned a vision. It was gone in a flash, but I had seen and heard enough. "Not at all well, sire. He will try, but he is a bad liar. Count Meinhard will not believe him. You should leave town while you can."

I wanted to scream at the thought of another winter day on horseback, but surely anything must be better than an Austrian jail. I went back to sleep while I had the chance. Perhaps I still hoped that I would be overlooked and left behind, but alas, I was the king's seer, and too valuable to abandon. I was even given a fresh horse, for the scouting party had managed to acquire around ten new mounts, and Richard now split us into two groups. Most of the best fighters were left with the exhausted beasts who had brought us from Aquileia, and they perforce lagged behind as a rearguard. The rest of us pushed on into the forest.

Count Meinhard dispatched the knights of his militia after us, and inevitably they caught up with the laggards. In the forest gloom they may have failed to notice that Richard was not present, but in any case, the king's men were not about to let the locals past, so there was a battle. Men were captured, wounded, or killed. I never learned the exact tally. They had done their duty and the Lionheart had escaped again.

After some hours that felt like the years of Methuselah, I disgraced myself by going to sleep and falling out of the saddle. Luckily, I broke no bones. After that, either William Legier or Conon de Béthune—or, when the road was wide enough, both of them—rode alongside, ready to catch me if I tried it again. If this sounds as if I were a soft-boiled, feeble, good-for-nothing unfit for such manly pursuits, that is exactly how I felt at the time. I was not the only one with fever by then—the king, especially, was suffering, perhaps in a relapse of a relapse of his serious sickness in Haifa. My only excuse, although I refused to mention it and no one else did, was that I was close to fifty. Richard was thirty-five, and very few of the others were older than he was.

The brief day ended but we pushed on by moonlight. Late in the night we found ourselves following an old Roman road, wide and straight. Like all such ancient highways it was in higgledy-piggledy condition, barely passable for long stretches, separated by patches of what it once had been, smooth and wide enough for four or five men to ride abreast. And after a while, the shade of Myrddin Wyllt came to our rescue. I have no memory of it myself, but I was told later that I suddenly pointed off to the right and declaimed, "Behold shelter and safe haven in the care of holy St. Gall!" If this is true and not just a joke made up later to tease the old man, I did it in my sleep.

Word was passed to the king and, sure enough, a track angled off to wind up the hillside. It was a steep climb, but we came at last to the Benedictine Monastery of San Gallo. We found the monks awake, having just completed their office of Lauds. I do have clear memories of Abbot Pio, tall and stark like a frosted pine tree, with an incongruous smile on his craggy face.

"All travelers are welcome, my lords, and especially those who have striven against the heathens in holy places. You may rest safe here in the Truce of God." He was telling us that Duke Leopold's warrant had been proclaimed even there, but he was going to ignore it.

He was as good as his word. The beds were hard but clean and the food plain but plentiful. We ate, slept, and prayed with the brethren. One of the novices found a stick with a branch that would make a handle, and shaped it into a cane for me. My other had vanished in the shipwreck.

We were all very grateful for such Christian charity, after the two counts' rapacious behavior. I know that the king left a sizable donation, and I added one of the coins that Queen Eleanor had given me so long ago, out of the few I had been hoarding. We waited until moonrise before leaving to continue our journey toward a fearsome mountain range.

I knew the little hills that the English call mountains, and had caught glimpses of real ones from afar since I embarked on crusading, but these looming peaks were close and menacing. If winter snows began while we were in their midst, we might be stranded there until springtime. The Lord answered our prayers by granting us dry weather. Our road followed the valleys, and we never had to tackle serious slopes. Moreover, the winds were growing colder—and continued to do so as we headed north— while we were mostly wearing clothes that had been brought from Outremer.

The villages were small and unimpressive, the people suspicious, but more surly than aggressive, so that I felt that they would be no more inclined to cooperate with our enemies than they were with us. Their fields were stony, their herds sparse. Early on our pilgrimage, they mostly spoke a form of corrupted Latin, but the German elements grew more pronounced as we progressed. As I have said, I already knew a smattering of the words, and rapidly learned more.

"Truly," the king said after we had bought some bread at a lonely inn, "you are a most useful tool, Lord Durwin—an ax, a sword, a scythe, and a razor, all in one." He had dropped back to ride beside me for a while, as he did with all of us by turns.

"Jack of all trades and master of none, Lord King."

"Nay, master of all. I am ashamed that I doubted you when we first met. You have amply proved your worth since then. I should have trusted my mother's judgment of you. Have you any new prophecies to impart?"

I shook my head. "Nay, sire, but that may be a good sign. They seem to come mostly in time of danger." One of Myrddin Wyllt's prophecies still remained unfulfilled, and that was my vision of Richard celebrating Christmas in Duke Leopold's castle. I did not mention that, but he must have been thinking of it also.

He rode in silence for a while, his face drawn, his eyes bright with fever. If Duke Leopold did not catch him, the fever might. Then he said, "Abbot Pio told me that it will take us at least a week to reach the great Danube River. That will be difficult to cross, for it is wide and our foes will be watching all the ferries. Another two or three days beyond that and we shall enter the realm of the Duke of Bavaria. He owes allegiance to the emperor, but they are not on good terms, and his lands run with the Duke of Saxony's, who used to be married to one of my sisters. So in ten days, God willing, we shall be able to hold our heads up and breathe freely again."

I had lost exact track of the date, but I was sure that ten days must put us past Christmas.

I kept expecting to see troops of armed men riding after us, or lined up across our path, but they did not appear. Our rearguard had never caught up with us, so they must have lost the battle outside Udine. Whatever the outcome, Count Meinhard of Udine would certainly have sent the news to his liege, so it probably passed us while we were taking refuge in San Gallo's monastery at Moggio.

We crossed a difficult pass, where the road was more mythical than passable, then descended into richer lands, although still mountainous. Here there were silver mines and prosperity, so there were more people in the valleys, with farms and even some grand houses. At every town gate, strangers were required to identify themselves before being allowed to enter, and we tried to pass as merchants. At a sizable town named Friesach, the trap was sprung.

Some hours before, William Legier had eased his horse close to mine, interrupting my daydreams of rest and hot food.

"From now on," he said, "whenever we enter a town, you and I are to stay close to the king. If necessary, the others will create a diversion to let him escape, but he wants us both with him."

I digested the news. Me, yes. I spoke the language—after a fashion, at least better than anyone else. But William was one of the deadliest fighters, so why not keep him in the rearguard?

We knew each other so well that he guessed what I was thinking and scowled. "You speak German," he said. "I speak Horse."

Ah, that made sense! Every knight in Christendom understood horses, but William was superb with them. Many years ago, back in Helmdon, I had seen him almost frozen with fear on a horse's back, but—with his usual talent of being outstanding at anything he tried—he had since mastered every aspect of horsemanship. No doubt he had benefitted from the experience he had gained while helping his father as King Henry's chief forester.

"But Richard only speaks King?"

He laughed. "He surely was not fluent in Merchant!"

We were allowed into the city, but throughout his life, the Lionheart was very rarely outwitted, and his contingency plan worked perfectly. He and his chosen two companions split off from the others, and the larger group made themselves conspicuous. Like a bull turning to a red rag, the Austrian troops pounced on them in the market square. There was a fight, and meanwhile the fugitive king, guided by his seer, slipped unnoticed out of town.

Friesach was obviously the last town we would escape, though. I was unarmed, and the king's distemper was waxing steadily worse. I think that any other man would have given up at Friesach or soon after. Not he! He set a merciless pace, so that for three days and nights we hardly stopped. It almost killed me, and was even harder on the horses. Without William's skill, I am sure they would all have foundered beneath us. He kept rotating them, so that each suffered an equal share of the king's greater weight. He gave them brief grazing breaks at night, but never enough to satisfy them. Despite his care, they developed saddle sores, and so did I. A couple of times we purchased human food at isolated inns or hamlets, eating it while we rode.

If you consider it impossible for three horses to have gone so far in so little time, I will admit that there were moments when I wondered about that myself. For instance, I found myself riding a piebald for some hours, and could not recall seeing it before— or, indeed, after. Sometimes, and especially at night, William would suggest that our mounts needed a rest, and he would scout ahead. When he returned, he was often astride something new. Neither Richard nor I ever spoke of the matter, for it would have been treasonous to suggest that the king of England was now a horse thief.

Following his lifetime practice of astonishing me, William had so distinguished himself in the Battle of Jaffa that he had become a royal favorite. He was almost as old as I, and thus around ten years older than the king, but it was his endurance and determination, as much as his horse sense, that carried us through that nightmare.

Everywhere I sensed eyes upon us. Every trudging, slope-shouldered peasant was a Leopold spy, every cottage held a garrison of his troops. Ironically, we were riding straight to the arch-villain's capital, for his palace is located in a town called

Vienna, and all roads led there. The flies were heading into the heart of the web.

You will understand that my memories of that hellish ride are very blurred. We bypassed towns whenever as we could, so I never learned their names. When we came to a ford, either William or I would scout ahead to make sure that it was not being patrolled. We dared not even trust monasteries then, in the heart of Austrian territory, for Richard's enemies had thoroughly blackened his name. Everywhere he was being proclaimed as a murderer and traitor, stained with the blood of Conrad of Montferrat and the Duke of Burgundy, loaded with bribes from Saladin, and would-be poisoner of the king of France. Can you doubt that William and I, who knew that he was guilty of none of these charges, were willing to do our utmost for him, whatever the cost?

On the third day we rode out of the hills and onto lush plains. At last—and we knew in our hearts that it was the end—we saw the mighty Danube ahead of us, and a mere glimpse of it was enough to drain the dregs of our hopes. At Vienna it is at least a mile wide, a moving lake, full of islands and sandbars. None of us had ever seen a river to match it, and I imagine that only the Nile of Egypt could.

Vienna is a sprawl of hovels on the nearer bank, with St. Stephen's Cathedral and the dukes' Babenberg Palace the only stone buildings. There are strict rules that only Austrians may trade within the city, so foreigners' markets have sprung up all around it. We turned aside to a hamlet called Erdberg, where there are a few inns, stables, and not much else, but it is close to a great market called Rochus.

I strained my rudimentary German to obtain lodging at a self-proclaimed inn, which was merely the back room of an old man's hut, where we had to provide our own food. William and

I put the king to bed and stacked the horses' saddles and other tack in a corner, which left little floor for us to sleep on, but to discard such valuable equipment might have attracted attention. Then William led the poor animals off to buy food, water, and shelter for them. I told him the words I hoped he would need.

I suppose I stayed behind as a guard over the king, but I was asleep when William returned. He nudged me awake with a good hard kick and I went staggering off down to Rochus to buy food. I saw many men there wearing strange clothes and speaking even stranger tongues, probably Hungarians, Byzantines, and even Russians, so I did not attract as much attention as I might have done, but my iron-reinforced shoe alone served to make me conspicuous. My attempts to bargain were rudimentary, and I could hardly speak any language at all through the flood of saliva that a glimpse of food produced.

I hobbled back to the inn, only to find my two companions already fast asleep. I ate one sour and shriveled apple, then lay down next to William, and joined in the snoring chorus.

That night I dreamed of Our Lord's Last Supper.

The next day, Richard could not stand, and was barely conscious. I watched over him while William went to scout the ferries. He returned shaking his head.

"It is hopeless," he told me. "The duke has posted a dozen troops at every jetty or pier. He has vastly greater resources than the counts who have accosted us to date."

I returned to the market and bought more food. But I also saw a gittern on one of the stalls and at once realized that it would make a good disguise for me—mine had been eaten by the Adriatic Sea. I asked to try it. It was old and battered, but once I had tuned it, it gave a fair sound, and I strummed a brief melody. That was rash of me, for it attracted attention, but when

I started to bargain with the crone who ran the stall, she took pity on this ragged old cripple, and let me talk her down. I slung the cord around my neck and returned happily to Erdberg, taking a roundabout way to our shack and keeping my eyes open for followers. I did not see any, and assumed that Leopold was confident that his ferry watch would trap the fugitives eventually. Rationally, he would not expect us for a few days yet.

The next day Richard seemed somewhat better, restored by rest and food. William and I both reported on the situation. He thought for a while and then nodded. He had been a warrior and leader of warriors since he was sixteen, and knew better than other men how to face unwelcome reality.

"Do you know if the duke is at home?"

William shook his head.

I said, "Likely he is, because his flag flies over the palace. People are buying their Christmas victuals, so the feast must be very close."

"And I should know by now to believe your prophesies, Lord Merlin." After a few minutes' thought, the Lionheart sighed and said, "I am worth a lot more alive than I would be dead."

Neither of us argued with that. William could guess where this was leading, and I had foreseen it in my dreams.

"How far is it to the palace?" the king asked.

I said, "Farther than you should try to walk, Lord King. You are very weak and might collapse in the street. One of our horses might carry you yet, but if you try to ride there you will surely be arrested. The patrols will have been told to look out for a very tall man with a red beard."

He sighed. "Then I shall not go, but my surrender must be voluntary. My two faithful barons, your service has been beyond praise. I have one last task for you, and I know you will find it the hardest of all."

William had gone rigid, looking as if he faced a death sentence, but when it came, it was only the second-worst order that his king could give him.

"William, go home. Tell them where I am, if they do not already know. If they do know, then you must not tell anyone that you came this far with me. And we three must agree on a tale such that neither of you will be accused of betraying me. I don't want you to be charged with treason after you have served me so well!"

Neither did I. A common penalty for treason is to be hung up by the ankles and flayed.

"Baron Pipewell," the king continued, "you are the troubadour; sing us a song of invincible faith and courage overwhelmed by fell circumstance."

"Aye, Lord King. Um . . . so it came to pass, that when you escaped the Austrian troops' ambush in Friesach, and the rest of your escort were slain or captured, that William and I were overlooked in the confusion. Knowing your destination, we followed you, but were unable to catch up, you traveled so fast. We arrived here, in Erdberg, just in time to see you being escorted to the palace by the duke's men-at-arms."

The king frowned. "I traveled all this way alone?"

"No, sire. Back when we tarried in the monastery of St. Gall, a young novice who knew the way offered to escort us. German was his mother-tongue and he conversed with you in Latin. Abbot Pio gave his leave. You and he found shelter here," I continued. "But today, when he had gone out to buy food, he somehow gave himself away. He was seized and beaten until he agreed to lead them to this shack."

I was rewarded with a royal smile. "Heart-rending! I shall set it to music when I have the time. But, in reality, one of you will have to inform that Leopold popinjay where he can seize me."

William now seemed quite sick with horror.

I set his mind at rest. "Don't worry. I will do this. I have ways of evading capture that you do not."

"I appreciate this sacrifice, Durwin," Richard said. "But be careful that they do not learn your true name, lest word get back to England."

He opened his purse and tipped out two heaps of coins, mostly silver, but also some of the Byzantine gold coins known as hyperpyrons. He must have brought them all the way from Ragusa or even Corfu. He poked at them with a finger until the piles looked about equal. I doubt if he realized, even then, that mere barons—and especially such unkempt rascally-looking vagrants as we had now become—who dared produce even one such coin, would at best be arrested as thieves, or more likely murdered for it.

Too overcome to speak, William scooped up his share, and tearfully saluted his liege. As he turned to the door, I stopped him with a prophecy, like an arrow through a hare. I did not know myself the words that I was about to utter.

"William, there is a boat with a furled green sail moored at a dock near the upstream end of the town. It will sail early tomorrow, when the wind changes. The owner will understand you if you use sign language and a little Latin, for there are many foreigners here. Pray book passage on it for both of us for two days. I will join you on board this evening."

After a moment's shocked silence, William nodded. The king managed to laugh in the middle of a coughing fit. "Oh, Merlin, I shall miss you! When you prophesy, I do feel like Arthur."

William said hoarsely, "See you then, my—I mean, minstrel." He almost ran out of the shack.

After that came my sentence. Richard brought out a ruby ring. It may have been the one I foresaw Count Engelbert refusing, for the count had ordered the messenger to return it, but whether he did so, I do not know. Either way, what the king handed to me was worth a small castle. He gave me some brief instructions on protocol and then told me to go.

As I took the ring, I recalled my dream of the Last Supper, where Jesus dipped a crust in the wine and passed it across to Judas.

"Aye, my lord. Saving Your Grace, it seems a little early in the day to call on a duke. First . . ." I dug under my rags to find the strip of silk I had been wearing as a sash to help keep me warm. On it were written half a dozen Release spells that I had often found useful during my travels. Lars had been carrying the rest of our collection when we parted. Our landlord was mumbling to himself in the other room, but I was confident that he would not understand Latin.

Richard had lain down and covered himself to keep warm. He was watching me curiously.

"Close your eyes, Lord King, unless you want to witness magic."

"Do it." He chuckled. "I shall not denounce you to the local sheriff."

He didn't truly believe me, but then I quietly sang the *Hic non sum* and disappeared.

"*God's legs!*"

I smiled, and instantly reappeared. "I just thought this might prove useful later, sire. It isn't as wonderful as it seems, because I am only invisible as long as I remain perfectly still." I never use that incantation without remembering how it saved Eadig's life in Lincoln Castle, many long years ago. Later it saved mine a few times, too. It remains responsive for four or five days after it is chanted.

I sang the *Præcipio tibi*, the *Fiat ignis*, and a couple of others that might come in handy. Then it truly was time to go. "God be with you, my lord. You have a Christmas feast to look forward to, but further than that I cannot see."

As a final precaution, before I left the hut, I went around to the back and hid my purse and my silken spell list in the tiny woodpile. Were I to be searched, that scroll would be enough to hang me.

I had not gone far before William accosted me, looking haggard—and dangerous. "I keep feeling that I should be doing that instead of you. But I don't know that I can bring myself to sell out my king."

"It isn't easy, even for an out-of-work minstrel," I assured him. "But Richard knows that I have tricks up my sleeve that you do not, and I am not selling him out as long as I am obeying his orders." I wondered how convincing that argument would sound if I were ever on trial before the privy council.

"But who will believe you?" he asked, being brutally realistic.

"We are both at risk. But I am going to go home to Lovise and my children, just as you must want to be reunited with Millisende and your sons. The lion is caged, William, or soon will be, but his enemies are surely plotting against him and I am still his enchanter general. Now, please—we are really going to sail away tomorrow, you and I, on that boat with the green sail."

Reluctantly, William nodded and stepped out of my way.

I doubt very much that my mission would have prospered had I been only the minstrel I pretended to be. Never had a little magic been more helpful. I trudged down the hill, through the sprawling market, and into Vienna. The city was unwalled, and in the busy Christmas throngs I was not challenged. With heavy heart I went on to the palace gate, where stood a pair of armored spearmen. The taller one, from the little I could see of his face, was not yet old enough to shave. The other was a grizzled veteran.

The trainee aimed his spear at my belly. "Password?"

"I am a stranger and know no passwords."

"Your name and business?"

"I am Blondel, a minstrel, and I have business with the duke."

The spear jerked closer. "Be off with you. The duke has far too many minstrels already."

"I bring a message from the king of England."

The boy turned and looked anxiously at his superior, who barked, "You know where he is?"

"He sent me, and I will speak with no one but Duke Leopold."

"No? Come with me." He gestured, and I preceded him through the arch into the courtyard, leaving palace security in the incapable hands of the boy hero. My captor shouted for his captain, and a potbellied giant of a man came striding out of the guardroom.

"A minstrel, sir, name of Blondel. Claims he brings a message from the king of England."

We eyed each other. He might be wondering why I wasn't cowering enough. I was wondering if he had enough authority to get me through the palace maze to Leopold.

"What is this message?"

"I will speak it only to the duke himself."

"You will speak it to me or I will have your teeth knocked out."

Some people believe that violence can solve problems, but in the long term it usually just creates more. I looked him straight in the eye and enchanted him into obedience with a whisper. "*Præcipio tibi!* Lead me to the duke."

"Follow me, minstrel." He spun around and we headed for the main door.

We were stopped twice more. The first time the captain bullied his way past a protesting steward. The second time our way was blocked by a dandified gentleman, who was addressed as "my lord" and obviously outranked my guide by about a thousand ducats a month. I could order the captain to kill him, of course, but that would cause trouble, or I could use the spell again. I was reluctant to do that, because this scented flunky would understand the Latin. He would still have to obey my orders, but he might guess why and scream for a bishop to anathemize me.

Instead I brought out the ruby ring. "His Grace Richard of England sends this as a token of friendship to his honored cousin, Duke Leopold."

He attempted to grab the ring, but I whipped it out of his reach. "You are not the duke!"

He snarled, but then swiftly led me into an anteroom. My wait there was brief. I barely had time to start appraising the architecture and artwork before another door was opened and I was escorted into a minor reception hall, complete with throne. I had seen grander, but not recently. An even fancier courtier demanded my full name.

I gave the first one that came into my head. "The minstrel Blondel de Nesle, Your Grace."

Word was passed, and in a surprisingly short time, Duke Leopold himself came marching in from a door behind the throne.

The Lionheart had spoken of him in such scathing terms that I expected a small, crooked man with a swarthy face and an annoying habit of wringing his hands. He was anything but— full-sized and handsome, clad royally in silks, fur, and jewels, with his hair and beard closely cropped, he looked every inch a duke. He was the same age as the Lionheart and almost as arrogant, which probably contributed to their mutual dislike.

Shuffling flatfooted behind him, though, came the largest priest I had ever seen, robed all in black, of course, monstrously bearded, carrying a jeweled crucifix in one hand, and a silver aspergillum in the other. He nailed me with arrowhead eyes full of hate, but he stopped a pace back from the duke and made no aggressive move.

I approached to a reasonable distance, knelt, and held up the ring. Speaking in Latin, of course, being unwilling to inflict my nursery German on him, I said, "Richard, king of England, offers this jewel to his cousin, Duke Leopold of Austria, in token of his friendship, and begs hospitality in the name of Jesus Christ, Our Lord."

Nobility often profess family relationships with noble strangers, but they make up for that by treating their true relatives worse than their enemies.

Leopold said, "Well, Father? Richard's pet witch is described as elderly, blond, and lame in his right foot. This one fits that recipe. Is he man or devil?" My first thought was that some of my former companions must have survived the battles, at least for long enough to be questioned, perhaps tortured. But it was also possible that knights returning from the crusade had been spreading stories about the Lionheart and his magical advisor.

The over-sized priest approached me, held up the crucifix, and gabbled Latin at me. He had a notably foul breath. Then he sprinkled me with what I assumed to be holy water. I did not scream and fly out through a window, which would probably have pleased him most. Instead I quietly recited the Nicene Creed and then made the sign of the cross. He backed away, baffled.

"He appears to be wholesome enough," Leopold judged. "We can examine him more closely later. Bring me the bauble."

A page approached me and nervously held out a silver tray at arm's length. I placed the ring on it and he transported it to Leopold, who examined it carefully, concluded that it must be genuine, and slid it onto a finger to admire. Then he raised shrewd gray eyes to study me, still on my knees.

"Truly a handsome gift to receive by the hand of a wandering, ragged minstrel. But not many minstrels are also sorcerers—as I know you to be."

"Only the credulous deem me such, Lord Duke. King Richard has sometimes honored me by listening to my counsel as well as my music."

The duke laughed. "Well, we can discuss that later. So where will I find that rogue who spat on my honor at Acre and now claims a right to my hospitality?"

"I can lead him to you, but he charged me to warn you that he is seeking Christian charity, as one crusader to another. If you require him to yield, he will do so only to you personally." This was a subtle but vital point. A guest is entitled to certain courtesies that a prisoner is not, and at some later date my king might wish to argue that he had surrendered voluntarily.

We all knew that any attempt to take the renowned Lionheart by force was certain to cost lives. I was confident that William Legier would still be lurking in the vicinity, and would come charging into any fight like a thunderstorm. And I was quite capable of setting a duke on fire if provoked.

Leopold rolled his eyes. "Then I had better come with you. I don't want him slaughtering a squad of my knights so near to Christmas."

We traveled on horseback, with an escort of a dozen mounted knights, one of them leading a spare horse. Aware that they were on their way to seize the most renowned warrior in Christendom, none of Leopold's men looked happy. When I pointed out the old man's shack, they dismounted and surrounded it. Then they waited for orders, fidgeting as if they held a wild boar at bay.

I said, "By your leave, Lord Duke, I shall inform His Grace that you have arrived."

Remaining safely mounted, Leopold nodded and I walked into the shack. The old man was not there, but the Lionheart was, seated on a stool with his sheathed sword across his lap.

I bowed. "Duke Leopold is here, Your Grace."

I did not know that those were to be the last words I would ever speak to him.

He nodded and rose. I saw him draw a deep breath before he walked out with head high. I remained inside, leaning against the wall where I had a view of events. The duke was still mounted, which was either a flagrant discourtesy or just cowardice. The Lionheart stared at him for a moment before speaking.

Then—"Your Grace, I crave hospitality in the name of Lord Jesus."

"And I declare you to be under arrest upon numerous charges."

Richard raised his voice so all the riders could hear. "Then you are breaking the Truce of God, and will be damned to Hell for all eternity."

Even Leopold flinched at those awful words. "But you are no true crusader, for you took the Devil's bribes to let Saladin hold on to Jerusalem. Your sword, renegade!"

Richard handed up his sword, sheathed and hilt first; Leopold took it. Then he beckoned for the spare horse and told a knight, "Fetch the witch."

I said, *"Hic non sum."* The man came in, inspected both rooms, and went back out again to report that I wasn't there.

Richard had moved out of my sight, but I heard his mocking laugh. "Make up your mind, Lord Duke! If he was only a messenger, then you have no further business with him. If he's a wizard, you'll never catch him."

Standing absolutely still is not easy, and I was afraid more men would be sent to make a more thorough search, for if anyone touched me or a draft even stirred my cloak, I would at once become visible again. I was counting on Leopold being too anxious to see his valuable prisoner secured behind bars to make a fuss over a mere flunky, and if I were the rumored sorcerer, then my magic might make him seem ridiculous. Sure enough, he told his escort to form up, and he rode off homeward with the most valuable moveable property in Christendom, the king of England.

It was the feast of St. Thomas the Apostle, December 21st.

I retrieved my purse and my silken grimoire and strolled down to the market to buy some dinner. I bought a pair of boots and a packsack to hold them, a warm cloak with a hood, and a clean shirt. That exhausted my usable money, because I could not imagine how I could change the gold into lesser coins without attracting suspicion. I still had the ruby ring that Queen Berengaria had given me, but for a ragamuffin like me to produce such a treasure would be asking to have the word 'Thief' placarded on my chest as I dangled in a hempen noose by the wayside.

In mid-afternoon I went down to the river. As I had expected, Leopold had withdrawn all his guards now that he had the boar in his net. I joined William on the boat.

We bedded down in a corner of the hold and conversed quietly in French. He asked about my Judas mission, and admitted that he had watched the king's arrest from a distance. He revealed his nagging guilt by saying, "I wanted to draw my sword, take them all on singlehanded, and chop that Austrian devil duke into cutlets. I just hope he isn't maltreating the Lionheart too badly."

I laughed. "No, the Lionheart's much too valuable for that! He's sleeping now, in a warm bed, having eaten a fine dinner. The duke's own doctor examined him and did nothing too barbaric to him. There are bars on his window and guards with drawn swords outside his cell, but that's all—no chains or manacles. And that Austrian devil, as you so rightly call him, is currently dictating a long, gloating letter to his liege, the emperor, bugling his triumph to the skies."

William groaned. "How do you know that? I've never known you just to pull prophecies out of the sky like this."

Considering the matter, I said, "Neither have I, now that you mention it."

With a chuckle that I knew well of old, William changed mood. "So just where are we going this time, Sage Merlin?"

"To a little place called Dürnstein. Leopold has a great castle there, where he will secure his prisoner for the present."

"Why should we go there? To do what?"

"I have to tell him that I know how we can rescue him! I only thought of it when I was already on my way to Leopold's shabby palace. I shall have to hurry back to England and collect the necessary enchantments, also a few helpers. And I am hoping that you can acquire some horses at Dürnstein, and that we will travel homeward together."

"There are better horse markets here in Erdberg, surely?" he protested. Yes, there were, and we were abandoning the poor, maltreated mounts that had brought us there. They were no longer worth much, but our saddles and other tack were.

"But we should still have the problem of crossing the river, and the boat will get us to Dürnstein much faster."

He gave up arguing at that point, because he could guess that I was foreseeing, being guided by Myrddin Wyllt.

During the night, the wind changed, as I had said it would. Downstream from Vienna the Danube is a moving lake, but upstream it is a well-behaved river, very wide, but confined within clearly defined banks. Its valley is likewise extremely broad, as you would expect. Our boat boasted a crew of six, three of them being owner-brothers. They would carry passengers as well as cargo, charging them by the day, for progress depended mostly on the wind, and also to some extent on the height of the river. At that time of year the water was low, the current slow, and the wind freezingly strong, but blowing out of the northeast. Consequently, we made very good time all the way to Dürnstein, arriving near to dusk. I spent the day strumming on my new gittern and trying to remember all the minstrel-type songs I could recall. I was seriously out of practice.

The hamlet of Dürnstein is on the northern bank, but is as close to negligible as anywhere can be. Its interest to me was the mighty fortress that stands high on the valley wall above it. The Danube bends there, giving the lookouts a fine view to both south and east. There was no real inn, but we were directed to a cottage that would take in boarders. We had to sleep on the floor, but only after being served an excellent supper. We rolled up in our blankets by the light of the fire's last embers.

"So what do we do tomorrow, other than break into that castle?" William demanded.

"I win my way in there with my charming smile and lovable personality. You stay on here and celebrate Christmas with the inhabitants. You also buy horses for us. Four, I think, would—"

For a moment I sensed the William of my youth, the monster eager to pounce. "Here? Where do I find those in a pocket-sized cesspit like this, you Saxon nitwit? I could count the houses in Dürnstein on the fingers of one foot."

"I have no idea where," I admitted. "That has not been revealed to me, but since the day I discovered that you could read and write Latin, I have never known you to fail me, William Legier, you old fraud. If I told you to fly, you probably would. Look after my packsack until I return, please. St. Stephen's Day is a big celebration here, it seems, but I will rejoin you on the day after—St. John's Day—and then we will ride off to England."

"This is devils' talk," William growled. He rolled over and went to sleep.

The trail up to the castle gate was long and steep. There were hints of snow in the air, but exercise and my new cloak kept me warm in the bitter wind. I arrived at the gate and humbly asked if a minstrel might be allowed to brighten the festivities. My foresight had told me that I would be accepted into Dürnstein Castle, and minstrels are always welcome over Christmas. Richard would be comforted to see that his whereabouts were known to at least one friend, and my offer of an eventual rescue ought to cheer him up.

I was passed to a steward and taken to be inspected by the lady of the castle, known as Hunde. She was large, intimidating, and harassed in the midst of the kitchens, arranging for the feast to come. She frowned at my accent, and demanded to know where I was from.

"Picardy, my lady. I am on my way home from the Holy Land."

"Huh! Another of those? Let me hear something."

I unwrapped my gittern and hastily tuned it. Then I played a verse. Music is international, but my repertoire of Austrian songs was scarcely greater than my experience of pearl diving. She nodded impatiently and gave me her blessing. So I had food and shelter for the next couple of weeks, had I needed that much. My only risk now was that I might be recognized by someone from Leopold's palace, possibly even the duke himself, accompanying Richard when he was brought to Dürnstein. Again, I gave my name as Blondel, although later I realized that I should have thought up a new nom de guerre.

The castle was huge, so I found an off-duty man-at-arms who would show me around in return for the latest tidings, for minstrels are the gossip carriers of the world. I told him that the word in Vienna was that the English king had been captured. He said that this was excellent news. When I inquired why, I learned that he had accompanied the castellan, Ministerial Hadmar von Kuenring, when he went to the Holy Land with his liege, Duke Leopold. Richard, in Dürnstein's opinion, was an arrogant thief who deserved to rot in jail, or worse.

I was most happy to be shown a place where I could wash properly for the first time in much too long. I would sleep in the hall, of course, with the foot soldiers and unmarried knights, but I was assured that good straw pallets were available for all. I was required to play at midday dinner, but I was fed amply afterward, in the kitchen.

The ministerial himself sent for me later. His title implies a nobleman who is vassal to a duke, a rank not much different from my barony. Hadmar von Kuenring was a big, coarse-featured man with a bullying manner, but I had already learned that his men respected him. He demanded to know where I had come from.

I told him Vienna and the tale of Richard's capture, which pleased him.

And before that? Originally from Picardy, I said, to justify my horrible accent. It is always best to stay as close to the truth as one's interests allow, so I told him most recently from Outremer.

Europe must be swarming with men returning from the crusade, but perhaps he saw the possible connection with Richard, for he frowned suspiciously. "What building guards the harbor at Acre?"

"The Tower of Flies, my lord." Right answer.

Later that day I met another minstrel who had found Christmas sanctuary in Dürnstein. He was much younger than me, darkly handsome and quick witted. His name was Jehan de Tours, which meant that he was a subject of Richard in his honor as duke of Touraine. That was no guarantee of his loyalty, though, for Richard as a ruler was more respected than loved and it was less than four years since he and Philip had been ravaging those lands to take them away from King Henry.

Jehan seemed somewhat puzzled when he heard my nom de guerre, and for a moment I feared that he was going to denounce me as a fraud, but he didn't, neither then nor later. Had he ever met the real Blondel he must have known that I was too old, but perhaps he had merely seen him from a distance and had possibly heard him sing. My accent was all wrong, of course, especially because we were speaking French and I spoke Anglicized Norman French, which was like no other version, but my hair was the right color for me to be called Blondel. Whatever he thought, Jehan accepted me and we set to work planning a partnership repertoire. He was very good at romantic ballads, and also on comic jingles.

We had quite enough work to do. The castle chaplain recruited us to sing at mass, of course, and we had to rehearse for that over the next couple of days. His deacon was young and jovial, and was to double as master of the revels for the festivities.

Near dusk on Christmas Eve, Richard the Lionheart arrived in Dürnstein under guard. I stayed well back in the shadows as he was marched in. He looked haggard—understandably so after a two-day ride from Vienna, but he was warmly dressed now and held his head high. To my great relief, Duke Leopold had sent him, not brought him, and I recognized none of the escort from my time in Vienna.

Christmas Day began with mass, held in the great hall itself so that everyone could attend, not in the ice-cold little chapel. After that, Jehan and I went off to do some more rehearsing for the dinner entertainment. In addition to our singing, there would also be performances by jugglers and acrobats recruited from the younger members of the staff and guard. If Richard were present, he would see me and know that he had not been forgotten. If he were left in his cell, I would try to slip away and speak to him during the meal.

I knew which I expected, though, for I had foreseen his presence at the banquet ages ago, and Myrddin had never let me down yet. Either Ministerial Hadmar or Fraulein Kuenring—or possibly both—had been unable to resist the temptation to entertain a king at their table. Quite possibly Richard had given them his parole, but there he was, up at the high table between them, being charming as no other deadly killer could be. To my practiced healer's eye, he still looked feverish, but I thought he was close to enjoying himself. After the last couple of weeks, food, warmth, and rest were great medications.

The enormous Yule log blazed on the hearth, and the hall was garlanded with greenery, especially holly with its brilliant red berries.

When my first turn to perform solo came along, I chose a song I had been taught by its composer, *L'amours dont sui espris*.

About the third line, I saw Richard's head swing around, so I did not look at him any more. When I had finished, the applause was scanty, for very few present would have understood the words or appreciated the subtle melody, but I knew I had passed my message, even if I had butchered the song.

I went back to the performers' table, where the jugglers were getting ready to perform and Jehan was busily chewing roast boar. He gave me a quizzical glance.

"That's a new one to me. Who wrote it, do you know?"

"Blondel de . . . I mean, I did. God's legs!"

He grinned.

"Listen!" I whispered. "All those stories about Richard are false! They're lies spread by the king of France, who broke his oath and sailed away. They are not true!"

"And the sorcerer with the limp, Durwin of Pipewell? He's not Merlin Redux?"

"If he is, I'll turn you into a slug!"

Jehan grinned again and reached for the beer. "My father fought under Richard. He would certainly agree with you."

"What's your father's name? I'll ask Richard about him if I get a chance."

I had known for days that I would make my way to Richard's cell that night to tell him that I could rescue him, but not right away. I even knew how he was going to react—first with disapproval because flight would give his enemies an excuse to kill him, then with reluctant agreement, because Philip and John must still be conspiring to steal his empire. I also knew that this visit was going to be dangerous, but Myrddin Wyllt had never let me down yet.

At last the host and hostess left the hall, together with their royal guest and his armed escort. Servants began snuffing candles and handing out sleeping pallets. I took one and spread it close by one of the doors, where constant streams of men were passing by on their way to or from the privies. I joined in and on the way back, deliberately took a wrong turning.

My tour of the castle had given me a fairly good idea of places where a noble prisoner would be held, and the most likely was the north tower, certainly not in one of the dungeons. I had not been shown inside that tower, but my hunch was confirmed when I heard guttural von Kuenring himself, stumping and grumbling his way down a spiral staircase that I was about to climb. I stepped into a shady corner, facing inward, and whispered *Hic non sum*. He and his companions went by without seeing me, growling in their version of German.

Now I had the problem of climbing that same staircase in the dark. The spiral wound to my right, which is customary in castles, so that an intruding swordsman, if right-handed, is at a disadvantage compared to a right-handed defender above him. I was no swordsman, but I had an iron lift on my right foot, so I had to go slowly and move with care. There was no banister, just a rope dangling around the newel axis to provide a questionable handhold. But that rope probably saved my life. As I ran my grip up it, preparatory to taking another step, I felt a sudden chill and pulled my hand down again fast. It tingled madly with pins-and-needles.

Cautious exploration told me that there was a horizontal warding across the shaft, like an invisible trap door. I do not know what would have happened had I penetrated that plane with my head, but even a mild surprise could easily have caused me to lose my balance and fall.

Or it might have just killed me outright. There must be a password, but I did not know it and I lacked a spell to disable the ward. So Duke Leopold employed sorcerers, too? I should not have been surprised.

I turned around, and went down, finding my way back to the hall without further trouble. My ambition to rescue my king would require further thought and probably much more magical ammunition. In the event, I never even tried, because he was moved from place to place so often during his captivity that it would have been impossible to plan the operation.

If Leopold's enchanter was present in the castle, he or she made no attempt to assault me or even make contact. Most likely he or she was being kept close to the royal prisoner and the trap

I had encountered was a permanent feature of the castle. But my visit to Dürnstein had taught me one important lesson—the *Myrddin Wyllt* was not infallible. Other magic could block it. As the Church insisted, prophecies could never be certain, because then they would limit the powers of God.

St. Stephen's day was quieter than Christmas, with many people nursing headaches or vengeful intestines, but Jehan and I were still expected to provide entertainment, because it was a local feast day. When the gate was opened at sunrise of December 27th, I departed, wrapped up in my cloak against the bone-cracking cold.

1193

anything that William Legier agreed to do, he did in style, and he had purchased not four but six excellent horses, together with fine-quality tack. Four spares would not be much harder to lead than two, he argued, and a purchase of that magnitude had let him pay with one of the king's gold hyperpyrons. An armed foreigner flashing wealth on that scale must seem suspicious, so now both of us needed to leave as soon as possible. I mounted and we rode off into the interminable forests of Germany.

"Do tell me, Baron," I said, "how you found such magnificent steeds in such an anthill of a village."

"I just whistled and they came," William said with unbearable smugness. But eventually he explained that a horse trader and his train had been passing through, on their way to Vienna. I retorted that Myrddin Wyllt must be looking after us, which put my companion into a two-hour sulk, because he saw that my statement might be true and he hated being beholden to magic.

I had taken the chance to pull on the boots I had bought in Vienna, putting my previous footwear in the pack sack that had held the new ones. Of course, I was now limited to a grotesque lurching walk without my iron step, but as long as I could stay mounted, only the horse would notice that one of my stirrups was higher than the other. I hoped that this flimsy disguise would deceive any guards who waited at city gates and might have been told to look out for me.

And so we rode off into the seemingly endless forest. At first, we headed upstream along the river, west and north, which we knew to be the right direction for England. Everything that lay between us and home was still a mystery to us. There was little traffic, and the weather stayed dry and cold for the first few days, and most nights we found shelter in some barn or woodshed, with or without the owners' knowledge. The land was hilly, the road a braid of trails, so that any pursuit would be lucky indeed to find us.

Out of the blue one day, William asked, "What's Lionheart doing now?"

"He's on his way to Regensburg. Leopold's taking him to meet the emperor."

"Durwin!" William shouted. "You're doing it again! Did you prophesy for the king like this?"

"Not often," I admitted. The late Myrddin Wyllt was keeping me informed in more detail than he ever had before. To my annoyance, he had no interest in Lovise or our children, and would show me nothing of their activities. Knowing that William had briefly considered becoming a sage himself and could be trusted, I then told him about the ancient appeal to Carnonos.

"Maybe they really should hang you as a pagan witch," he said, but I knew he did not mean it. William was a very practical man, and I was much too useful to be wasted on a gallows.

As much as the terrain allowed, we stayed close to the Danube. If you wonder why we did not travel on the river itself, the answer is that very few craft sail upstream on it. The river people build their boats in the headwaters, then float them down to Vienna, where they sell both their cargo and then the boats themselves, for lumber. Then they walk home.

The weather turned bad after the first few days, and few things are more unpleasant than a day on horseback in drenching rain. Thereafter it varied between horrible and even worse, but the German Empire has much colder winters than England does. Also miserably hot summers, so I have been told, but William and I did not stay around to find out. There were many days when I could envy King Richard, warm and dry back in Dürnstein, for Myrddin Wyllt kept me aware of his condition. I was happy to see him recovering his health, although returning strength brought the torments of boredom and impatience with it.

In effect I was the best-informed man in Christendom, and I passed on all the news to William. Leopold's letter announcing Richard's capture reached the emperor just a week after the event. Henry at once wrote to Philip of France, whose joy at the news was even greater. I saw him dictating a reply, so excited and close to drunk that his scribes could barely make out his Latin. He reminded Emperor Henry of the agreement they had made in Milan, and of his relative, Conrad of Montferrat, who, so he claimed, had been murdered on Richard's orders. The fact that there was not a shred of evidence that the Lionheart had been involved in that crime in any way was completely irrelevant, of course.

One day soon after that, William saw me with tears in my eyes, and I explained that Queen Eleanor had just learned of her son's imprisonment. She and Justiciar Walter of Coutances would now be faced with the problem of raising the money to pay Richard's ransom. Fortunately, at that unhappy moment, they had no idea how enormous that ransom would be.

By then the bargaining was underway, with letters flying back and forth between Vienna, Paris, and wherever the emperor happened to be, for he had no fixed capital. William and I traveled fast, considering the state of the roads, but we could not match the pace of the imperial couriers. We avoided the cities as much as we could. It was only two days after we passed by Regensburg that Leopold arrived there with his prisoner to show him to Henry.

The emperor, who ruled even more of Christendom than Richard did, was a much less impressive person. His grandiose raiment and high heels failed to hide the fact that he was of short stature, and seemed excessively so compared to the English king, or even Leopold. He wore no beard, and his enemies whispered that he could not grow one. As successor to Charlemagne and all the Caesars, he liked to regard himself as rightful ruler of the entire world, but his mind was fast and his eyes were never still.

Believe me when I say that the prisoner was not allowed to remain there for long, because the duke was frightened that his liege would steal his treasure away from him. So once Richard's identity had been confirmed, he was packed off back to Austria, while the other two settled down to do some furious arguing. My German wasn't up to understanding much of what was being said, but the sheer loudness of most of it was enough to convey the emotions involved.

We had already learned—because it was on everybody's lips—that the emperor was in grave danger of seeing his empire fall apart. Half or more of his greatest vassals were in open revolt, including a couple of archbishops. His attempt to retake Sicily from the usurper Tancred had been a military disaster. The prospect of a king's ransom must seem like a gift from Heaven to him right then.

Near Regensburg, William and I fell in with a band of merchants heading the same way we were. At first, they were suspicious of us, naturally afraid that we might be spies for a gang of outlaws that preyed upon innocent travelers, but they eventually accepted our story of being honest crusaders on our way home. By then I had gone back to wearing my iron shoe, having traded my matched boots to a village blacksmith in return for a sword. It wasn't much of a sword, and I was never much of a swordsman, but I was able to show the merchants' paid guards that I could wield it passably well, if not as well as I played my gittern. However ancient we might seem to these youthful huskies, two extra swordsmen were a welcome addition to the company.

Of course, we were often questioned—at bridges or fords or even upon entering small villages. Usually our stories were believed. When they weren't, I used the *Præcipio tibi* spell to compel obedience. Our merchant companions knew the country, and led us away from the Danube and over the hills to Nuremberg and so into the drainage of the Rhine, which flows into the Narrow Sea in the Duchy of Brabant, another part of the German Empire. That was a comforting thought, but we were still a very long way from home.

I had given up worrying about my king by then, being convinced that he was a lot safer in prison than he would be at liberty, when he would most certainly ride off to fight someone, probably either King Philip or brother John. I had taken instead to keeping an eye on that treacherous John. A year had passed since I warned Justiciar Walter Coutances and Queen Eleanor that he was heading over to Paris to conspire with Philip. Then she had managed to keep him in England. She couldn't do that now, since he had learned of Richard's capture. Convinced that his hour had come, the faithless worm insisted to anyone who would listen that Richard was never coming back. To Paris he went, and that morning, as my horse ambled along a grassy trail, I was watching a great ceremony in the Louvre Palace. Fortunately, but as usual when I was foreseeing, my riding companion was

William, who was accustomed to my long silences and knew what they signified. On this occasion I exploded in a string of foul oaths. The couple ahead of us looked around, but did nothing more.

"What's eating you?" William asked. "Seen your own funeral?"

"I think I would prefer that. I've been watching Lord John doing homage to King Philip for all of his brother's lands in France—the duchies of Normandy, Aquitaine, Brittany, the counties of Anjou, Touraine, and Maine. I know that last night he swore to marry the wretched Aalis and give the Vexin territory back to Philip."

William spat. "Does this surprise you? Loyalty has never been an outstanding attribute of the Plantagenet tribe."

"But then he did homage for England itself!"

He actually lost color. "God's teeth! His father never did that. Philip has no claim on England!"

"He does now." This was by far the worst treason yet.

"If that scum ever becomes king, then Lord Jesus help us all."

I had known that my companion had no love for Lord John, but now he told me why, and even on that forest trail he lowered his voice. "A friend of mine . . . I won't mention his name. He has no title beyond his knighthood, but he inherited a goodly estate by marrying a rare beauty. She was sixteen and could have stepped right out of a dream. I doubt if he even bothered to ask what her dowry would be. But one night, a couple of weeks after the wedding, who should ride in but Lord John and a troop of armed men. He demanded hospitality, and when your king's brother does that, you don't tell him to say 'Please.'

"My friend obeyed, and tried to play the gracious host, although the banquet must have cost him a month's rents. That was bad enough, but right after the meal, John announced that he would sleep with his hostess that night. My friend refused, of course. John had him beaten up—ribs and both legs broken, fractured jaw, and so on. Then he dragged the girl into the bedroom by force and kept her there for the night. That's the sort of belly worm that stands next in line for the throne of England."

"I've heard similar tales," I admitted. I'd also heard many stories of Richard seducing pretty girls, but never by outright rape. With his attitude to money, he could buy the Queen of Sheba for a night or two.

"We ought to round up Queen Berengaria and send her to that Dürnstein place to give the king something to do in all this spare time he has."

"Good idea," I said. Of course, I thought of the king's worries about his own fertility, but did not mention them.

The sooner the Duke and the emperor could agree on an asking price for their prisoner, the better it would be for the peace of Christendom. Why wasn't the Pope thundering about their violation of the Truce of God?

That night we slept at one of the better inns we had encountered. William and I shared a bed, for neither the first nor last time in our lives. I was weary and hoped for sleep, but it failed to come. I tried to see my dear Lovise, but Myrddin Wyllt refused me. He sent instead a view of King Philip and Lord John celebrating their new relationship—just the two of them, plus a couple of busty wenches, all four of them well lubricated by wine.

This was of no interest to me. I tried to withdraw, but Myrddin Wyllt seemed determined to keep me there. What was I supposed to see?

Suddenly another figure appeared in the room, facing me and apparently unnoticed by the others. Tubby, swarthy, with a forked beard and a curious sort of tonsure, Bran of Tara bared his teeth at me in triumph, and made a strange two-handed gesture. The seeing vanished.

The shock of it jerked me out of my trance. I cried out, wakening my bed mate.

"What's wrong?" demanded a sleepy voice.

"Lots," I said. "Lord John is using magic. I always suspected, and now I know."

"I'm not surprised." William rolled over, back to his previous position.

But it was a serious development. Once again the *Myrddin Wyllt* had been overruled by opposing magic. And John would not take kindly to being spied upon. I must hurry! I was needed back in England, and if any serious magical contest developed, I must have the use of all those spells I kept in my workroom in Oxford.

On the 14th of February, Emperor Henry VI and Duke Leopold signed a treaty in Würzburg, Bavaria. They agreed that Richard would pay a ransom of 100,000 marks, an amount so mind-boggling that William refused to believe me when I told him. The two kidnappers were to split this loot equally. Of course, they did not call it a ransom, because then they would fall afoul of the Truce of God. Instead they agreed that one of Leopold's sons would marry one of Richard's nieces, a daughter of the late Duke Geoffrey and sister of the infant Arthur. The 100,000 marks was to be her dowry. Even Helen of Troy had not cost that much.

They also tagged on a lot of petty conditions that Richard must agree to, such as providing galleys and troops for Henry's re-conquest of Sicily, and persuading the Pope to absolve them of any breach of the Truce of God. Also, Richard must stand trial for his alleged crimes. That clause worried me a lot, because how could he prove that he had *not* poisoned the Duke of Burgundy, or hired the Old Man of the Mountain to have King Conrad stabbed?

By then, William and I were making better time, because we had reached navigable water on the Rhine. We sold our horses at a small profit and bought passage on boats. Our travel was still not trouble-free, for every town and petty baron along the way expected to be rewarded for the trouble of watching us go by, but most of the time we could stay out of the wind and snow, which was more than could be said for horseback.

The end of the month brought us to Antwerp, the main port of Brabant. March is not a good time for sailing, but we still had much of the money the king had given us, and enough money will buy anything. We sailed on the third, and four days later landed safely in a village called Grimsby. I won't describe the voyage, except to say that the moment we set foot on dry land we both fell on our knees and gave thanks to God. And when I stood up, the first thing I saw was Lars's wildly grinning face.

"There's a church here," he said. "You're too late for mass, but at least you could say your prayers out of the wind." In our embrace, he lifted me clear off the ground. When he set me down, he said, "You're lighter than you used to be, Father. God save you, too, Godfather."

"And you, Godson," William retorted. "You've grown a span since I saw you last."

"It's these boots, my lord." He hadn't lost his jackanapes sense of humor.

"You also seem to have inherited your father's skill at prophesying."

"I rummaged through his grimoires while he was gone."

"How did you get here?" I asked, although I knew that Myrddin Wyllt must be involved.

Lars shrugged, and then shivered, for the wind on the beach was biting. "The Queen sent me. As soon as I told her you would be landing here on Sunday, she threw gold at me and told me to get here and bring you to her as fast as you could travel. They have a meal waiting for you over there at the inn," he added hopefully.

William chuckled. "Good planning! At the moment, hot food counts for more than the queen's nightmares. Your father hasn't kept one mouthful down since Wednesday, and I could eat a harbor seal myself. Lead the way."

Like a common porter, Lars scooped up our—admittedly scanty—packs and led the way. The inn was merely the front room of some fisherman's house, but his wife was a good cook. I hadn't known I was hungry, but after draining a horn of watered ale I changed my mind. Lars had eaten earlier, so he did most of the talking, while William and I gulped her excellent herring and onion potage.

"So how long have you been spying on us?" I asked.

"About a fortnight. Before that you seemed to be outside my range. As I told the queen." I suspected that Lars was lying, at least to some extent. He had lied to the queen, too. What I wanted to know was whether he had seen me betraying King Richard to Duke Leopold. If he had, and had let anyone else know, there was either an ax, a rope, or a skinning knife in my future.

He glanced uneasily at William, and obviously decided that he could be trusted—and would have to be, since he knew that Lars could not have known of our arrival by any mundane means.

"Yes, I used the same enchantment you did," he went on. "But it is finicky, you know? It wouldn't show me anyone but you, Father, and nothing before you took to the river."

"That's good. And how is Her Grace?"

"A lightning bolt in a wimple, as always. The justiciar held a meeting of the great council in Oxford last week, and she sent for me. That was when I told her that you were to be landing here today. She tore chunks out of my hindquarters for not keeping her better informed."

"The council was called to consider the ransom demand?" I was very glad that I had not been in England to attend.

"I suppose so. It's rumored to be a weighty one."

"It's very close to impossible," I said.

Sunday or not, our business seemed so urgent that we decided to start our journey south immediately. As soon as we were on our way, riding three abreast, I asked what news there was of Lord John, for I had not dared try to farsee him since Bran of Tara had disrupted my vision. Lars recounted very much what I had espied that day—that John had done homage to Philip for all his brother's domains in France and also, or so it was believed, England too. After that, I now learned, the renegade had tried to seize the crown by force, hiring some Flemish mercenaries and bringing them across the Narrow Sea in an armed invasion of England.

The traitor had marched on London, but the city had rejected him and remained true to the king. So had the great majority of barons and other landowners. The privy council had raised an army to oppose him, and was meeting with much success. He was now believed to be holed up in either Windsor or Tickhill castle, both of which were currently being besieged by government forces.

William promptly asked Lars what he was doing for a living these days, which I should have done sooner, of course. With an admirable effort at modesty, my son revealed that he was now the nation's expert on the treatment of diseases found in Outremer. Employed by the college, he lectured both there and in provincial chantries on that topic, and he was also in demand by returned crusaders whose fevers had recurred, as many of them did. He didn't say that he was raking in money like heaps of autumn leaves, but he certainly gave that impression.

He then mentioned in passing that he was betrothed to the most beautiful girl since Helen of Troy. She had been widowed at sixteen when her knight husband died of wounds received in the siege of Acre. And, since he, Lars, had foreseen my return, he had assumed my approval and arranged for the wedding to be celebrated next Monday. He was, after all, *very nearly* twenty-one, and her parents were agreeable. I asked what his mother thought, and he smugly reported that she was enthusiastic about the match. She had helped him choose the house he had bought—in Oxford, a short walk from Beaumont Palace. At that point I most happily gave him my blessing.

After the first day's ride, William left us to head for his own seat, near Loughborough, and I was free to question Lars about his use—or abuse—of the *Myrddin Wyllt* enchantment. I was reassured as much by his air of hurt innocence as by his words.

"We were all worried to death, Father! The whole country, I mean. We didn't know if the king had left Outremer, and even Myrddin wouldn't tell either me or Mother anything. Nothing! We were terrified that your ship had gone down with all hands. But then rumors began to circulate that King Richard had been taken prisoner somewhere in the empire. I tried the *Myrddin Wyllt* again, and this time I saw you and Baron William riding with a group of merchants. After that I checked on you every few days. I told no one except Mother, honest! Two weeks ago I saw a vision of a boat arriving in Grimsby with church bells ringing for Sunday mass. I don't know how I knew it was Grimsby, I just did. And the queen sent for me . . ."

And he hadn't been able to resist impressing the queen with his prophetic powers.

"All right then," I said. "There are times when that enchantment seems to think for itself. It was very wise to blank you out for so long, because I think our old foe Bran of Tara may be able to eavesdrop on what it tells us. Believe me, Lars, I have done nothing I am ashamed of—nothing at all—but some of my actions could be badly misrepresented, with disastrous results. The important thing is that the king is alive and well, and he was not captured by King Philip." Possibly thanks to me and Myrddin Wyllt. "The French dog has a personal hatred for Richard, but the emperor is only interested in money, and Richard has lots of that."

Lars and I spent our second night at Pipewell, with Harald and Hilda, who rejoiced at my safe return, and were certainly planning to attend Lars's wedding. Our third day brought us to Oxford. We deliberately arrived there too late to call on the queen, but no hour would have been too late to waken Lovise, who would have sat up until dawn, waiting for us.

It had been a long year since I rode out of her life. I won't try to recall everything we said to each other that night. I doubt if I could, for most of it was incoherent baby talk and mumbling, during fondling and between kisses. Some sorts of happiness can't be fitted into words.

Clad in my best clothes—which were very loose on me now— and with my hair and beard newly trimmed, I presented myself in the morning at Beaumont Palace, where Queen Eleanor had waited for me ever since Lars had foretold my return. I was shown at once into her private withdrawing room, with no one else present, not even the normally inevitable Amaria.

Eleanor was showing her age at last. There were lines around her eyes and mouth that had not been there when I left her, a year ago. I knelt to kiss the fingers she offered.

"My Merlin! You are most welcome back." She waved me to a chair.

"And happy to be so, Lady Queen, but I fear that I failed in my mission. You ordered me to bring him home, and that I did not do."

"But he is well?"

"He was grievously ill several times, but he has recovered his strength now. Prison boredom torments him, of course, but his captors are very careful to keep him from harm."

"His captivity is monstrous! I have written several very strong letters to the Pope."

I could imagine. "And the ransom the scoundrels are demanding is beyond belief." I was still a member of the privy council and thus entitled to know what it had decided, but I dared not put direct questions to the queen dowager.

"It may be beyond what his dominions can raise," she said. "It seems likely that we shall have to tax every man in the kingdom a quarter of his income and a quarter of his movable property, men both in England and across the seas. Churches and monasteries will be melting down their plates. Can you wave a magic wand and create thirty-five tons of silver for me, Lord Enchanter?"

"I don't think so, Your Grace. I shall have to read over my spell books and see." In fact, I was fairly sure that there were such enchantments in my collection, but at the moment I was trying to estimate what a quarter of my income would be. Certainly a lot less than the tax collectors would believe.

Speyer is located on the Rhine, upstream from Worms. It is a small town, but much more imposing than the sprawling shanty clutter of Leopold's Vienna. It boasts a magnificent cathedral, built of brown stone in traditional style. The long, high nave must always be breathtaking, and on the morning that Myrddin Wyllt showed it to me, it glowed with imperial majesty. Tapestries bedecked the pillars, trumpets blared and echoed responded. Emperor Henry VI himself was there, crowned and bejeweled on his throne, while the electors of the empire were assembling in their robes and riches, a feast for the eyes—the dukes and prince-bishops who select the emperors, gathered now to sit in judgment on Richard of England. Some were his enemies—Leopold of course, and Boniface of Montferrat, brother of the murdered Conrad. Some were his friends and even relatives, like Otto of Brunswick, the nephew who had ruled Aquitaine in his absence. The two dominant clerics of the empire, the archbishops of Mainz and Cologne, were there, and both must be very unhappy at the conflict between this trial and the Truce of God.

A host of lesser grandees flanked them, including observers from England and some of his French lands, including the dwarfish William Longchamp. I also saw some of the companions who had survived the shipwreck but failed to complete the trek to Vienna. They were exhibited as prisoners, of course. I did not get a clear enough view of them to count them, and had no way of knowing how many of the missing were still alive, if any.

And there was Richard, the tallest man there, clad in simpler clothes, but still projecting the royal authority of the anointer, as if he knew that God was on his side and would stand by him. There was no precedent for such a trial.

When the crowd had settled and the opening prayers been said, the charges were read: that Richard had sold out the crusade to Saladin, had failed to attack Jerusalem, had ordered the walls of Ascalon dismantled, had tried to poison King Philip, had arranged for King Conrad to be assassinated, had supported the usurper of Sicily, Tancred, to the detriment of the island's rightful overlord, the emperor. And so on. There was no mention of a flag being thrown into the moat at Acre, which would have seemed a farcical trifle in such a context. Nor did anyone mention that the emperor desperately needed a lot of money to glue his empire together again.

Calm, assured, and kingly. Richard rose to answer the charges. One by one, he demolished them. He described the events of the crusade, mocking Philip for deserting it in abrogation of the many oaths he had sworn. As for Tancred, he had been holding Richard's sister, Joan, prisoner—what would any honorable knight have done except take up arms against the man? And when that problem was resolved, of course Richard had had to make peace with him so that he could journey on to the Holy Land and fight the Saracens. Hour after hour he spoke with such royal poise and majesty that he won over the entire assembly. The simmering antagonism of the opening faded into admiration, and Philip was exposed as the cowardly renegade he truly was.

Last of all the accusations came the assassination of Conrad of Montferrat, and it was then that Richard pulled out a letter, written on a scrap of parchment bearing traces of Arabic writing from an earlier use. It was signed by Sinan, leader of the Hashshashins, and it witnessed—in very bad Latin—that King Richard had had nothing whatsoever to do with the death of Conrad. This was all true, but I had written this tract months ago to Myrddin Wyllt's dictation in the priory on the island of Lokra, off Ragusa. Richard did not say so, and its evidence was accepted by his judges.

This final revelation completely won over his audience. He walked forward and knelt to the emperor, who raised him and gave him the kiss of peace. The congregation cheered, and the vision faded.

I had never been as proud of my king as I was at that moment.

"Aha! So you're back," Lovise said. "I was about to send for the embalmers."

She was seated in my favorite chair at my desk in the workroom—portraying anger, but not quite masking the relief that underlay it. I lay stretched out on the couch, although I had no memory of arriving there. All I could recall was waking before first light, pulling on a woollen robe, and coming downstairs. A glance at the windows told me that I must have been there all day, for it was now evening. I decided that I was very hungry, and my mouth was drier than the hills of Outremer.

"I am sorry if I worried you," I mumbled, struggling to sit up. "You know I never come to harm in these trances."

"No, I do not know that! Did you plan this one, or did it 'just happen,' as you call it?"

"It just happened. Today was the day of the trial. Oh, Lovise, it was marvelous! Richard utterly—"

"I don't give a fig for Richard! It is you I worry about, you, my husband. That damnable *Myrddin Wyllt* enchantment has enslaved you. You don't summon it anymore; it summons you! You're not trailing around after the king now, you're home in England, and what does it matter to you what happens to him half a continent away?"

I looked around in the hope that I might see a flask of something to drink, moving my tongue and lips in an effort to produce some saliva. "It matters to me whether our liege is Richard or that damnable treacherous brother of his. Oh, darling, he was magnificent! All those dukes and archbishops and the emperor himself, sitting there ready to condemn him as a criminal—and he won them over, every one of them! I thought he was going to steal Henry's empire away from him."

"*So?*" my wife shouted. "What does it matter to you? Why does that devilish Merlin ghost have to pick on you? What does it expect you to do about this vision it has given you, anyway?"

"I'll send a note to the queen, and maybe Walter, telling them the good news. Those scoundrels have no excuse to hold Richard prisoner anymore! Under the Truce of God they have to release him now."

My wife spat out an oath I had never heard her use before. "Truce of nothing! You are as naïve as a baby! He won't walk free until they've bled him of every penny they can squeeze out of him. And even then, King Philip may still put in a higher bid."

She was absolutely right, of course; her common sense was prophesying as truly as Merlin ever did. I did not argue with her, so I must have known then that she was right. She had foreseen Philip's subsequent efforts to buy the prisoner, but fortunately even the emperor didn't dare back out of the agreement he had made. Yet it was to be almost another year before Richard stepped ashore in England, a free man again.

I stood up and stretched painfully.

"Burn it!" Lovise stormed.

"What? Burn what?"

"The *Myrddin Wyllt*! Burn it and every copy and note you've ever made on it. Maybe then you will be free of it."

That would feel like tearing my eyes out. I shuddered and did not answer. "I must find a drink," I said, moving toward the door.

"Not so fast!" Lovise had not moved from her seat—my seat, at my desk.

I realized with dismay that we were having our first real quarrel in twenty-six years of marriage. I stopped and said, "Yes, dear?"

"I want to know what all these incantations are here for." She gestured at the spell rolls I had been working on the previous day and had intended to work on today, had Myrddin Wyllt not carried me off to Speyer. Lovise had had hours, perhaps all day, to read them, and she must know exactly what they were for.

"They're alchemy spells," I said. "I've had them for years and never really had time to—"

"To start turning lead into gold?"

"Well, I was afraid all England would have to pay ransom to

get its king back, but now that the German princes have found him innocent, we shouldn't have to—"

Lovise's icy blue stare never wavered. "The last time I suggested we magic up some money to pay taxes, you told me that this would be dabbling in black magic. Suddenly the ethics of counterfeiting have changed?"

Realizing that we must talk this out, however dry my mouth, I sat down on the edge of the couch. "Yes, dear. They have changed. In the first case, we were being taxed to send our king off to the Holy Land to recover Jerusalem from the heathens. That was money for a holy cause. But the ransom the Germans were going to demand would be against the Truce of God, and therefore a very unholy cause. I would happily cheat them."

"You are splitting hairs. You think the Germans won't think to test the coins to make sure they're genuine silver?" Lovise's voice drooled contempt.

"They can try. First, they'll scratch a coin or two to make sure they aren't just lead with a wash of silver on top. And then they'll weigh them against a standard weight. Every metal has its own density, as you know. Ordinary counterfeits are easy enough to detect. But the alchemists know how to combine metals so that the mixture weighs exactly what that same volume of silver would weigh, and how to enchant it so that it has the same bright luster. If the Germans do persist in demanding a ransom as if Richard had been captured in a fair battle, then their cause is ungodly and we need have no scruples in paying them with fake coinage."

For a long moment my wife just stared at me. Then she said softly, "We discussed this with Lars once, remember? The three of us. We discussed the danger of the slippery slope? You are sliding, Durwin! What once you saw as utter evil now just seems like bad taste to you. Suddenly ends justify means. Black magic is only a darkish gray. Fall into that pit and you will never emerge again."

I rose and held out a hand. "The point is moot, darling. They won't dare demand a ransom now, so the council won't have to wring out the country's lifeblood. I promise that I'll tuck all that alchemy lore back in its chest in the crypt. Let's go upstairs."

I was wrong, of course. Richard had to agree to contribute that gigantic "dowry" to marry off his niece, and the council had to find the money somehow.

I was called to attend the next meeting, and I had never seen so many glum faces. As the queen had predicted to me, every man in England would be required to pay a quarter of his annual income and the value of a quarter of his movable property, while the country had not yet recovered from the brutal "Saladin tithe" of two years ago, levied to pay for Richard's crusading army. There would be many hungry bellies come next winter.

Furthermore, since there could be no hope of raising such a sum without Lord John's six counties paying their share, a truce had to be arranged. An uneasy and unhappy peace settled over the land.

Near the end of June, I was called to Westminster for another meeting, but the news was no more cheerful. Money was coming in so slowly that it might be years before we could buy our king back. No truly helpful ideas were presented. Earlier, I had requested a private audience with Queen Eleanor. As soon as we adjourned, she received me in a small and heavily perfumed dressing room, where a Moorish girl was trimming her nails for her. She had said very little at the council meeting, and her face had given away nothing at all, but it was an easy guess that she was very unhappy at the current situation. She addressed me in Latin, which the slave girl would not understand.

"Have you brought any cheerful prophecies, Lord Durwin?"

"No, Your Grace. My sight has been neglecting me lately, but it does that often. I did bring you these, though." I handed her six silver pennies, each inscribed *Henricus Rex*, because Richard had not yet changed the coinage.

The queen examined them, holding them at a distance as many elderly folk do. "It always flattered him, you know. He was never this handsome." She was referring to the gross caricature of Henry on the obverse of the coins. "These are very welcome, my lord, but taken all together they will not scratch the total of our needs."

"This is true, but I merely wondered if you could tell which are genuine, and which ought to bear my likeness instead of your late husband's?"

Her eyes flashed with delight, and something like her old smile returned. "I certainly can not! But others more skilled than I will surely examine what we offer."

"I have a friend who is an expert in money, ma'am. He lends it, so he must be careful that what he gets back is of true value. I asked him the same question, and he had to admit that he could not tell the real from the false."

Her smile grew even brighter. "And anything that can fool a Jew will certainly fool a rabble of greedy Germans?"

"A reasonable hope."

"You truly made some of these by your magic?"

"A little magic, Your Grace, and a great deal of hard work. I had to mold a freshly minted coin, and those are not easy to find. Then I had to make the necessary stamps, and melt metals in a crucible. As a child I used to watch my father at work—he was the farrier in Pipewell Abbey—so I am familiar with forges. Those six took me almost a month, so to make a large number will require a team of skilled workers. Even imitation pennies have a cost, although they come much cheaper than real ones."

Mostly they were composed of lead, which is much cheaper than silver, with a proportion of tin, and enough magic to give them the right glitter and ring, because every type of money has its own voice when dropped on a hard surface. I had rewritten several incantations to create the effect I needed.

The queen asked no more questions about sorcery. She spread her fingers to inspect her manicure. "This was prettily done," she said in French. "Go now and find Francois and tell him I need him."

As the Moor left, the queen gathered up the coins and turned back to me. "How many of these six are fakes?"

"Five, my lady. I marked the real one with a scratch so I could know it."

She laughed. "You truly must be Merlin Redux! Here, take them. You have my royal permission to spend them, but you must break your stamps and make no more. I could appoint you a moneyer, Baron Durwin, and let you take over one of the king's mints. The one in the Tower would be the most suitable, I should think. Because," she added with a mischievous smile, "if you got caught counterfeiting, a dungeon would be ready to hand! But no, we must not do this. If it ever became known that my son had been paying off his ransom with false coin, he would be both furious and chagrined. He would have your head, and perhaps mine as well."

I bowed. "I confess that I am relieved by your decision, Lady Queen, and my wife will be even more so. She knew what I was doing, and despised it."

I was genuinely happy, yet I could not but think, as I took my leave, that queens never go hungry, never have to walk behind a plow in leaky shoes, never have to listen to their children crying themselves to sleep on empty stomachs. Let the people pay the ransom. He is their king, after all.

The next day I rode home, eager to tell the news to my wife. Knowing how much it would please her, I did what I had not done in nigh-on twenty years—I rode the whole way in a single day. I changed horses at every posting house, of course, so I did not have to exhaust a single mount, just myself, and it was midsummer, when the days are long. The sun was resting on the horizon as I rode up to the Oxford post. After so many hours in the saddle I would have enjoyed a walk to my door, but I had baggage, although not much. So I accepted the normal offer of an escort, and a groom rode alongside me for the short journey across town to Beaumont Palace. I dismounted at the gate and shouldered my bag. As he led my weary horse away, I felt a sudden flash of warning, like the silent flicker of summer lightning.

I paused, looking around. There were no lights in windows yet, no children still playing on the palace grass, and the streets of the town had been deserted. Most people would already be in bed, if not asleep. Nothing seemed wrong, but . . .

"Myrddin Wyllt?" I whispered. No one answered, yet I felt even more confident that danger was lurking somewhere close.

I think I mentioned earlier that I had learned long years ago never to travel without a few defensive spells, usually memorized Release spells. I had none stored in my head that day, but I did have a few parchment incantations at the bottom of my pack. I knelt, scrabbled through my laundry, and found what I wanted— the *Præcipio tibi* that had served me so well on my travels in Germany. I read it through quickly. Then I rose and banged on the gate with my cane. In a surprisingly short moment, a youthful but whiskery face appeared in the grill. It belonged to no one I recognized, so I leaned close and softly spoke the charm to enslave him. His eyes iced over.

"Whose man are you?" I asked.

"Lord John's, master."

"Tell me where Lord John is right now."

"I don't know, master. The captain didn't tell me."

"Tell me what the captain did tell you."

"He told me to mind the gate, and be sure to admit an old man with blond hair and a limp, wearing a faded blue jerkin, who would be arriving shortly."

I had already assumed that Bran of Tara must have been spying on me, to have foreseen my all-day trek and late arrival. That mention of my blue jacket confirmed it.

"Tell me where are the real guards are."

"In the guardhouse, master. Asleep, but not harmed."

So I had Bran himself to deal with here, plus an unknown number of others.

"And who is in charge?"

"Lord John, master."

"Let me in!"

I told him to leave the gate open and precede me to the guard room, a few paces away, where two men I did know lay prone and unconscious. I told my temporary slave, "Now lie down beside them and sleep until dawn."

I might have tried to waken the two genuine guards, but that would take time I did not believe I had, and might not succeed anyway, because I knew my opponent was a very powerful sorcerer. The man from Tara and the Plantagenet monster were in control of my house, my servants, and worst of all, my wife. Leaving the sleepers in peace, I rummaged in my pack once more, until I found a parchment scroll bearing a spell I had never used. The glosses on the original had warned that it was hugely dangerous, even to read aloud. I had chanted it once, and the acceptance alone had scared me so much that I had never spoken the release, letting the power die away over the next couple of days. It was listed in my files simply as the *Achilles*.

Peering in the fading light, I read it over in a soft whisper, and was appalled again at the violence the words threatened, but I felt no acceptance. I took some calming breaths and tried again.

This time acceptance came in a rush, speeding my heart, banishing the fatigue of my long day's ride, and making my whole body quiver with a lust for battle. I sent a quick prayer to Heaven that I would not need to invoke this monstrous incantation.

I hobbled swiftly through the dusk to my front door, which was unlocked, contrary to all my standing orders. Fearlessly I went in, dropping my pack and shouting as one does on returning home after an absence. Nobody answered, but there was light in my workroom, so I headed that way. The door stood open; in I went.

Only three candles lit the long chamber. The first thing I saw was Lovise in the center, gagged and bound into a chair with ropes like those we used in our stable. Her gown had been ripped open to expose her breasts. Her eyes were wide with horror at the sight of me walking straight into the trap. Behind her stood Lord John, clutching a gleaming knife long enough to carve meat off a roasted ox.

A few feet to their left, my right, was the portly shape of Sage Bran, leering at me through his forked beard. I did not doubt that he had foreseen my arrival and had some deadly spells ready to cast. The rest of the big room was crowded by seven or eight men-at-arms holding naked blades—swords or pikes—and two more who were aiming spanned crossbows in my direction. I barely noticed any of them. They would do nothing until the order was given. John and Bran were the danger.

"Welcome home, Baron Durwin," the prince said, unable to resist a slight sneer.

"Get out of my house and take your dogs with you."

"Watch your tongue, Saxon. First, you will give me the stamps you used to make those coins you tried to bribe my mother with yesterday."

"I threw them in the Thames. Go and look for them yourself."

John pouted. Without taking his eyes off me, he said something in a language I did not know. Bran replied briefly, but he also shook his head, so he had probably been asked if I were lying.

"Foolish of you," John said. "You will have to make replacements for me. You clearly do not understand the gravity of your situation, Durwin. In the short term, I have your wife here, at my mercy, such as it is. She's too old for my taste, but my gallant lads, here, would enjoy sharing her. In the longer term, I have Father Ferdinand. You do remember Father Ferdinand? A very large man—wasted as a priest, ought to be a woodcutter or a blacksmith. He has already described for us, in writing, the elderly blond minstrel with the crippled right leg who sold King Richard to the duke."

I felt a chill and, at the same time, a rush of fury that almost overcame my grip on the incantation I was holding in. Obviously, Bran of Tara had been spying on me for a long time. I ought to feel flattered, but for the first time in my life I was seeking violence—deadly, personal violence. I seethed with it.

"If Father Ferdinand's affidavit is not enough," Lord John continued happily, "then his bishop and Duke Leopold have given permission for him to travel to England to testify at your treason trial. He will be accompanied by some other witnesses. You made a fool of the duke, and Leopold is a very touchy man. Now do you understand your problem, Durwin?

Had his knife been under my throat instead of my wife's he couldn't have frightened me by that time. I was infused with the soul of Achilles, and Achilles never knew what fear was.

Biting my words, I said, "I understand more than you do, Lackland. I order you to leave my house at once and take all your flunkies with you."

John considered my defiance for a moment, then asked Bran another question. Again the answer seemed to be negative.

"First," the prince continued, "I want the password to release those." With a nod of his head he indicated the wall of scrolls where I stored my collection of incantations.

"You shan't have it."

"I will count to three and then cut off one of your wife's nipples. If you still refuse—"

This had gone far enough. I could no longer resist the raging of the Release spell still throbbing in my head. I spoke the trigger words, *Magna qualis Achilli*, and at once it made me, as directed, more terrible than Achilles.

If you are reading this, I assume that you are familiar with the hero of Homer's *Iliad*, the greatest of all war stories, so you are already aware that "Fast-footed" Achilles was not only the swiftest warrior in the Achaian army, but also the greatest of all human killing machines, unmatched and utterly ruthless. I spun around and went for the nearest of the men-at-arms, a green youngster whose chain mail hauberk looked too big for him; he also held his pike as if he'd never touched it before. That was not what made him my first victim, though, but the fact that he was standing in front of the wall of scrolls, so when the ferrule of my cane stabbed him in the eye, he fell back against it.

The resulting flash of lightning and clap of thunder almost drowned out his scream. He dropped the pike, which I caught before it hit the floor, discarding my cane. At a length of eight feet, it was clumsy for indoor fighting, but it had both a stabbing blade and an ax. In two unequal steps I reached Bran of Tara, who was not wearing armor. I cut his throat with a single slash. Sharp cracks indicated that the two crossbows had loosed, but both quarrels missed me by a yard. The next to die was the other pikeman, who hadn't even started to react.

The two crossbowmen to my left had barely begun to reload, so I rushed them while they still had their mouths wide open, which made good targets for my stabbing blade. That left the swordsmen, and by then they had awakened to their peril. They all tried to flee. I got two of them before they reached the doorway and the rest jammed in it. The last one standing did turn and try to parry, but he was far too slow, and my weapon had much greater reach than his. I stabbed him right through his chain mail, which broke the point of my blade, but by then I had no more need of it. This slaughter could hardly be described as a battle. Achilles had merely executed a dozen or so sluggards. I ended where I had begun, with the pikeman who had been felled by the wards on my library. He was starting to sit up, so I cut his throat also.

To Lord John, the only survivor, my move along the big room must have seemed little more than a blur. I slowed down to human speed and came at him with my pike leveled.

"Cut off a nipple, would you?" I roared. "Guess what I am about to cut off?"

He screamed, slashed Lovise's left breast, and fled, howling in terror at the miraculous change in fortune and leaping over corpses, some of them still twitching.

I let him go because attending to my wife was far more urgent than trying to curb a cur like John. I had never intended anything else, because nothing would save me if I were convicted of injuring the king's brother. After half a year in the Holy Land, I knew the enchantments for wounds by heart. The spiteful gash was not deep, so I easily closed it and stopped the bleeding. Then I took up Lord John's knife and cut her bonds. I pressed down on her shoulder when she tried to rise.

"Sit a moment," I said. "Take some deep breaths. There may be a slight scar, I'm afraid."

"But you will be the only one who will ever see it."

I was reassured that her ordeal had not driven her out of her wits. My gentle wife was as tough as any veteran campaigner, a descendant of Danish raiders. "I hadn't expected such a welcome."

She leaned against me. "I wish you hadn't had to kill them all, but I know you had no choice. I am enormously proud of you, dear Durwin, my most perfect knight."

"I am just as proud of you. Most women would still be screaming their heads off."

"I just have to catch my breath first."

Then she did rise, and we embraced. I led her off to bed, for she had lost blood and endured a traumatic experience. I cast a gentle relaxation spell on her, one I often used to help patients sleep.

Then I went downstairs to see what other trouble I had. My alertness and general well-being surprised me, for marginal notes on the *Magna qualis Achilli* scroll warned that it was always followed by a major reaction. I found our servants on the dining room floor in the same sort of induced coma as the guards at the gate, so I left them to sleep it off. I still had to decide what to do with the bodies in my workroom, and the ghastly pools of congealing blood. Strangely, I felt no guilt and no regrets. That was Achilles' doing.

The prudent Lord John, I assumed, would certainly have kept a saddled horse handy, so he was doubtless fleeing away under the stars, faster than a terrified owl. There was no moonlight, so I could only hope that he would fall off and break his neck. I wasn't about to twist his luck—not yet, anyway, but clearly our feud was not over.

Killing people was against the law, usually, and major crimes were the business of the sheriff. I knew that Baron William Brewer, then high sheriff of Oxfordshire, was currently on his way to Germany to help negotiate the king's ransom and release, but he would have left someone to look after his larceny business while he was away, so I strolled over to Beaumont Palace itself, which was where he was most often to be found. A few windows were lighted and the lantern by the door was lit, so I applied the knocker with some vigor.

The shutter opened and a frown appeared behind the grille. "Yes?"

"Fine evening. I am Baron Durwin."

"Oh! What can I do for you, my lord?"

I held up a bloody hand. "I've just killed some men, and I'd like the bodies removed, please."

That brought me to the attention of the deputy sheriff, Sir Richard Brewer, son of the high sheriff, a fat-faced youngster with a straggly mustache and an air of horrified desperation at having to deal with a peer of the realm come to confess to a major crime. Worst of all, I even seemed to be sober, which precluded the most obvious excuse. He wasn't stupid, though, and as soon as he recovered from his initial disbelief, he acted as reasonably as possible under the circumstances.

He gathered some men with lanterns and a cart. I noticed a blanket tossed into the cart and guessed that it probably concealed chains, in case I turned violent. I led him and his helpers to the main gate to see the two supposed guards fast asleep, and the snoring stranger, whom I identified as the only one of the gang I had spared. I insisted that he could be safely left there in the meantime, and he would probably turn out to know nothing.

Then we went to my house. Even I was appalled when the lanterns revealed the abattoir that I had made of my workroom, with a dozen corpses lying in a congealing lake. I warned everyone not to touch the warded wall of scrolls. Of course Brewer was strongly disinclined to credit my story.

"You expect me to believe that you slew all these men singlehanded?"

I was old, and a cripple.

"I expect you to believe that I am the king's enchanter. The spell is mightier than the sword."

He again surveyed the carnage. "Who's the unarmored one?"

"Bran of Tara. He was a sorcerer in the service of the man who initiated all this horror, the man who led it."

Young Brewer thought for a moment, detecting more trouble in the guarded way I had spoken. "So who was this leader?"

"The one who wounded my wife? He escaped, unfortunately."

"His name, my lord?"

"You are happier not knowing his name, son. Let's just say that in the poor light I did not recognize him, but don't ask me to repeat that under oath."

At that point young Brewer decided that he had both a duty and the authority to perform it. He flared. "I ask you again—who led these men when they invaded your house? I am aware that you both are a nobleman and a royal confidant, my lord, but you are not above the law!"

I wondered if he really believed that homily, because in practice it would rarely stand up to scrutiny. "He was man far above your reach, Sir Richard. Even the great council dares not obturate him at the moment."

His lips shaped the name of Lord John, but only his eyes dared speak it.

I nodded, and with that my night's work was done. The Achilles enchantment released me and reaction set in. Every joint and muscle in my body seemed to scream, as if I were being torn apart. I would have fallen if Brewer had not caught hold of my arm.

"You all right, my lord?"

"No," I muttered. "I am going upstairs to bed. Kindly remove the carrion, wash the floor, and lock the doors when you leave. You can return the keys in the morning."

I crawled up the stairs and went to sleep on the rug beside my bed.

It took me three days to throw off the effects of the Achilles incantation. On the first day, Lovise and Lars managed to rouse me enough to get me into bed, and once in a while push some food and water into me, but the rest of the time I just slept. On the fourth morning she cuddled up close and asked if I were ever going to wake up.

"No. Well, maybe tomorrow. How are you?"

"I am well, thanks to your tender loving care."

I managed to roll over to kiss the end of her nose. "Your sarcasm is what I love most about you."

"That's not what you used to tell me. Oh, Durwin, you were marvelous— Sir Lancelot to the rescue! You looked so calm and confident when you walked in . . . and so horribly vulnerable! But the trouble isn't over yet, love. Men from the privy council arrived last night. They're staying in the palace, of course, and they'll to want to hear from both of us."

"Don't worry, dear. No one else in the kingdom could get away with blatant sorcery like that, but I can." I wasn't quite as confident as I tried to sound. It was one thing for King Richard to butcher 2,700 Saracens in cold blood, but for an elderly cripple to take on eleven armed men and an alleged sorcerer singlehanded and kill them all must seem an intolerable insult to chivalry and the Christian faith.

Three days in bed without proper sustenance had left me very shaky, but I managed to rise, make myself presentable, and in due course receive the delegation from London. One of them was William Marshal, who thoroughly disapproved of my style of fighting and was always inclined to put much more trust in Lord John Plantagenet than I ever did. Yet he had to agree that I was entitled to defend my wife and home against armed intruders. In the end they all came around to this view, and congratulated me. They went back to London with the surviving thug, the one I had put to sleep. I later heard that he had been hanged, but I suspect he had a very nasty time in the Tower first. Even if his testimony implicated Lord John, which I doubt, that couldn't bring down the villain. Justice must wait until King Richard returned.

"And what happens if he doesn't come back?" Lovise asked me that evening, as we were relaxing after the long summer day and celebrating life with a fine French wine.

"Then we shall have to hide from King John. Lord in Heaven, what a horrible sound those two words have!" I drank some wine to take away their taste. For the first time I thought seriously about what else Lord John had said.

"On second thoughts, my angel, we had better go into hiding right now and stay there until the king does comes back. It seems that John had his pet sorcerer spying on us like I sometimes spied on them, at least while we were in Austria. You remember Lackland mentioning a Father Ferdinand?"

Lovise nodded, regarding me carefully.

"Father Ferdinand will have described a blond, aging minstrel with a lift on his right shoe, who sold Richard to Duke Leopold."

That admission made even my own wife stare at me in horror. "You didn't!"

"Yes, I did, because the king ordered me to. He was sick, exhausted, and trapped. He judged it better to give himself up than to be arrested in the street at sword point like a common pickpocket. So he sent me to negotiate his surrender."

"But if John has that evidence in writing, he'll give it to the privy council! He may have done so already. He's as spiteful as . . . as . . ."

"As an adder?"

"Thank you. Why don't you fetch the *Loc hwær* scroll and we'll ask where he is at the moment?"

Good idea. I began to rise and then fell back in my chair . . .

I saw a vision of a spacious hall, with tapestried walls reaching to an arched ceiling. The windows were high and glazed, the floors covered with carpet instead of rushes. On a table in the center stood a bowl of Easter lilies, so I knew that this was a foretelling. A man in rich clerical robes was standing with his back to me, flanked by a couple of less senior divines and three or four well-garbed laymen, but only the central figure was distinct, and the vagueness of the others was another sign of prophecy. They were facing the open doorway, so it was a reasonable guess that they were about to receive special guests.

That entrance hall was very familiar to me, but it took me a minute or two to place it. At last I recalled being a guest there more than a year earlier, on my way to the Holy Land. So the man in the ornate costume with his back to me must be John of Alençon, archdeacon of Lisieau, and this was his palatial "house." I knew then exactly who was expected. This was springtime, next year.

A herald in bright livery entered and proclaimed the name I had already guessed—Richard, king of England, duke of Normandy, et cetera. Freed from his captivity and back in his own domain, he was restored to his former Herculean majesty, no longer the ragged invalid I had parted from in Vienna. The infamous emperor must have fed him well. And on his arm stepped a diminutive but graceful and dauntless old lady—Eleanor, dowager queen and duchess. She looked years younger, now that her favorite son was restored to her.

So I knew that the Lionheart would once again be at liberty and, since he would never dare journey through lands ruled by King Philip, he would have visited England on his way to Lisieau, in the heart of Normandy. The greetings that followed were warm and genuine, for the archdeacon was an old friend.

Gradually the minor characters faded away, even the queen, until a later hour darkened the sky beyond the windows and I was seeing only Richard and his host seated across an empty fireplace, drinking and reminiscing. The king was leading the conversation, as kings always do, and I was granted snatches of it. He had been delayed by bad weather in the Narrow Sea, and was worried about some place called Verneuil, which Philip was besieging. He said little about the ongoing treachery of his brother in league with Philip. When he did mention it, it was more in pity than in anger.

Suddenly he stopped talking about that and looked quizzically at de Alençon. "You are jumpy, old friend. Something troubles you?" He laughed. "You have seen my young brother!"

de Alençon nodded. "Indeed I have. I told him that I thought you would be lenient with him, and treat him much better than he would treat you if your positions were reversed."

"I am sure you are right. I will not harm him. Send for him if he is here."

The archdeacon rose, but instead of pulling a bell rope to summon a servant, he hurried out of the room. In a few moments Lord John came in, shaking and cowering, as well he might when faced with the king and brother he had betrayed so abominably.

"John!" Richard held out his arms.

John rushed forward and dropped before him, groveling and weeping on the king's boots. John of Alençon followed him in, shaking his head at the spectacle.

Richard bent and raised his brother. "John, John! Fear not. You are only a child, and you have gotten into bad company. It is those who misled you who will be punished. I forgive you." Then they embraced.

Unnoticed except by me, de Alençon rolled his eyes. At twenty-seven, Lord John was no child! But I thought I knew the speech that the Lionheart had been quoting. As an adolescent he had joined his brothers Henry and Geoffrey in rebellion against their father, King Henry. Henry had won, but he had forgiven their treason, and what Richard had just said sounded as if it might be the very words he had heard when he was pardoned. John had been only an infant then and would not have been present, but he had probably heard the story many times. Richard had been sixteen. He would have remembered his father's leniency.

The scene wavered and faded away. I was back in Oxford, in the previous summer, and Lovise was frowning at me.

"What did you see?"

I reached for my wine. "Disaster. Richard is going to forgive Lord John. The traitor will be allowed to live."

"That's crazy!"

"I suppose it's good Christian charity—or family solidarity. It shouldn't make any difference to us, though." Or would it? If John had already put Father Ferdinand's evidence before the privy council, when Richard returned, would he support my version of events or his brother's? The more I thought about it, the more I began to doubt. Would I even be alive by that time to receive a royal pardon?

Then I felt another foreseeing coming.

The time was again spring, but the landscape was farther south than Lisieau and unfamiliar to me. I was facing a small castle encircled by a besieging army, which had worn the grass underfoot to dust and was fouling the air with the inevitable stench of latrine pits. The castle flew a baronial pennant I did not know, but I recognized Richard's lion banner above the largest tent, although the lazy afternoon breezes hardly stirred it.

The siege was ending even as I watched. A passable breach had been battered in the wall and orders were being shouted to hold any further shots from the trebuchets. Angevin forces were streaming in the gates that now stood open. In a few moments the pennant was hauled down. I could hear cheering, and then a bugle.

I made my way through the camp toward that big tent with the banner. Men were going in and out a lot, but I could see no sign of Richard himself. Suddenly uneasy, I willed my invisible self to move faster, and was delivered instantly to the center of the crisis, where the Lionheart reclined on a bed, propped up on pillows, horribly pale. His left arm was supported by a sling and that shoulder was heavily bandaged. Even in the dim light I could see white streaks in his hair and beard; his face was twisted by pain, but also aged. He was several years older than in my previous vision. Doctors and aides hovered around, helpless to relieve the situation.

"Can I bring you anything, sire?" one asked.

The king made a feeble attempt at humor, as men will do to demonstrate courage. "Baron Durwin is what I need most. No, no—do not send for him. He cannot possibly get here in time."

I wanted to scream that I was there already, but I produced no sound, because in reality I wasn't. Nor could I sing the incantations that might save the patient, but he was right to say I could not be sent for and arrive in time. I knew some of the men crowded in the background: William the Marshall and Walter Hubert, now archbishop of Canterbury, who looked as dusty as if he had just spent hours on a horse. If people like those two were being summoned, then the crisis was extreme. A deep shoulder wound is almost always a sentence of death, not immediate, but in a week or ten days, when the gangrene spreads. I had little hope that the Lionheart had three days left.

"Lord King!" A young man-at-arms streaming sweat pushed his way in from the doorway, shouting. "Chalus-Chabrol has fallen! Your banner flies there now."

The dying man nodded. "We heard the bugle. Falk, give this man a silver mark for bringing us these happy tidings."

The messenger gabbled thanks. Then, perhaps hoping to increase his sudden wealth, he added, "And we got the archer what shot you, Your Grace!"

"Well done." The king looked around the fence of faces and spoke to an older man I did not know. "Bring him here. Don't let them hurt him."

Why was I seeing this? Where was Chalus-Chabrol? Was I supposed to warn Richard never to go near it? I had learned back in Dürnstein castle that the Myrddin Wyllt prophecies were not carved in the rock of destiny. Some of them were written in smoke and liable to change. This tragedy was located years ahead of my seeing it.

A few minutes later a prisoner was manhandled in and slammed to the ground near the king's bed. One bystander aimed a kick—

"Leave him!" Richard barked. "Stand up, lad. What's your name?"

The captive rose, rubbing his wrists and ribs to soothe bruises. He wore no armor and his clothes were threadbare. He looked like a sixteen-year-old who had eaten very little recently, and whose efforts to seem defiant produced no more than a childish pout.

"Bertrand de Gourdon." He omitted any term of respect. When addressing a king, that required either considerable courage or extreme folly.

"You've killed me, you know," Richard said gently. "My wound is festering, so within a week, I will be called to my Maker. What have I ever done to you that you should want to kill me?" He spoke in the southerners' Occitan, which I had trouble following.

"You killed my father and my two brothers."

The dying man smiled wanly, surveying the grim faces of the audience. "That's a fair answer, is it not, friends? And this young man is not just an expert crossbowman, he was the only defender on the battlements at the time, the only one brave enough to make a show of defiance and take me on in an archery contest. He had no shield except an old frying pan. That is true manhood! Bertrand de Gourdon, I forgive you! Fulk, give him a purse of silver. You are free to go, Bertrand."

The boy accepted the purse disbelievingly and looked around at the watchers' scowls. Then he made an awkward bow, thanked the king, and went. None of the onlookers shifted, though, so he had to push his way through. He disappeared under the flap, but I doubted very much that he would walk out of the Angevin camp with his bag of silver.

Richard sighed. "Walter, I must rest now. We will talk at length later."

The tent began to empty. William Marshall caught the eye of Archbishop Hubert, who nodded. The two of them took their leave of the king and went out. I followed as they strolled over to a deserted area where they thought they would not be overheard. Beyond them, at the far edge of the camp, I saw Bertrand de Gourdon, now naked, tied between two posts, and gagged. His captors were sharpening knives, while other men were gathering to watch him being flayed. Probably both Marshall and Hubert noticed, but neither commented.

"No hope?" Hubert asked.

Marshall shook his head. "When they unwrap his bandage, they can smell the rot in Limoges."

"Donkeying around without any armor, I suppose?"

"Of course. He just thought he'd get off a few arrows one evening."

The archbishop growled like a hound. "Even Saladin warned him against tomfoolery like that! So who's it to be—Arthur or John?"

"He won't say. He may decide later, or he may leave it to us. John's starting to make trouble again. But Arthur's only twelve years old, and his mother won't let him out of Brittany."

"Not even to inherit an empire?" the archbishop said skeptically.

"Well, perhaps, but Philip must have heard the news from his spies by this time, and if he isn't readying his army already, I'll eat my castle."

"John's shown that he's not much of a fighter."

"He couldn't be worse than a twelve-year-old."

"You could be Arthur's regent."

"No! It has to be John," Marshall insisted.

And I, the unseen listener, wondered whether the flawless Sir William had already sent notice to John that the throne was about to become vacant. Hubert was silent for a long moment. Perhaps he was wondering the same, but he did not ask.

Finally he shrugged. "You will regret this, William," he said.

I was given no time to consider this dread vision, or what I was supposed to do about it. The *Myrddin Wyllt* whirled me away like an autumn leaf. Uncertain cheering assailed my ears and I found myself in a church I knew, Rouen Cathedral, in Normandy. John sat on the throne—a plumper, older, and more heavily bearded John than I knew—and Archbishop Coutances was just placing a coronet on his head, making him duke.

I groaned a silent *No!* and was instantly swept away.

Westminster Abbey came next, where Archbishop Hubert was anointing the new king with holy oil. If Arthur was currently the age I had heard William Marshall give him, then it was ten years since I had foretold that John would one day wear the crown of St. Edward. Oh, poor England!

Enough! Surely that is enough?

No, Carnonos had yet more horrors to show me.

The prisoner was secured by three chains—to both wrists and his neck—although they had enough slack to let him move around his cell. Yet it was a cell, with a tiny barred window and a door of massive timbers. His clothes had once been those of a nobleman, although now they were filthy and torn in places. He had a bench to sit on or sleep on, a water bottle, and a bucket, nothing more, not even a candle or a blanket. I viewed him by the fading light of evening, seated on the bench, legs outstretched, leaning back against the cold ashlar blocks of the wall, tortured by the slow creep of empty time. That was no way to house a prisoner of quality, perhaps a hostage who should have been treated with honor.

Only when I realized how young he was—sixteen?—fifteen?—did I guess his name. I also guessed why I was being shown his torment, and then I cried out silently to Myrddin Wyllt to spare me from what I was certain must be about to happen. But I was not spared, and neither was the boy.

Metal clanged and squealed; the door opened. The prisoner's chains clattered wildly as he swung his legs to the floor and stood up. A man appeared in the entrance, and for the moment came no further. He was finely garbed in an ermine-trimmed robe of scarlet, but he had a sword belted on over it, and those do not belong together. He stared sullenly at the prisoner, and belched.

The boy made a slight bow, little more than a gesture, for he never took his eyes off his visitor. "God preserve you, Uncle."

"But not you," John said. He was drunk.

The resulting silence might have been intended to terrify the youth, but it did not seem to. Eventually he was the one who broke it.

"To what do I owe the honor of this visit, Lord King?"

"A problem. I have a problem. Two problems. I mean you are a problem, but I have another problem—can't find anyone willing to rid me of the first one. Problem, that is."

Arthur's fists clenched. "You mean no one is willing to blind me and castrate me as you ordered?"

"Never did," his uncle said, slurring the words. "Mean we talked a lot about it, but I didn'in't sign that."

"And now you have signed my death warrant but can't find an executioner willing to shed royal blood?" His voice was admirably controlled.

"Got no choice. You swore allegiance. You agreed I was rightflull king. Thenyou 'scaped. You led'n army 'gainst me."

"Escape?" Arthur snapped. "If I *escaped* from Le Mans, then I was a prisoner, and if I was a prisoner, then any words I swore were sworn under duress. I am the rightful heir!"

"Tha's the problem—words! Words!" the king muttered, and walked into the cell, drawing his sword.

Durwin! Durwin! What's wrong? Wake up! Wake up!

For a few seconds I heard Lovise's voice as she tried to rouse me, and then I slid back into Myrddin Wyllt's sty of nightmares.

I was in a town I knew quite well, Le Mans, in Anjou. Some houses had been smashed by rocks that trebuchets had thrown too far, and there were fires burning in the distance, but the inhabitants must have taken refuge elsewhere, for the only souls I saw were a troop of soldiers marching along. In their midst rode King Philip, triumphant.

I saw Chateau Gaillard, King Richard's masterpiece of a castle overlooking the Seine, only 25 miles from Rouen itself, a stronghold he had sworn could never be taken. I saw it with a breach in the outermost wall, and a French flag flying above the keep.

And so on. City after city, stronghold after stronghold, I was shown the fall of the Angevin empire. Henry II and Richard the Lionheart must have been weeping in their graves. But then came something different.

I stood by a marshy, reed-infested river under a summer sky, almost certainly back in England. In the distance stood a castle I recognized as Windsor, not far from Westminster, so the river could only be the Thames. When I turned around, I faced an astonishing sight—a great array of baronial pavilions, each in its own colors and flying its distinctive pennant. There were several dozen of them, each guarded by knights and squires, but the greatest and most impressive boasted the three-lion standard of the king of England. I had seen similar gatherings in the Holy Land, but much more diluted, scattered throughout an army camp. Here there was no army, just the assembled nobility and senior clergy of England.

I moved in closer. In a central clearing between the royal pavilion and the host of barons' tents, a meeting was in progress. King John was instantly recognized on a throne, although he was older and fatter than the last time I had seen him, while he was murdering his nephew. The extra years had just added to his look of dissolution. He was flanked by high-ranked clerics in their finery, and a few—astonishingly few—loyal supporters. William Marshal was with him, and some men arrayed like bishops.

Looking along the rows of benches occupied by the opposing nobility, I recognized many I knew, all of them older than I remembered. Among them sat unfamiliar, younger men, probably heirs of those who had died in the generation that had passed since the crusade. And all of them were grim-faced and purposeful, as they must be if they were in revolt against their liege lord the king. What in the world could have brought about this rebellion?

A stocky herald in gaudy tabard arose on the rebels' side and began to read from a large sheet of parchment. He was facing the throne as if dictating terms of surrender to the king, but his text was worded as if spoken by the king himself. That confused me for a moment, but then I realized that the rebels expected John to sign and seal this tirade as his own proclamation.

> JOHN, by the grace of God King of England, Lord of Ireland, Duke of Normandy and Aquitaine, and Count of Anjou, to his archbishops, bishops, abbots, earls, barons, justices, foresters, sheriffs, stewards, servants, and to all his officials and loyal subjects . . .

If my preceding visions had been correct, then most of those titles were historical fictions by now.

> . . . that we have granted to God, and by this present charter have confirmed . . .
> Heirs may be given in marriage, but not to someone of lower social standing. Before a marriage takes place, it shall be made known to the heir's next-of-kin . . .
> If a man dies owing money to Jews, his wife may have her dower and pay nothing towards the debt from it . . .
> No man shall be forced to perform more service for a knight's fee, or other free holding of land, than is due from it . . .
> The city of London shall enjoy all its ancient liberties and free customs, both by land and by water. We also will and

grant that all other cities, boroughs, towns, and ports
shall enjoy all their liberties and free customs . . .

"Father! Father, wake up!" A heavy hand slapped my face. Unable to rouse me from my long trance, Lovise had sent for Lars. "Wake up, Father. You've been gone for hours."

"Lars? Where . . ." I was in my chair in Oxford. Wasn't I?

No. I was standing on high battlements, and a quick glance around told me exactly which castle they belonged to, because I knew it well, having almost died in a cellar there, long, long ago. Lincoln is one of the largest, strongest, and most strategic fortresses in England. But I had seen it only in days of peace, in the reign of Good King Henry. There was no peace now, with arrows flying and the battlements manned by troops in armor. *Crash!* The masonry trembled under my feet as a missile struck the walls.

Sheltering behind the merlon next along from mine, a man was shouting orders in a shrill voice. He was not tall, and wisps of white hair hung from below his helmet, yet he seemed to be in charge, for men ran to carry out his orders. Then he turned to peer out the crenel at the enemy, and I saw that he wasn't a he at all. She was my old friend, Nicholaa de la Haye, hereditary constable of the castle, a woman quite as tough and determined as Dowager Queen Eleanor. Nicholaa would not surrender to God himself, even if the walls were collapsing around her. She was old now, but chain mail suited her.

So who were the enemy? I looked out upon Lincoln market square, crammed with troops and two small trebuchets. Ha! They would need a lot more artillery than that if they were to take Lincoln Castle. The last time there had been a Battle of Lincoln had been during the anarchy, the civil war that I recalled from my childhood. Had John's misrule brought those terrible days back again?

Then I saw that the besiegers' flags bore the yellow fleurs-de-lis of France. Merciful Heavens! A French army in the heart of England? Oh, John, John! What horrors have you wrought?

I saw no more, because Lars tipped a jug of water over my head and yanked me out of my trance. He had solved the problem by means he had been taught in the College, but with the caveat that they should only be used in grave emergencies, because such sudden withdrawals can be dangerous to the subject. One such emergency is a state of trance lasting more than two hours, which mine already had. I survived unharmed, although I was confused at first. I forget what I babbled while Lovise wiped my face and Lars poured me more water, this time to drink.

"Whenever you've been to, Father, here it's still 1193. King Richard is still a prisoner in the Empire. Remember now?"

I drank a bucketful and then nodded. "Um. Yes. But I have been shown a terrible, terrible future."

Lovise fetched dry clothes for me, and went to find some food while I changed. Then the three of us settled into chairs, and between mouthfuls I outlined what I had witnessed. I had seen Richard die, which he must do eventually, of course, but the death I envisioned would be due to his own folly and when he had reigned only ten years. He would die childless, because John was going to succeed. There would be some dispute about that, and later John would personally murder Arthur, his nephew. In subsequent years he would lose all or most of his lands on the continent, and his barons would rise in revolution. And after that the ultimate disaster of a French invasion.

There was a long silence. Bats were chirping in the darkness outside.

"Advise me!" I pleaded. "I trust you two more than any else in the world. If I tell all this to anyone else, I will be chained to a wall in some prison for the insane. Why have I been shown all this? What am I supposed to do about it?"

"You haven't told me everything that happened here the night that Lord John came visiting," Lars said.

I let Lovise tell him, for I was hoarse. I could not shake the certainty that all this outpouring of foresight had been vouchsafed me so that I could do something with it, but I could not see what that something might be.

"Well?" I said at last. "What does it mean? What must I do? Why me, and why now?"

"I think that 'now' is important, Father. But first, who is sending you these visions, and are they good or evil?"

My wife and son then stared at me as if I were a criminal on trial.

"The visions must come from either Heaven or Hell," I said, "but that isn't very helpful, is it? Either will act through an agent, a saint or a devil."

"Do they lead you to do good or evil acts?" Lovise asked, ever logical.

"Good, I think. With my foresight I helped the Lionheart strike a couple of deadly blows against Saladin. I probably saved him from falling into Phillip's deadly clutches. I count those as good."

"But your visions have never failed! You think that now you can change the future?"

"They failed once," I said. "In Dürnstein Castle." And suddenly I understood. "No! The future can't be changed by ordinary means. But it can be changed by other magic!"

"Lars?" Lovise said. "You think you know the answer." Mothers are good at making statements like that.

Lars, of course, was no longer the boy who had scrumped the deacon's apples and battered the school bully to jelly. He was a prize graduate sage, an experienced traveler, and he had been quietly nodding for some time as I recited the wisdom I had received from the *Myrddin Wyllt*.

"Merlin? Are you truly Merlin Redux, Father?"

"No!" I insisted. "If I were, I would surely have more control over the seeings. But Merlin's ghost may be sending me these visions. Or Merlin himself, in his lifetime, may have foreseen the need for someone to . . . oh, such twisted speculations must drive a man mad."

"That makes more sense, I think. He could have foreseen the need for you to recover ancient, forgotten magic. He's been training you for this all your life. Have you ever had a whole gallery of visions thrown at you like this? Like tonight's collection, I mean?"

"Never. But it varies. Sometimes there is no vision. I remember Baron William asking me questions and I would tell him the answers without having been aware that I knew them. But this entire wagonload of sordid future history dumped on me all at once . . . no, never."

"I said early on that I thought this foreseeing of yours would lead to something important. And now I think that what happened tonight is important. You have been shown the stakes. The time has come for you to do what is required of you."

I shivered. Lovise said, "Do you think Lord John really has a letter from this Father Ferdinand describing you playing Judas?"

At that we had to explain to Lars about John's threats and my actions in Vienna. He pulled a face as if he'd drained a horn full of lemon juice. He thought for a moment and then suddenly lost color.

"You've found the answer?" his mother asked.

He nodded. "Merlin! Tell me, Father, what name do you most associate with Merlin—the original Merlin, I mean?"

"King Arthur, of course."

"The once and future king!"

Lovise whispered, "Oh, no!"

"It makes sense," our son insisted. "Merlin has trained Father to see the future as he did, and the future is a tyrant so terrible that the earls and barons of England revolt against him. A tyrant who is defeated in battle, who brings back the horrors of the Anarchy, when Stephen and Maud fought for the throne. A tyrant who murders the right-wise born king, Arthur of Brittany. This revelation comes immediately after that same villain threatens to destroy Father, so that they are now mortal enemies—literally *mortal* enemies."

I was appalled by this logic. "And what am I supposed to do? Challenge John to a duel? Ambush him with a crossbow? Poison his wine cup?"

"I think your method of attack is obvious."

"My powers do not extend to murder."

"Of course they do," Lars said. "Murder by magic. And if you review Lord John's horoscope, I'm sure you'll find that he is in a very vulnerable period just now. The brother he has betrayed is alive after all and about to be either released outright or ransomed. Three nights ago, he led a band of men-at-arms and a sorcerer against a low-born Saxon cripple and suffered total defeat. We must strike while the stars are against him, Father!"

I shivered, recalling some of the atrocities I had witnessed in my long war against the Sons of Satan. Must I now change sides? But my son had said *We*, and I took comfort from that.

But not much comfort. "You both know that to commit the horrible crime you propose would require full-blooded black magic performed at midnight on a pentagram. I should need four accomplices, and all five of us would be risking our immortal souls." Years ago, Lord John himself had predicted that such would be my fate.

"Count me as one, of course," Lars said.

"And me as another, dear."

"Lovise! You're not serious!"

"I am serious. You think I am that flighty Queen Eleanor, to betray my husband? I have not forgotten my wedding vows. Besides, I think Lars is right. You are Merlin's successor, and Arthur Plantagenet is to be Arthur Pendragon's. Why has it taken us so long to see this? Your destiny and duty is to secure his path to the throne of England—*Arthur* Redux!"

"There are still only three of us. We must have five. Who will believe our story or volunteer to imperil his soul? Do you expect me to go around the College asking who would like to join in a jolly pentagram party to kill the king's brother?"

Lovise stood up. "It is obvious that we should all sleep on this. Lars, do you want to go home for what's left of the night or would you rather stay in your old room here?"

Sometimes ideas that have seemed too horrible to contemplate will suddenly metamorphose into obvious truths, and this was one of them. A man who would take a sword to a chained and unarmed youth would certainly not hesitate to revenge his humiliation at the hands of a despised Saxon wizard. I now considered my danger from Lord John to be both clear and imminent. And so must Myrddin Wyllt—whatever mysterious entity lay behind that name—because he, or it, had rushed me through the rest of the evidence at breakneck speed. John no longer had his tame sorcerer to hand, but he might have a back-up for all I knew. If he truly possessed a letter signed by Father Ferdinand—or had counterfeited such a letter based on Bran's farseeing—he might drop it on the privy council's table at any moment, although he would more likely recognize that anything coming from him would seem tainted, and find some crony to deliver it for him.

Someone, for instance, like William the Marshall? I shivered all over at the thought.

The next morning, therefore, I was abroad at first light, saddled up and riding north. Late on the second day, I reached William Legier's seat outside Loughborough and was relieved to find him at home. They all made me welcome: William himself, Millisende, and their surviving sons, Enguerrand, Frank, and Guiscard, who was very nearly a young man now and enjoyed hearing me confirm his own certainty that he already was.

Millisende had suffered a bad crusade, losing four children at a single stroke, plus living for two years in the dread that her husband might never return either. She was thinner, although her black mourning dress contributed to that impression, and her hair was white as ivory. My arrival must serve to remind her of the losses she had suffered that Lovise had not, yet she greeted me with unaffected joy.

William himself showed me to my usual room. Then he closed the door, leaned against it, and said, "What's wrong? You look like a three-day-old corpse."

"A week old at least. William, old friend, I have a very great favor to ask, something I never thought I would ask of anyone. I also have a long story to tell you, so that you will understand my need."

He folded his arms. "I will never, ever, suspect you of lying to me, friend Ironfoot, so just tell me in two short sentences."

"A few years from now, King Richard will die childless. John will inherit the throne and run the country into utter ruin. He will lose—"

"Two sentences, I said. So what are you planning to do about it?"

"Kill John. Now."

"A very good plan, I'd say. Count me in. But I foresee trouble when his big brother returns to his realm."

"My way of killing can get around that problem. I shall use black magic. But I need two helpers to complete the pentagram."

His face darkened. "And what happens?"

"Lord John suffers a fatal accident, wherever he happens to be at the time."

William laughed then. "Is that all? Happy to oblige. I wouldn't call that black magic at all—more a public benevolence. And I think I know someone else who would happily make up your five."

"I thought you might. You told me his story once, remember?"

William's brewer makes the finest ale in the county, and the two of us consumed a lot of it far into the night as I told him the entire story, in detail. I had judged him correctly. Above all, William Legier was a fighter, and any true knight must despise the conniving, faithless John Plantagenet. As I had been, he was disgusted to learn that Richard was going to give his shameless brother a pardon instead of the hempen collar he deserved.

We drank our final toast of the night to "The once and future king."

By the second sunset after that, I was home again. Lovise gave me a worried look, but did not verbally compare me to a corpse of any vintage. Instead she showed me four spells that she had selected from our black magic collection in the crypt. I read them through with growing revulsion. Each one seemed worse than the last, and the fourth made my flesh creep. I had confiscated it from the Sons of Satan, and they had possessed nothing worse. It was short and infinitely vicious.

"This one?" I said, looking up. "The others are all too long to expect two amateurs to manage."

"I thought so," she said. "If that does not ruin him, I can't imagine what will."

"We'll have to write out the parts before William and his friend arrive." If his friend declined to cooperate, we would have to find another fifth voice.

My dear, lovable wife smiled grimly. "I already did. We just have to proofread them against the original."

William arrived about an hour later, accompanied by a man he introduced merely as Rolf, which I was certain was not his real name. He was in his early twenties, younger than I had expected, and must have been strikingly handsome before Lord John's thugs worked him over. Now he was lacking half his teeth, his nose was twisted, and he walked with a cane, as I do. That damage alone would have justified his hatred of the prince, even without the subsequent rape of his wife. He assured me that he was eager to help with my project.

"It must be done at midnight," I explained. "If you are not too weary from your journey, I can send for my son and we can chant the spell tonight. It won't take very long."

"And what will it do to the subject?" William asked.

"That is not specified, but it will be both fatal and humiliating."

Again, I recalled Lord John warning me in Winchester that one day I would be enlisted by Satan. Now it was happening and I might rue the consequences through all eternity. I considered that John himself had long preceded me.

At midnight, in the crypt, lit by the spooky light of only five candles, we assembled at the points of a pentagram that Lars chalked on the paving for us, and we sang the enchantment. We had already read it over five or six times—backward, as is usual in rehearsal.

It was written in a version of Parisian French, but the spell itself was much older, translated from Old Norse. I could have guessed that from the content, and Lovise could tell from the curious word order. We five, who all liked to think of ourselves as good Christians, solemnly beseeched the mischief god Loki to wrack shameful destruction on John Plantagenet, Count of Mortain. As I had predicted, the invocation did not take long, and I felt acceptance like peals of divine laughter, mingled with an upsurge of personal shame.

Judging by a complete lack of comment, the others felt much the same. Lars set to work with a mop and a bucket that he had arranged beforehand, washing away the pentagram. Lovise took up a candle and led the way upstairs. We burned our song sheets in the fireplace.

"How long until it acts?" Rolf asked.

"Impossible to say," I said. "But I am sure we will hear when it does."

Personally, I expected news of a shipwreck or a fall from a horse, but two days later Oxford buzzed with word from Dorset that Lord John, indulging in his beloved sport of hunting, had somehow managed to get bitten by a rabid fox. The details of the encounter were never entirely clear, but I did admire Loki's panache. John died about three weeks later, insane and convulsive.

So we had cleansed the world of a great evil. But two days after the state funeral—which I naturally attended—Lars, Lovise, and I began carrying all the black magic scrolls and grimoires up from the crypt, and methodically burning them. Now we need never be tempted to use any of them in future. Knowing how animate some of those spells could be, we made sure that not a single page survived. The last to burn was the *Myrddin Wyllt*. I was very happy to watch it go.

epilogue

In March of the following year, King Richard stepped ashore in England, a free man at last. He had himself crowned again in Winchester Cathedral, but Philip was creating trouble in France without any help from the late and unlamented John, so Richard wasted little time in crossing the Narrow Sea yet again. In the five years remaining to him, he busied himself in his dukedoms and counties, and never returned to his kingdom.

Within a month of John's death, Arthurian supporters in Brittany had smuggled Dowager Duchess Constance, together with her daughter and her six-year-old son, out of France, and brought them safe to England, for there was now no denying that young Arthur would be his uncle's heir presumptive until such time as Queen Berengaria produced a son. She never did, and Richard died at Chalus-Chabrol in April, 1199, in the manner I had foreseen. I had never tried to warn him of my vision. He had never sent for me or consulted me. Our last glimpses of each other had been on Christmas Day in Dürnstein Castle.

At his own request, the Duke of Brittany, then aged twelve, was crowned as Arthur II in Winchester, not Westminster as was customary. Winchester was renowned as an Arthurian town.

Archbishop Walter Hubert of Canterbury was appointed regent until the new king should came of age, two years later. Much to my surprise, Regent Hubert left me in the office of enchanter general, but I believe this was at the insistence of the king himself, who is much taken with the exploits of his great namesake. He always addresses me as "Merlin."

If he continues to reign as well as he has done these last five years, he will be well remembered and England can expect many more kings of his name in the future.

reality check

Yes, there really was a Prince Arthur, posthumous son of Geoffrey, Duke of Brittany, and thus grandson of King Henry II of England. He was born on 29 March, 1187, and died in early April, 1203, while a prisoner of King John. The manner of his death is unknown, although there were rumors that John killed him personally in a drunken rage. As there had been fighting between their factions, John may have staged a secret trial and convicted him of treason. Arthur's sister Eleanor was another victim of John's savagery—she may have been starved to death in Corfe Castle, in Dorset. These disappearances did not improve the king's already odoriferous reputation.

The scene where William Marshal and Archbishop Hubert decided Richard's succession is taken from the historical record, but personally I do not believe it. Richard had had several days to contemplate his coming death, and would have named his own successor.

There is a strong modern belief that Richard was homosexual. This might explain his lack of children, but I prefer my theory of sterility. If his sexual behavior had been unorthodox, then surely Philip would have added that to his catalog of accusations?

John was even nastier than I have represented him, and likely insane by our standards. He repeatedly broke the chivalric standards of the day, which held that commoners didn't matter but members of the nobility could only be killed in battle. If captured, they must be ransomed or at worst held captive indefinitely. On one occasion John sent twenty-two high-rank prisoners across to England and had them starved to death. Eventually the earls and barons rebelled and forced him to sign the *Magna Carta*, affirming some "rights" they claimed, or made up. As he always did, John soon broke his word, and then the barons colluded with the king of France, who sent his son over with an army and a very nebulous claim on the English throne. John died before the issue was settled, so the barons then evicted the French and did homage to John's son, Henry III, who reined for 56 years.

There is a curious parallel here between John Lackland and the last of his Plantagenet line, King Richard III, the one who was recently dug out of a parking lot in Leicester. John was believed to have killed a niece and nephew, and Richard two nephews, "the princes in the Tower." In both cases, England seems to have reacted with abhorrence and eventually revolution. In both cases, foreign armies invaded. Richard died in battle, and John of eating too many lampreys. I have long wondered who cooked the lampreys, and was tempted to have Durwin do so, until Prince Arthur walked on stage and suggested a better ending. (Richard III lost to Henry VII, the first Tudor king, who named his firstborn Arthur. That Arthur didn't live long enough to reign either.)

More than half the characters mentioned were real people, although my descriptions of their appearances are mostly fictional. If you take out Durwin and his doings, the storyline sticks very close to history, even in many details. The first inspiration for this book came when I read of William Marshal being sent from France to Winchester to inform Queen Eleanor of her husband's death. When he arrived (with injured leg) she already knew. That is possible in real world terms, but it reads better as magic. I appropriated to Durwin several other historical details, such as the caravan ambush at Tell al-Khuwialifia. Yes, Richard would have sent spies out, but fiction is tidier than fact. And there were two shipwrecks.

Christians in the Middle Ages were religious to a degree rarely professed today. Relics of saints were more precious than gold. I tried to make Durwin seem devout, but not obsessively so. Thus he felt justified in murdering Lord John because, when he became king, he would lose most of the Angevin lands in France and alienate the barons so much that they would force him to sign a charter limiting the powers of the monarchy. To a patriotic subject like Durwin, these failures would have seemed catastrophic. Ironically, although John was undoubtedly a sadistic tyrant, by our standards the loss of the French domains was an improvement, because it made ruling England a full-time job and forced the nobles to choose between their French and English lands. And the *Magna Carta* is honored today as the first tentative step toward democracy, parliamentary government, and the notion of human rights.

Life was short in the Middle Ages. Kings came of age at fourteen, youths of sixteen led armies, and girls were allowed to marry at twelve. At forty-eight, Durwin would have been an old man. Saladin died in 1193, Leopold of Austria in 1194 (of gangrene after crushing his foot in a tournament), Emperor Henry VI in 1197 (of fever contracted during his re-conquest of Sicily), and Richard I in 1199, as related above. Historically, John then ruled until 1216.

As in the earlier books of this series, all the towns and villages mentioned are genuine and still survive, although much has changed. Only Pipewell has disappeared; it remains a name on a map—pronounced "Pipwell" by the locals.

acknowledgments

i have used (and in some cases abused) the books listed below. I am especially grateful to David Boyle's *The Troubadour's Song*, which I discovered by accident after I had begun writing my story, and which I recommend as not just fine history, but as a great true-life adventure story. Boyle has researched King Richard's itinerary from the Holy Land until his capture in Vienna, so I am indebted to him for many of the details.

Asbridge, Thomas	*The Crusades*
Boyle, David	*The Troubadour's Song*
Duby, Georges	*William Marshal*
Gillingham, John	*Richard I*
McLynn, Frank	*Lionheart & Lackland*
Miller, David	*Richard the Lionheart: The Mighty Crusader*
Morris, Marc	*King John, Treachery and Tyranny in Medieval England*
Seward, Desmond	*The Demon's Brood, A History of the Plantagenet Dynasty*
Warren, W.L.	*Henry II*
Weir, Alison	*Eleanor of Aquitaine*
(also)	*Britain's Royal Families*

about the author

Dave Duncan was a prolific writer of fantasy and science fiction, best known for his fantasy series, especially The Seventh Sword, A Man of His Word, and The King's Blades. He was both a founding and an honorary lifetime member of SF Canada, and an inductee of the Canadian Science Fiction and Fantasy Hall of Fame. His books have been translated into fifteen languages.

Dave and his wife Janet, his in-house editor and partner for fifty-seven years, lived in Victoria, British Columbia. They had three children and four grandchildren. Dave passed away in October 2018. *Merlin Redux* is one of the last novels he finished.